The Edge of the World

Bill Wahl

RAVEN CREST
BOOKS

ISBN: 979-8-572253-51-1

DEDICATION

For my brother Tommy, who, despite the many cruelties life threw at him, always kept us laughing.

"Rebellion cannot exist without a strange form of love."
Albert Camus

SIGNIFICANT INDIVIDUALS

Liz Burton	Narrator and journalist
Max Henderson	Owner of Henderson Nautical Works
Dominic (Dom) Delfino	Head of Security/Max's best friend
Sheila Taylor	Max's PA
Hedvika Zavatsky	Max's solicitor
Peter Henderson	Max's son
Violeta Henderson	Max's wife
Winston Godfred	Devotee of Max
Sunrise70 (Laura Beech)	Radical
Jean-Pierre Lavelle	Captain
Alexis Girard	Chief Engineer
Hugo Dubois	Chief of Aeronautics
Margaret Williams	Prime Minister
Jared Philcox	Home Secretary
Ronald Hudd	Defence Secretary
Barnard Roux	French Naval Chief of Staff
Philipe Dupont	French Secretary of State
Candi (Susan Marshall)	Prostitute

PROLOGUE

People think they know the story of Max Henderson. This is understandable. What happened to Max was so far beyond normal I suppose everyone was glued to the TV and newspapers for a while. The problem is that the public knows that story *too* well. But the truth is that when these incredible events played themselves out, few people understood Max. Come to think of it, when people say they know the story, what they really mean is that they know *the events*.

And the things people said about Max were all over the spectrum. He has been called an anarchist, a hero to the people, a criminal, a visionary, and mentally ill.

You may well ask – what right do I have to tell the story of Max Henderson? My name is Liz Burton. I'm a journalist, and I'm probably less experienced and qualified than most of the journalists and news crews that got involved. But I was there, right at the beginning, before anyone knew there was a story to tell. I was the girl standing at the gates of Henderson Nautical Works at 7:00 AM, coffee in hand, waiting for a chance to speak with Max. Because of that, I eventually got let into Max's world in a way that no other journalist did.

So I saw a lot of what happened… first-hand. And some of the people who were close to Max spoke to me. And what did I see? An anarchist? A hero? A criminal? Someone with a mental illness? Those are difficult characterisations to respond to, but I will say this – as I got to know Max, I formed the impression that he was a person more like you and me than anyone ever imagined. In the pages that follow, I'm going to tell you the story of Max Henderson with all the intimate detail it deserves, and you can decide for yourself.

CHAPTER 1

Officers Jennifer Stanbury and Dennis Clark are cruising down Walker Road. It had already been a tough shift. They'd dealt with an aggressive drink-driver, a domestic violence call, a drugs arrest, and they had just finished investigating a break-in at a junior school. It's 10:40 PM, and with twenty minutes left on their shift, they want nothing more than to ride around, drink coffee, and pass some idle conversation.

The police radio spits out static, and then, "All units in the North Portsmouth area, we have a citizen report of a 10-56A on the A275 Bridge."

Dennis has only been on the force for three weeks, so Jennifer has something of a teaching role with the new recruit. She brakes, begins a K-turn, and looks over at Dennis. "10-56A is code for what?"

"Suicide," says Dennis.

"Almost. It's a report of a suicide attempt. Radio dispatch and tell them we're responding."

Dennis grabs the radio. "Dispatch, this is Unit 36 — we are responding. ETA is three minutes."

"Copy, Unit 36. The citizen report indicates a middle-aged man wearing a blue suit and standing on the railing of the bridge. The individual may be intoxicated."

"Copy, dispatch."

Jennifer concentrates, accelerating and braking hard as she weaves the car through traffic. "We'll blue light this, but I'm not putting the siren on because the jumper will hear that a mile off." She glances over at Dennis. "There's something strange about this call. Any ideas?"

"Yeah," says Dennis. "The A275 Bridge isn't really the right bridge if you want to kill yourself."

Jennifer brakes hard. "Come on, move it," she hisses at a car in front of her. "Correct, it's not the right bridge. I mean, you might kill yourself, but it's not really high enough. If you want to kill yourself, there are better bridges in southern England. Most of the successful suicides around here happen at the Itchen Bridge up near Southampton."

"So, what does this mean?" asks Dennis.

"Well, it might mean that whatever is happening with this guy is impulsive rather than something which has really been thought through. But who knows?"

Jennifer punches the engine down the slip road and onto the A275, and then slows as she makes her way onto the bridge. The bridge is well-lit, and both Jennifer and Dennis can clearly make out the male figure. Jennifer brings the patrol car up onto the curb about twenty metres from the man, and for a brief moment, they examined the scene. The man is standing on the top of the railing and leaning against a support cable, which he clutches with one hand. The man stares down into the harbour water and appears oblivious to the police car.

Jennifer looks over at Dennis. "Okay, let's approach, but slowly."

They close the car doors carefully and begin to walk towards the man. When they are ten feet away, they stop. The squad car's flashing blue lights sweep the area and cars pass but are clearly slowing as drivers take in the scene. "Good evening, sir," says Jennifer. "I'm Officer Stanbury and this is Officer Clark."

The man gives no indication that he is aware of the officers. Jennifer notices that the man holds a beer in the hand which is not clutching the bridge cable. She tries again, raising her voice slightly. "We're a bit worried about your safety, sir. You're awfully close to the edge."

The man slowly turns his head towards them and becomes less stable against the cable, swaying and adjusting his feet on the railing. "Careful, sir," says Jennifer.

The man's expression carries a sad smile and his features are flaccid and dopey. "I sorry officers," the man says through slurred speech.

"That's okay, sir," says Jennifer. "You're not in any trouble. We just want to make sure you're gonna be safe. Do you mind if Officer Clark and I help you off the railing?"

The man looks down into the darkness and Jennifer's heart pounds faster. She takes a tentative step forward and does a quick calculation, realising that if he lets go they aren't close enough to grab him. The man looks back at her and nods slowly. The officers walk to the man and Jennifer climbs up two of the railings and puts an arm around the man's shoulder to steady him. Dennis gets up onto one of the railings, takes the beer bottle from the man's hand, and grips his right arm. "Sir," says Jennifer, "see if you can step down onto the next railing – we've got you."

The man tries to step down but slips on the lower railing and falls forward. Jennifer and Dennis instinctively tighten their grips and yank backwards. The weight of the man is taken by Dennis, and they fall, landing together on the pavement. Jennifer jumps down from the railing and is aware that her partner has absorbed much of the man's weight in the fall. "You okay, Dennis?" she asks. Dennis nods but looks a bit stunned as he slowly pulls himself up onto one knee. The man lies still on his back, his glassy eyes searching the officer's faces. Dennis and Jennifer make eye contact and then help the man into a sitting position, his back against the bridge railing.

"You okay, sir?" asks Dennis.

The man nods groggily. Jennifer gets down on one knee and looks the man square in the face, making sure she has his attention. "Sir, can you hear me alright?" Again, the man nods. Jennifer notices his blue suit for the first time – the tie is loose and material wrinkled. "What's your name, sir?"

"I'm Maxwell Henderson," he says, his words slurred. "People call me Max."

"Okay, Max. It's not really safe sitting here on the pavement, so we're going to take you back to the squad car for a moment, okay?"

Max nods. Jennifer and Dennis help him to his feet and walk him to the patrol car. They get him into the back seat and Jennifer leans in. "Have you got any ID, Max?" He nods, and, with some difficulty, pulls at a wallet in his back pocket. Cars continue to slow as they pass, drivers craning their necks. Jennifer looks over at Dennis. "Officer Clark, would you mind keeping these cars moving – one of these rubberneckers is gonna fender-bender in a minute." Dennis nods, walks to the back of the patrol car, and begins waving at the curious faces as they drift past.

Max hands Jennifer his entire wallet. She opens it and pulls his driving licence out, scanning it. She looks back at Max. "Mr Henderson, can I ask what you were doing up on the bridge railings?"

Max shakes his head groggily and looks up through bleary eyes. "I'm sorry to waste your time officer. I didn't mean for this…"

Jennifer waits, but Max seems to have lost his train of thought. "Have you got a car somewhere, sir?"

Max shakes his head. "I was in a taxi."

"Mr Henderson, can you just sit tight for a moment. I need to have a word with my partner, and we'll get you sorted out." Max nods, and Jennifer shuts the door. She locks the car door and motions at Dennis. They move a few feet down the pavement.

"So, what's the protocol?" asks Jennifer.

"I think we should take him to Accident and Emergency, right?"

"Yeah. We can't know why he was up on that railing, and he isn't saying anything to reassure us. He really needs to be assessed by the psychiatry liaison team."

"Y'know something," says Dennis. "I think I might know who that guy is."

"What d'ya mean?"

"I mean, I don't know him personally," says Dennis. "But I think he might be some sort of celebrity – or maybe somebody important."

Jennifer looks down at the licence in her hand. "Maxwell Henderson," she says thoughtfully.

"I've got it," says Dennis. "He's the guy who owns that huge shipyard – Henderson Nautical Works. Down on the harbour."

"Oh yeah. That makes sense." Jennifer looks at Max through the squad car window for a moment. "He must be seriously wealthy. I wonder what the hell he's doing on a bridge railing?"

Jennifer stares down at the pavement for a moment before looking up. "I think I better have a word with the Chief about this."

"Why's that?" asks Dennis.

She grins at Dennis before continuing. "Because there's always a little bit of politics in policing. You might as well learn that sooner rather than later."

Dennis and Jennifer hold Max by the arms as they walk through the door of his home. Max swipes at a wall switch and the large foyer fills with light. The officers cannot help but look around the entrance as they hold onto Max. There are several intricately crafted models of ships on display. Jennifer identifies a sixteenth century galleon, a large steamship, a dreadnought, and a World War Two battleship and aircraft carrier.

"So, it's just your wife at home?" asks Jennifer.

"Think so," says Max.

Jennifer squints in the foyer light. "You think so?"

Max shrugs. "Sometimes she might have… a guest."

Jennifer faces Max. "What?"

Max looks at them, his eyes bleary. "It's okay… I'm very grateful officers, and I'm sorry to cause trouble. I'm okay now." He staggers as he reaches into his pocket, and the officers hold him up. Max places keys on a side table.

"Chief says we need to make sure you get into bed safely, Mr Henderson," says Jennifer.

Max grins dopily and shrugs. The three of them climb slowly up the wide spiral stairs to the landing, the officers each gripping an arm. Max leads them down a hallway and the sound of a man's voice is heard as they pass a door. Then, a playful female shriek and more laughter from the man. Dennis and Jennifer glance at one another. They make their way to a bedroom at the far end of the hall and Max turns on a table lamp. He pulls clumsily at his jacket and Dennis helps him get out of it, placing the coat on the back of a chair.

Max sits down heavily on the bed and gazes up at the two officers, a sad smile on his face. He shakes his head. "I don know what happened tonight."

"That's okay, sir," says Jennifer. "We can all have funny moments."

"Yes," says Max. "That's what it was."

"Shall we get those shoes off, sir?" says Dennis.

"Oh yes." Max leans down, yanks off a shoe, and Dennis catches him when he slumps over. Dennis pulls off his other shoe.

A particularly loud shriek of female laughter drifts down the hallway. Max suddenly gazes into space and begins to sing in a muted tone, "There's a love that knows no end… and that is all… there is to know. I'll tell you this my loyal friend… take your chance… before you go."

Max shakes his head. "It sounded better when she sang it in Spanish."

"Sorry, sir," says Dennis. "Who sang it?"

Max looks from one officer to the other. "Well, that was twenty-five years ago, and you can't get my wife to sing much these days."

The officers gaze back at Max, confusion written on their faces. Max raises both of his hands and gazes at them, as if remembering his circumstances. "I am wasting your time with empty stories."

"That's okay, Mr Henderson," says Jennifer. "A proper night's sleep will do you good."

"Of course," says Max. He makes a concerted effort to shake both of their hands, crawls on hands and knees to his pillow, and collapses into sleep.

CHAPTER 2

Dom Delfino pulls his black BMW X7 SUV into Max's driveway at 7:45 AM and kills the engine. He drops down onto the pavement and makes his way to the front door. Six feet six inches tall, he's a little softer than he was twenty years ago, but he's still more muscle than fat. Dom adjusts his silk tie and inserts a key into the door. He is surprised the door is unlocked, and he enters the foyer. Dom walks to the large and sunlit kitchen and stares at a handsome young man who is pouring coffee into a mug. The man looks surprised and uncertain.

Dom smirks at him. "Make yourself right at home, mate."

The man looks confused and offers an apologetic expression. "I have small angielski." The man illustrates by displaying a one-inch gap between his thumb and forefinger.

Dom laughs. "Angielski? You got small angielski? Maybe your English is shit, but I bet you got a big dick, right?"

The man raises his hands to display his incomprehension.

"Right," says Dom, moving towards the man and gripping him under an arm. "It's time for you to fuck off." He takes the coffee cup out of his hand, places it on the table, and ushers the stunned man into the foyer. Dom opens the door, points outside, and offers the man a practised sarcastic grin. "Go."

The man appears frightened but doesn't leave. "Pieniadze," he blurts out.

"What?" says Dom.

The man rubs his fingers against his thumb. "Pieniadze," he says again.

"Oh for fuck's sake – she didn't pay you?"

The man raises his hands again and makes a face. Dom smirks, retrieves his wallet from his back pocket, and begins to fish out notes. He holds the bills and stares at the man. "Romanian? Czech?" The man appears confused. "Polish?"

"Yes, Polskie," the man says, smiling with enthusiasm.

Dom takes the man's wrist and shoves two hundred pounds into his palm. He points out the door and grins. "Okay, now fuck off you dirty Pole." He turns the man towards the neighbourhood, gives him a little shove, and closes the door.

Dom enters Max's bedroom and is surprised to see he's still in his clothes. He pulls the curtain open and light floods into the room. Dom sits on the bed and gives Max a gentle shake.

Max groans and opens sticky eyes with some difficulty. He sighs heavily. "Am I alive, Dom?"

"'Fraid so boss," says Dom. "And the news gets worse – we gotta leave in thirty minutes. Time for a shower."

Max and Dom enter the large conference room at Henderson Nautical Works, a tumult of conversation already at hand. Max offers the dozen executives and heads of departments a wave and walks over to the large plate glass window. Max and Dom gaze across the estuary to Gosport Marina, where they can see perhaps a hundred sailing yachts. Sunlight glints off the green water. Gazing across the estuary is something of a meditative ritual for Max and Dom.

Dom leans in close to Max's ear. "You okay?"

Max nods. Sheila Taylor, Max's PA, enters the room carrying a tray with three large cafetières of coffee. She puts them on the large oval table and then stands next to Max, studying his face. Sheila is seventy-five years old and was the first Henderson Nautical Works employee. A few years ago, a newer member of staff asked her when she was planning to retire. She said, *I'll retire you*. For those who know Sheila, retirement never occurs to them.

Sheila studies Max closely. "What you been up to Max? Something's not right with you."

Max frowns at Sheila. Dom leans across Max and whispers, "he had a few beers last night."

Max looks between them. "God, you two are like gossiping hens."

Sheila casts a critical eye over Max's appearance, and frowns. "Max, your suit is a mess."

"It's fine, Sheila."

"It's not fine, Max – it's wrinkled." She rolls her eyes and looks over at Dom. "Lot of good you were this morning."

"Hey, I don't tell the boss how to dress."

"Just wait a minute," says Sheila, and she disappears from the room. A moment later she returns, carrying a jacket. She removes Max's jacket, puts the fresh one on him, and straightens his tie. Dom makes a show of appearing to brush something off the shoulder of the new jacket, and

Sheila glares at him. "There's nothing there," she snaps.

"Right, would you two stop it please," says Max. "I need coffee and I want to get this meeting started. Where's Hedvika?"

The three of them face the room and see that Hedvika Zavatsky, Henderson's legal counsel, has just sat down at the table and is pouring herself a cup of coffee. Max sits at the head of the table, Hedvika to his left, Sheila to his right, with Dom sitting next to Sheila. The tumult of conversation subsides, and several faces smile in Max's direction. Sheila pours coffee for Max and adds milk.

The seating arrangement at the conference table was never formally designed, but it's no accident. The dozen execs and department heads in the room are essential for the productive running of Henderson Nautical Works, but these people come and go as careers develop. The three individuals sitting near Max are, for him, the loyal ones. Hedvika, Henderson Nautical Works' attorney, has been with Max for eighteen years. Growing up in the Czech Republic, Hedvika had a successful modelling career before she read Law at Cambridge. Slim and standing six feet tall without heels, her beauty remains strikingly apparent. Dom has worked for Max for fifteen years and seems to have so many roles it's often not clear what he does. Personal security, driver, fixer, adviser, friend, and whatever else might be necessary. Sheila, of course, has been Max's PA from the very beginning.

Max and Hedvika make eye contact. "Morning, Max," she says.

"Morning, Hedvika."

Max looks over at Sheila and nods. "Okay, everyone," says Sheila, her voice shrill and loud. "Let's get started. I'll assume you've all read the minutes of last week's meeting." Sheila pushes a button on a remote and projects the agenda for the meeting onto a screen. "Financial report," says Sheila.

The Director of Finance, a thin and nervous woman, projects a series of graphs and pie charts onto the screen and gives a report. Three minutes in and Max's vision begins to glaze. Ten minutes later, and Max touches Sheila lightly on the wrist. "That's wonderful... thank you," says Sheila.

"Oh... okay," says the Director of Finance. "Are there any questions or comments?" The room is silent for a moment, and a few heads turn in Max's direction. "So..." says Max, "plenty of money then?"

"Ah, well... yes," says the Head of Finance. "As I mentioned, revenue is up six per cent this quarter and our stock price..."

"Thank you," says Sheila.

The Director of Finance sits down. "Nautical works proposals," says Sheila.

The Director of Project Acquisitions, a plump young man, pushes himself out of his chair. He walks to the front of the room. "There are three potential projects we've been approached on. Two are possibilities, and the third is a rather odd case which is unlikely. I'll start with the unlikely proposition so we can get it out of the way. Image number one please, Sheila."

Sheila punches at her laptop and projects an image onto the screen. There are a few sniggers and some murmuring. The Director of Human Resources says, "What the hell is that?"

"That," says the plump man, "is a French nuclear-powered aircraft carrier." He stands closer to the screen and points to the image. "It's *Joan of Arc*. Laid down in 1978 and launched in 1983. It's a big bastard — 42,500 tons. The Americans had launched the first nuclear-powered carrier in 1961, so this was the French trying to keep up. *Joan of Arc* was decommissioned four years ago. And… it's a real problem for the French government. Some press reports are saying that the ship is contaminated. Some say asbestos, some say worse. The French authorities say the reports are complete nonsense. It's moored at the Cherbourg Naval Base and there have been student protests recently. The French would love to get rid of it."

"What's the job?" asks Dom.

"Well, they want to tow it here so we can break it down."

"What are they offering?" asks the Director of Finance.

"14.5 million, which seems like a nice payday but, believe me, it's not. It's an enormous job and the political headaches with our own government and the public don't even bear thinking about. The French are basically looking for someplace to dump this albatross."

"I've had a cursory look at the project," says Hedvika. "Financially, I have no idea. But politically and legally, it's a nightmare. I'd think it would probably take six to twelve months to even get permission from the government to bring it over. And they may say no.

"Okay then," says Sheila. "Do we move on?"

The room is silent for a moment, and then the sound of Max clearing his throat is heard. Heads turn towards Max, who is gazing up at the carrier. Max looks at the image a moment longer, and then examines the others around the table, faces all staring back at him. Max takes a sip of coffee and then slowly pushes himself out of his chair and stands in front of the image, his arms clasped behind his back. He continues to examine the ship for a full minute, silence heavy in the room. The image shows *Joan of Arc* steaming out at sea, a third of its deck displaying jet fighter aircraft.

"Max?" says Sheila.

Max turns and faces the room, raising his eyebrows. "Yes, I understand. Reports of contamination. Bad deal. Political problems. It's just that…" Max turns and gazes at the image again. He traces an index finger along the ship's hull, turns and faces the room. "She's a stunning ship, isn't she?"

"Well, maybe, but…" starts the Director of Project Acquisitions.

"Hold on a minute," says Dom. "What is it Max?"

Max turns to the image again and clasps his hands behind his back. "I suppose we and the Americans refer to her as *Joan of Arc*," he says, "but of course the French call her *Jeanne d'Arc*. I like thinking of her as *Jeanne d'Arc*. There's more romance in that. I've kept an eye on her over the years. Her service has been about as glorious as can be expected during the post-war years." Max turns and gazes at the faces in the room, as if suddenly realising he has been speaking out loud. He turns again and stares at the image. "You know, she did very well supporting the Americans with Afghanistan. She launched hundreds of sorties against the Taliban. She offered support during the Indian-Pakistan crisis of 2002 and helped protect a no-fly zone over Libya in 2011. I think she launched planes in the Persian Gulf against Islamic State, just as that problem was starting up. She did very well, really." Max turns and faces his staff again before continuing. "We often think of battleships or maybe submarines as the really beautiful ships. You know, their lines and the way they move through the sea. But this ship… she's just so pleasing to look at."

"But sir," says the young man. "That's a very dated photo. *Joan of Arc* is decades old. It's been moth-balled for four years."

Max takes a step towards the young man and stares at him for a moment, as if seeing him for the first time. "*It's* been moth-balled?" asks Max. "Y'know, we didn't use to refer to capital ships as an *it*. We're not talking about a pair of your underpants, are we?"

There is some laughter from around the table and the young man looks confused. "I didn't mean to be disrespectful, Mr Henderson. I'm just saying that… *Joan of Arc* was decommissioned at least four years ago, and there are these reports in the press."

Max looks back at the image. "Well, I'm sure she probably needs some tidying up."

The young man's mouth drops open and he stares at Max, confusion written on his face.

"Sir, the French aren't asking us to repair or refurbish the ship – they want us to break it up."

"Oh," says Max, as if waking from a dream. He looks around the room for a moment and then claps his hands. "Well, isn't that odd." He looks at his PA. "Sheila, can you please send that image to my email?"

"Of course, Max."

Max sits down again and takes another sip of coffee. Sheila looks at him tentatively, and then Max waves a hand at her.

"Right," says Sheila, looking at the young man. "What's the next project request?"

The plump man walks to the front of the room, uncertainty written on his face. "Can I have image number two please?"

Dom walks into Sheila's office and sees that Max's PA is speaking on the phone.

"Climbed over a wall?" Sheila says. "Okay, I'll let Mr Henderson know… yes, thank you."

Sheila hangs up and looks at Dom. "Peter has escaped from rehab again."

"Shit," says Dom. He stares into space, trying to recall how many times Max's son, Peter Henderson, had absconded from heroin rehab programmes. "Is this the third or fourth time?" Dom asks Sheila.

"I'm not even sure," says Sheila. "I hate having to tell Max."

"Max has asked me to see him. I'll tell him."

"Thanks," says Sheila. "He's free now – go on in."

Dom walks into Max's office, closes the door, and sits across the desk from Max, who is gazing at a sheet of lined paper in front of him.

Max looks up at Dom. "Thanks for coming down, Dom."

"No problem. What's up, boss?"

Max looks down at the list of names on his desk, then back at Dom. "So, you know I had a few beers last night, right? Well, it was a bit worse than that."

"What do you mean, boss?"

Max blows out a large breath. "A couple of police officers helped me home."

"What? What happened?"

"Nothing. Like I said – I was drunk and they gave me a lift home and... helped me into bed."

An expression of concern and hurt crosses Dom's face. "Boss, why didn't you call me?"

"Oh, I don't know. Things just sort of happened. Anyway, the two officers, they were very helpful. I mean, I'd like to... express my gratitude. Maybe some sort of gift."

Dom studies Max for a moment and thinks the situation over. "Sure, I can sort out a gift, but I'm worried about exposure."

"What do you mean?"

"Cops are always getting badgered by journalists and paparazzi. Some cops will take money for leaking a story, anonymously. Who were the cops?"

Max looks down at the names. "One of them was a guy named Clark. His first name begins with a D. Maybe David. The other one was a woman. I think her name is Stanbury, but I can't remember her first name.

"I never heard of a David Clark," says Dom. "The woman is Jennifer Stanbury. She's a good cop – not a leaker. But the guy, I don't know."

"Okay. Look Dom, these officers... they were just very kind, y'know. I want them to know how grateful I am."

Dom looks at Max for a moment. "Sure, boss, leave it with me. I'll sort something out."

"Thanks Dom... something nice, okay?"

Dom nods and gazes at Max for a moment. "Boss, if there's a problem, you call me, right?"

"Yeah yeah. Of course, Dom."

Dom gazes at Max for a moment. "There's something I need to tell you."

Max looks down at his desk, takes a deep breath of air and then blows it out. "It's Peter, isn't it?"

"I'm afraid so, boss."

"He's escaped from that rehab centre, right?"

"He has," says Dom.

"Damn it," says Max. "Peter was doing so good. I visited him two days ago. He'd been off that shit for three weeks. He was putting on weight." Max looks up. "Can you find him again, Dom?"

"Of course, boss. He's probably using the same dealer. He'll be somewhere around Guildhall Walk."

"Dom… I'm worried this time. I got a bad feeling."

"I'll get him, boss." There is a pause. "What do you want me to do when I find him? Should I take him back to the rehab centre?"

Max thinks for a moment. "Nah, screw that place. It never works. Just bring him to me, okay?"

"You got it, boss."

CHAPTER 3

Max sits in his car and gazes across the water of Portsmouth Harbour at Portchester Castle, taking in the light and the way it glints off all that ancient stonework and the huge turrets. There is a four-pack of cold and hoppy pale ale sitting on the seat next to him. Max opens up the glove box and pulls out a pint glass, and then slowly pours a can into the glass. If he's gonna get a bit drunk in his car and look across the Solent Estuary at 4:30 PM, he might as well do it the right way. Maybe he's cracking up, but he's not an animal. He inhales the tropical fruit aroma of the hops and takes a swig of beer. He's aware of this painful physical ache in his chest, which feels like emptiness or an absence of something. A memory comes to him. His son has overdosed and he's lying on his back in Max's driveway, which is where some junkies had dropped him off. Max has administered three doses of Narcan to Peter, just like the nurses had told him to, and Peter is coming around. He forces the images from his mind.

Max kills the rest of the pint glass of pale ale and studies the castle closely, trying to remember its history. The French besieged the fort and took it off us in 1216, but we got it back of course. Max closes his eyes and works his way through some of the history of the fort, remembering that several maritime campaigns against France were launched from there. He knows he's thinking about that because it's easier than anything else he might think about. He reaches for another can when his phone rings through his car's speaker system.

"Hi Sheila," Max says.

"Max, I just want to make sure you remembered your medical appointment."

Max sighs heavily. "Bollocks. I forgot. What time is it?"

"It's at 5:10 PM. You should probably head straight over."

"Okay. You know, Sheila, people tell me I have a good mind – you know what I say?"

Sheila already knows the answer to Max's joke, but she asks anyway. "What's that?"

"I say, thank you, but it belongs to my PA."

Sheila laughs. "Funnier every time Max."

"Yeah."

Max sits in the waiting room, collecting his thoughts. He feels like maybe this is a bad idea, and perhaps he should have just kept the issue to himself. Max thinks that probably lots of men his age have dick problems. He doesn't like talking about it, even with Dr Anoop. And besides, what his GP had asked him to do seemed pretty strange. Dr Anoop had told him to wet some stamps and to wrap them around the base of his dick before he went to sleep, the edges of the stamps overlapping with one another. It seemed strange there wasn't a test that was more sophisticated these days.

Max's name is called and he walks down the hall and enters the consulting room. The older Indian gentleman stands and offers his hand, which Max shakes. They sit down.

"Okay, Max. So how did the erection self-test go?"

"Well, I did it like you said for three nights in a row, and the stamps were broken every morning."

His GP smiles and claps his hands. "Excellent, Max – that's very good."

Max feels confused. "I don't get it, Dr Anoop. Why is this good?"

"Max – you have a problem getting a good erection, right? This test tells us if there is a physical reason why you are having the problem. A man your age will have maybe three to five erections a night, while you are sleeping. If there is something physically wrong with you, you won't have those erections and the stamps won't break. So, you are having some nice erections. You see?"

Max doesn't really appreciate his GP talking about his nice erections. Max sighs. "Okay, so why isn't... my dick working better?"

Dr Anoop smiles. "Are you having some stress, Max?"

"Of course I'm having stress. Life is stressful, right?"

"Well, yes, Max. But is anything especially difficult these days?"

"No, not really. Just the same shit as normal."

"And how are things with your wife? With... um..." his GP scans his notes, "... how are things between you and Violeta?"

Max looks at his hands for a moment and then shrugs. "You know how it goes – I mean, when you've been married for years. It just happens less often, right?"

"Max, do you think some couple's counselling might help?"

"What? No. Definitely not. Not a good idea."

Dr Anoop gazes at him, and Max feels like he's supposed to say something else. "What about those pills men take? You know – what are they called?"

"Viagra."

"Yeah. Viagra. What about that?"

"Max, you don't need a doctor to prescribe that anymore. You can buy it over the counter. But you shouldn't need it. There's nothing wrong with you physically. Max, I think you need to relax, okay? Maybe you are working too hard. How about a holiday? Women love to plan holidays, right? Tell Violeta to find a nice place to go. Warm. Lots of sand and sun. You see?"

Max gazes at Dr Anoop for a moment and realises there is nothing more he wants to say. He nods. "Okay. You're probably right."

His GP places a hand on his shoulder and gives him a warm smile. "Good," says Dr Anoop.

Max stands up and walks to the door, then turns and grins at his GP. "So, the NHS owes me a few quid for stamps, right?"

Dr Anoop laughs. "Oh no, you can still use the stamps for mailing letters."

Max's grin broadens. "Yeah, I don't think I could mail someone a letter with a stamp that's been stuck to my dick all night."

"Sure you can, Max. Everyone gets letters mailed with erection self-test stamps."

Max laughs, offers a wave, and heads down the hallway.

CHAPTER 4

There is a knock at his office door, and Max looks up from his paperwork.

"Come in."

Sheila enters and then closes the door. She is holding Max's work overalls, which are on a hanger and covered in plastic film.

Every Thursday afternoon, Max exchanges his suit for work overalls and goes back to the shop floor. You can't run a shipyard just from an office. But there is another reason, and employees who have been around for even a month understand it. Max enjoys getting his hands dirty. He worked in a shipyard from the day he left school, and the wonder of building and repairing ships, big and small, has never worn thin.

"Where you working today?" asks Sheila.

"They cast a propeller last week for *The Tangier*. They should be breaking it out of its mould today."

"Is that the big cargo ship we're building?"

"That's the one," says Max.

Sheila is pulling the plastic wrap off Max's work overalls. "Sheila, I appreciate it, but you don't need to get my work overalls professionally cleaned."

"They were just really dirty this week."

"I know, but I don't like my work clothes to look too clean."

"Max, that doesn't make any sense."

"They notice."

Sheila makes a face at Max, hands him the hanger and leaves the office. Max changes into his work overalls and puts his hard hat on. He opens his office door and catches Sheila's eye. She walks into his office and sits next to him in front of his computer.

"You want to review names?" she asks. Max nods.

"Which workshop are you visiting?"

"*The Tangier* is in Workshop B," says Max.

Sheila taps on a few keys and brings up the images of staff which were taken when work badges were made for each of the employees. Sheila has organised the images for Max by worksite. She opens up a file labelled Workshop B. About eighty-five images come up on the screen, with names under each photo. Next to many of the names is some piece of personal information. Max begins scanning through the images and then points at a photo of a man. Under the image it reads, *Martin White, Engineer. Supports Liverpool FA. Wife pregnant.*

"Did Martin's wife have the baby?"

"Yeah," says Sheila. "You gave him a bottle of scotch and a baby tula."

"What's a baby tula?"

"A baby sling – for carrying the kid around."

"Oh." Max nods and scans through more of the images. "Max," says Sheila, "you have more than eight hundred employees. I don't think they expect you to know all their names."

"You're right. They don't expect me to know all their names. Which is exactly why it's important that I do know all their names."

Max continues to scan the photos, making sure he is connecting faces with names correctly, while Sheila updates the information on Martin.

When Max is satisfied, he makes his way out the front door and along the main gates of the shipyard. He is surprised to see a couple of security guards holding a rough-looking young man by his arms. He approaches, working to recall the security guards' names.

"Hi, Ted... and is it... Mark?"

"Yes, Mr Henderson," they answer in unison.

Max looks at the man and guesses he's been sleeping rough for a while. "What's going on?"

"We found this guy in one of our sheds," says a guard. "Looks like he's been sleeping there. Trespassing. We've called the police. They're on the way."

Max looks the man over. He seems to be in his thirties, dishevelled, unshaven, cuts on his hands. "Why are you sleeping in a shed, son?" asks Max.

The man shrugs. "I've had some problems."

"Problems?" asks Max.

"Lost my job." The man looks at the ground. "Wife left me."

Max looks at his security guards. "I know you guys are doing your job, but I don't want to hand him over to the police. He's got enough problems."

"Okay, Mr Henderson," says one of the guards. "What do you want us to do with him?"

"I'll take care of it," says Max.

"Are you sure, Mr Henderson?"

"Yeah, it's fine." Max turns to the man. "Walk with me, okay?"

The guards release the man, who follows Max through the gates of the shipyard. Max walks with him down the street, towards the inner city. A police car passes them and Max looks over his shoulder. "Well, that was close," says Max.

The man looks at Max, a confused expression on his face. "Where are we going, sir?"

Max points up to the next block where three taxi cabs are waiting for fares. "Just there."

They stop when they reach the first taxi and Max looks at the man, squinting in the early morning glare.

"There's a homeless shelter on Kingston Road."

The man nods his head. "Thank you..." the man says, but he hesitates. "I drink," he says. "I can't stop."

Max pulls his wallet out and opens it. He holds one hundred pounds in bills out to the man, but the man just stares at the money. Max takes the man's dirty hand and pushes the bills into it. "You always have a choice," says Max. "Don't ever think that you don't have a choice." The man opens his mouth, but no words come out.

Max leans into the cab window. "Can you take my friend to the homeless shelter on Kingston Road please?"

"Sure," a voice says. Max hands the cabbie a twenty.

He looks the homeless man in the eye and offers his hand. The man shakes it and nods, a silent acknowledgement of gratitude in his eyes.

Max watches the taxi drive away and then makes his way back through the gates of his shipyard. Max enters Workshop A and then scans a medium-sized ferry called *The Amethyst*, which is up in dry dock. She's an older ship, and he helped out with blasting and painting a few weeks ago. He wonders why she's still up in dry-dock.

"Hey, Bobby," he calls out. A foreman walks over.

"Hi, Max."

"How's Richard doing in the ring – he had any more fights?"

"He fought a Scouser last Saturday. Knocked him out in the third round."

Max claps him on the shoulder. "You must be proud of that boy."

"Oh yeah." Max imagines the foreman is looking at his work overalls. Max points to the ferry. "How come she's still here?"

"The paint job is done but the owner asked us to check the valves on the diesel engine, so we did. I told him the whole engine needs an overhaul, but you know how they are. He says the engine don't need an overhaul – just sort the valves. So I says to him, come down and I'll show you myself. So he comes down and I explained everything. But he doesn't know shit about diesel engines, and you know how they are?"

"Is it the condenser?" asks Max.

"Condenser, heat exchanger, compressor. It all needs work. So he finally agrees to let me do a proper overhaul."

"That's good, Bobby. They hate to pay for a proper overhaul but when these older ferries conk out, you know just when that's gonna happen."

"Right in the middle of the English Channel."

"Exactly. Every time, right?" says Max.

"That's just what I said to him, Max. I said she's gonna conk out right in the middle of the English Channel, and how much is that gonna cost you?"

Max nods at him.

"Nice overalls," says the foreman, smiling.

"Oh, shut up," says Max, giving him a grin.

Max exits the workshop and walks across the dockyard. He stops between a couple of ships that are up in dry dock and reaches down to the ground. He runs his hands over dirt and gravel and then rubs his hands over the front of his overalls. Max walks into Workshop B, thinking about Sheila and feeling a little guilty about messing up his overalls.

Max scans the room. There are a few men and one woman inspecting the twenty-three-foot propeller, which is still in the casting mould. The woman is the yard's first female foreman and Max supported the promotion. He thought it was important. He reminds himself of the metal composition of the casting. Eighty per cent copper, nine per cent aluminium, four per cent nickel, four per cent iron, and one per cent zinc. You have to keep this stuff fresh in your mind or someday it will be gone. He walks up to them. "Hello Mark… Peter… Sharon… Steve."

"Hi, Max," they say, nearly in unison.

"Is she completely cool now?"

"She is," says the woman.

Max reaches out and feels the mould. "It's a good-looking job," he says. Max looks over at the two diggers equipped with drills. "We breaking the propeller out of the mould, then?"

"Just about to, Max," says the woman. She points at a digger. "You want to take a turn?"

"I don't know… I don't want to damage it."

"You won't hurt it," she says. "Just go slowly. I'll guide you."

Max nods and they walk toward one of the diggers.

CHAPTER 5

Max looks up from his office desk at the clock on the wall – 5:50 PM.
He thinks that he should probably go home, but he still has half a beer
in his glass and, besides, he doesn't want to go home. He takes another
sip and continues to stare at the images of *Jeanne d'Arc* on his computer.
Doing some further research had seemed like a good idea right about the
time that opening his first beer had seemed like a good idea. There were
three empty beer bottles on his desk, and he tries to remember how many
beers are left in his office fridge. He realises he is hungry, gets up from
the desk, and makes himself a plate of cheese and crackers.

Max has followed the developments of the great capital ships for
years, in part for business purposes, but mostly just because he likes
knowing what's happening. As he gazes at the image of *Jeanne d'Arc*
steaming at sea, it strikes him as just wrong that a ship like that would be
pulled into pieces, as if it had never existed.

Max takes another long sip of beer. Even though he'd followed the
carrier like other capital ships, Max hadn't looked into the detail until this
evening. She was a smaller version of America's flagship carrier at the
time, *The Enterprise*. But at eight hundred and fifty-eight feet, she was still
huge. She could take a complement of 1,950 men and as many as forty
aircraft. Ship-to-air missiles, eight twenty-millimetre cannons and, of
course, those two nuclear reactors which could drive her at twenty-seven
knots... forever. For Max, she had function *and* form. She was just so
beautiful to look at.

Max finishes his beer and wonders what to do. Without making a
decision, he opens his fridge and pours himself another beer. He sits
down and wonders if Hedvika has gone home. Normally, Max wouldn't
bother his lawyer at this time of day but the beer is warming his head and
making him feel like he needs to work his thoughts out with someone he
trusts. He punches her office prefix into his phone and asks her to come
down.

Ten minutes later, Hedvika enters the office, closes the door, and sits
opposite Max. She brushes her blond hair from her face and adjusts her
glasses. "Hi, Max. Gloria wanted me to thank you for the birthday gift.
She loves cashmere. How did you know?"

"Sheila knows everything, right?"

Hedvika had been with Gloria for several years now. Not many people knew Hedvika was a lesbian, but she been open with Max many years ago.

Hedvika notices the beer bottles. "Rough day at work, Max?"

"I'm okay. You can have a glass of wine, right?"

"Just a small one. I have to go to a dinner party later."

Max gets a bottle of Chardonnay from the fridge, pulls the cork and pours her a glass. She takes a sip and Max studies her chiselled features and full lips for a moment. She seems a little tired and Max feels bad dragging her in here at this time of day but he is sick of being alone with his thoughts.

"Can I talk to you about the Jeanne d'Arc?"

"That big carrier? Sure, if you like," says Hedvika, her Eastern European accent chipping at the vowels.

"I know it seems like a ridiculous proposition," says Max, "but I just can't stop thinking about her. She's such a beauty. And I don't see why we need to see her as old, you know? I mean, hell, nuclear propulsion can drive a ship forever, theoretically."

Hedvika takes a sip of wine, her eyebrows coming together in a state of confusion. "Max, I'm sure *Joan of Arc* is a nice ship, but what are you saying?"

"Well, I'm just thinking, maybe we could help the French after all. They want to get rid of *Jeanne d'Arc*, and maybe it would be nice to have her."

"What do you mean *nice to have her*?"

"You know, look after her. Maybe sort her out. I don't think she needs breaking apart. I think she's got a lot of life left in her. Can you imagine what it would be like to tour a ship like her?"

"Not really, Max, because I don't know anything about nuclear aircraft carriers. Besides..."

"Look at this," says Max. He turns his laptop around so Hedvika can have a look at the photo. The image shows the inside of the carrier's bridge. Hedvika leans forward and scans the photo. The bridge is large with several leather seats, banks of sophisticated-looking equipment, and windows all around. It reminds her of the bridge on the Starship Enterprise.

"Okay, Max, that's impressive. But I don't understand. I mean, where are you going with this? Like we said in the meeting, the only conceivable commercial interest in this project would mean breaking the ship down. And even that doesn't make sense for us."

Max looks down at his hands for a moment, thinking. He gets up from his chair and looks into space, and then back at his lawyer. "Hedvika, haven't you ever just wanted something. Y'know?"

"Well sure, Max. I'd like a new car right now. I'm doing some test drives. I think I might get something sporty."

"Okay," says Max. "Forget about Henderson Nautical Works accepting *Jeanne d'Arc*. Forget about breaking her down. What if I accepted her? The French would love to just give her away, right? What if *Jeanne d'Arc* was sort of like... a personal project?"

Hedvika stares at Max for a moment, too stunned to reply. "Max," she says finally, "repairing old watches is a personal project... coin collecting is a personal project. Nuclear carriers are not really a personal project."

"Why not?"

"Because..." says Hedvika. She stares into space. "Max, I don't even know where to begin. For one thing, our government is not going to give you permission to take possession of this carrier."

"Really? Let me ask you this. Who says we need permission from the government? Ships are dropped off here all the time. Huge ships. We don't ask the government for permission."

"Max, this is a capital warship. It's different."

"You know something, Hedvika? The French want this beautiful ship broken into pieces. And I just feel like there is something else... something..." Max seems to lose his way. "I don't know. Just something."

Max slumps down into his chair and takes a large swig of beer. Hedvika stares at him, trying to read his expression. "Max, we've known each other a long time, right? Is something wrong?"

"No, I'm fine," says Max. "I wish people would stop asking me that."

They are silent for a couple of minutes, Max drinking his beer, Hedvika sipping wine and trying to organise her thoughts. "Max, I can see this is important for some reason, but it *is* crazy, and here's why. A private British citizen cannot hold a standing army. The government doesn't allow for this. We haven't had a civil war in a while, but when Britain has civil wars, they are bad. Very bad."

Max looks up at his lawyer. "Hedvika, it's not a standing army. It's a boat."

Unable to help herself, Hedvika laughs, and she is relieved when Max smiles. "Max, *Joan of Arc* is not a boat – it's a nuclear-powered warship."

Max sips his beer and then raises his glass. "Semantics, Hedvika, semantics."

"That's not how the government will see it."

Max gazes at Hedvika for a long moment. "Well… fuck 'em" he says.

Hedvika laughs but feels uneasy, and she suddenly isn't sure she knows Max as well as she imagined. They are quiet for a few moments. Max notices that Hedvika's wine glass is empty. "I'm sorry to keep you, Hedvika. You need to go to your party."

Hedvika walks to the door and looks back at Max. He seems sad, and she doesn't like to see him like this. "Max, if you really want me to look into this, I will."

Max nods. "I'd appreciate that, Hedvika."

"Max, maybe this is something we should just keep between us, you know? I mean, if you need to talk with Dom or Sheila, okay, but otherwise… yeah?"

"Sure," says Max.

CHAPTER 6

It was right about the time that Max was having this conversation with Hedvika, that I was getting involved with the story of *Joan of Arc*. I was working for *Britain Today*, a national paper, but I had only just finished my journalism degree, so none of the editors were letting me near the bigger stories. It's hard to believe it now, but at that time the story of a French warship no one wanted was getting very little interest in Britain. But it was a story they let me have. I remember the words of my editor to this day: *There's a carrier the French want to get rid of. You can have that if you want.*

I made a trip to the naval port of Cherbourg to get a look at *Joan of Arc*. There, I'd spoken to protesting students and listened to their theories of how the carrier was contaminated by nuclear material. I'd spoken to French authorities who said that this was nonsense. I'd asked everybody I could talk to about what the French Government was going to do, and whether they were trying to get the British involved. Everyone had an opinion, but no one seemed to know anything for sure. All of this was apparently so dull, my editor gave me six lines on page ten of our paper.

But I got a small break when I returned from Cherbourg to my office in London. I knew a secretary who worked for ASB Nautical Systems, Britain's largest shipyard. She called me and said that the French had asked ASB to take *Jeanne d'Arc*, and ASB had refused. So we knew the French *were* trying to unload the carrier on a British firm. This got me about eight lines on page six of the paper, but it also gave me an idea. The only other British yard capable of handling the carrier was Henderson Nautical Works. I phoned and got as high up the food chain as Max Henderson's PA, Sheila, who said she didn't know anything about it. She wouldn't put me through to Max, and I had the feeling she was 'playing dumb'. So I got up at 5:00 AM the next morning, put on my best skirt and jacket, and drove down to Portsmouth. At 7:00 AM I was standing at the gates of Henderson Nautical Works, coffee in hand, waiting for the chance to speak with Max (as I've said).

The employees coming to work had been well-coached about dealing with reporters and they probably didn't know anything, so I was getting nowhere with them. And then, at 8:45 AM, I spotted Maxwell Henderson. I'd committed his face to memory from photos I'd found. He was walking with this big guy, who I later learned was Dominique Delfino. It was odd seeing those two together because Dom wore this sharp suit whereas Max's suit was wrinkled, his trousers were too short and he wore tennis shoes, which looked very odd. Unless you knew better, you would mistake Dom for the owner. I stepped forward as they approached.

"Good morning, Mr Henderson – my name is Liz Burton. I'm a journalist with *Britain Today*. Can I have one minute of your time, please?" I hold my badge up for them to see.

Dom steps between Max and I and takes Max by the arm. He's whispering into Max's ear and is guiding Max away from me, but Max stops. "It's okay, Dom," he says.

"Liz Burton, you say," says Max, and he offers me his hand, which I shake. "When Dom and I were driving in, security told us there was a young woman who had been standing at the gate since early this morning. I guess that's you."

"Yes, Mr Henderson."

"So, what's so important?" he said.

"I'm covering *Jeanne d'Arc*. I've been to the naval port at Cherbourg, and she's a real problem for the French. I've had a report that ASB Nautical Systems has turned down the carrier. Can I ask, sir, have the French approached Henderson Nautical Works?"

I noticed Dom's hand move up Max's arm. Max studies my face. "Tell me something, Liz," said Max. "How close did you get to *Jeanne d'Arc*?"

"You can't get that close, but with a pair of binoculars, you can get a good look at most of the ships."

"And what did you think?"

"She's impressive. Huge. No planes on the decks, but she's a beautiful ship."

Max smiled at me and nodded, and I was going to ask my question again when Dom spoke.

"I'm sorry, but Mr Henderson is going to be late for a meeting." He tightened his grip on Max's arm and ushered him towards the gate.

"But Mr Henderson..."

At the gate Max turned and looked back at me. "It's Liz Burton, you said?"

"Yes. Mr Henderson..."

But Dom ushered him along and the conversation was over. He did give me a wave and I felt I'd made a connection, even then. I didn't have anything they would let me print, but as I drove back to London I was sure there was a story. Of course, I had no idea how right I was.

CHAPTER 7

Max and Sheila sit in front of Max's computer. Max receives, on average, two hundred and twenty emails a day, so part of Sheila's job is to screen and prioritise each and every one. Once a day they sit together and talk through the ones Max needs to deal with personally.

Sheila points to an email from the Head of Accounts. "Pontus Cargo is six weeks behind on payment for the repairs we made to one of their ships last quarter. Accounts has written to Pontus Cargo and left messages, but they're not paying up. We're doing repairs at the moment to *The Leviathan*. Accounts think we need to do something about this. Like we should threaten to stop work on *The Leviathan*."

Max shakes his head. "No. I don't wanna do that. The cargo industry is good at the moment. Pontus Cargo is owned by Richard Ambrose, but his son is running things these days. Richard always paid his bills on time, so something isn't right. Set up a call with Richard. I'll sort this out."

"Okay," Sheila says, making a note on a pad of paper.

Sheila points to the next email and opens her mouth, but there is a knock on the door. "Come in," says Max.

Dom enters and closes the door. "Excuse me, guys, but I need to speak with Max."

"Sorry, Sheila," says Max. "I'll give you a shout when we're done."

Sheila leaves and closes the office door, and Dom looks at Max. "Sorry to disturb you, boss."

"Are you kidding? I'm dying in here. What have you got?"

"I found your son."

Max takes a deep breath and blows it out. "Is Peter okay?"

"Pretty much. He's well out of it right now but he seems alright."

"Where is he?" asks Max.

"He's in my office."

"Your office?"

"You said to bring him to you, right?" says Dom.

"Yeah, I did. But you can't leave him alone, Dom. He'll just run off again."

Dom smiles. "Trust me – he's not going anywhere right now."

They walk down the hall together and then enter Dom's office. They stand and stare at Peter, who is sitting in Dom's desk chair, his right wrist handcuffed to a large desk drawer. His head has fallen back, his eyes are closed, his mouth open, and he appears to be asleep. Max moves closer and inspects his son. Peter's face carries a scraggly beard and there are cuts and bruises on a cheek and forehead. At twenty-four, he is handsome, despite his dishevelled appearance.

Max shakes his son's arm. Peter grunts and opens his eyes. "Peter, wake up."

Peter makes an effort to focus. "Dad?"

"Yeah, it's me Peter."

His son shakes his head groggily and looks down at the desk. "I'm sorry, Dad. I fucked up again. I really fucked up."

Max holds his son's chin and pulls his head up so they look at one another. "Jesus, Peter, look at you. You smell like a toilet."

"I know."

"Your face is all messed up. What happened?" asks Max.

Peter shakes his head slowly. "I don't know, Dad."

Max feels his son's shoulders. "You've lost weight. You were looking better in rehab."

Peter tries to raise his arms, but the one which is handcuffed to the desk catches. "Ow," he says, looking down at his wrist. Peter gazes at his dad. "I'm handcuffed? How did that happen?"

Max glances over at Dom. Dom pulls some keys out of his pocket and removes the handcuffs, which he slips into his pocket.

Max leans closer. "Peter, what the hell am I supposed to do with you? I thought maybe this time was it. Maybe my son would be dead."

Peter looks down at the table, long greasy hair hanging over his face. He's shaking his head slowly, and then Max and Dom begin to hear sobs. Max puts his hand under Peter's chin and holds his face up. Peter's eyes are closed tight in an expression of anguish, and tears are running down both cheeks. Max looks over at Dom, who shrugs.

"Oh hell," says Max, and he pulls his son into him and hugs him tightly. Peter continues to sob and Max holds him for another couple of minutes. The sobs subside and Peter just looks down at the table. "Just give us a minute, Peter," says Max. He moves to the door, motioning to Dom.

They walk down the corridor and stop. "I don't know what to do. What do you think, Dom?"

"I don't know, boss. Sometimes I think he needs a good kicking."

Max shakes his head. "He's sick, Dom. It's a real sickness, y'know?"

"Yeah. Sorry, boss. It's just that I see how frustrating it is. Should I take him back to rehab?"

"He's been there three times. He gets better, he puts on weight, and then he's back on that shit. It doesn't work. When I visit Peter in rehab, y'know what they're doing? Those junkies are sitting around in their pyjamas playing cards. Or some fucking board game, maybe. It's pathetic." Max gazes at Dom. "Peter needs a job. Something to do. Let's put him to work."

"But what can he do?"

"I don't know – sweeping up, taking the rubbish out, painting. There's plenty of shit needs doing around here."

"But won't he just run off, boss?"

"You're security, Dom. Figure something out. I don't care. Tie him to a goddamn anchor if you need to."

Dom laughs. "Okay, so I figure out some way of making him stay put. But what about the medical side of things. He's been back on the gear for a couple of weeks now, right? I think he's supposed to have medical help. I'm sure you can't just come straight off H."

Max stares at the ground, thinking. "Dom, keep an eye on Peter for a minute."

Max sticks his head into his PA's office. "Sheila, can you call that Occupational Health physician we got. Dr Tucker, right? Can you tell him to come down to Dom's office? Tell him it's important, okay?"

"Sure, Max," says Sheila.

Max enters Dom's office and they stare at Peter for a while, who has fallen asleep again with his face resting on his arms. Ten minutes later, Dr Tucker knocks on the door, and they let him in. Max shakes his hand and introduces Dr Tucker to Dom.

"How can I help, Mr Henderson?" says Dr Tucker.

Max points at Peter. "This is my son, Peter. He's a heroin addict. He was clean for a while and in rehab, but he left rehab a couple of weeks ago and he's been using again. So, he's gonna need medical help, right?"

"Well, yes. Will he be returning to a rehab centre?"

"Nah," says Max. "I'm fed up with those places. We're going to hire Peter, so he'll be working for us. He's just going to need a bit of medical support to help him along."

Dom can't help grinning at the expression of surprise on Dr Tucker's face. "He's going to work for Henderson Nautical Works?" the doctor asks.

"Sure," says Max. The doctor looks down at Peter, seeming to inspect him. There is a viscous string of drool hanging from Peter's open mouth.

"I don't know if he's fit for work, sir."

"Well, Peter's normally more dynamic than this. He's just a little tired right now. So what do we do, Dr Tucker?"

Dr Tucker looks at Max and then Dom. Dom shrugs, and grins. "Well," says Dr Tucker, "I'm not an expert on managing heroin withdrawal, but he will need to be put on an opioid agonist such as methadone to help him come off heroin safely. But, even if Peter is an employee of ours, I don't write prescriptions for that. I can only advise his GP, who would provide medical care."

Max moves close to Dr Tucker and then puts his hands on the doctor's arms. "That's a real relief for me, Dr Tucker. I'm very grateful for your help."

"Um, well… okay. Of course, I'll need to assess your son. And I can't assess him until he's properly employed."

"Of course," says Max. Max looks over at Dom. "Take Peter down to Human Resources and get him employed, okay. Then take him over to Occupational Health so he can see Dr Tucker."

"Okay, boss."

"Um, Mr Henderson," says the doctor. "My schedule is completely full this afternoon."

Max takes a step forward and smiles at the doctor. He puts a hand on Peter's shoulder. "Dr Tucker. I love my son very much. Are you a father?"

"Yes, Mr Henderson. I have two girls – about Peter's age."

"Then you know, right?"

Dr Henderson nods. "Okay, Mr Henderson." He looks over at Dom. "Bring along the paperwork from HR with you as well, okay? And, after I see him, he's going to need to see his GP either later today or tomorrow morning. Withdrawal symptoms begin six to twelve hours after the last fix, and they get worse over the next few days. He needs to start medication soon. Also, he won't be signed as fit to work for at least a week."

Max moves a step closer to the doctor, smiles, and offers him his hand.

Dom sits next to Peter in the Human Resources waiting room. Dom is

33

paging through a copy of Elle magazine because it was either that or something even less appealing. He looks over at Peter, whose eyes are half-closed, greasy hair hanging over his unshaven face. "Hey," says Dom, elbowing Peter. "Brighten up, yeah?"

Peter looks over, groggy. "What are we doing here, Dom?"

"Are you kidding me? This is your big moment. You got an important job interview in a few minutes."

"What? Why?"

Dom takes a more careful look at him – the scraggy beard growth, cuts and bruises and dried blood on his face, the greasy uncombed hair and, of course, the drool. Dom smiles and points at an article in the magazine. "Maybe you should give this a read."

The title of the article is *The 10-minute beauty trick that transforms your look*. Peter looks confused. Dom stands up, takes Peter under both arms, lifts him out of his chair, and ushers him into a nearby toilet. Dom locks the door and then runs water over some paper towel. He washes Peter's face with the towel, scrubbing hard to remove blood, grime, and drool. He then runs the tap. Dom cups his hands and fills them with water, and then runs his hands through Peter's hair. He dries Peter's face with another towel and turns him so he is facing the mirror. Peter smiles dopily.

"Right," says Dom. "Y'know what that was?"

"What?" says Peter.

"That was the two-minute beauty trick that transforms your look."

"Okay," says Peter. "Am I really getting a job?"

"It seems so," says Dom.

"Does that mean I don't have to go back to rehab?"

"Probably – as long as you don't fuck-up. Right?"

"Okay," says Peter. "I don't wanna go back to rehab."

When they emerge from the toilet there is a formally dressed female HR officer standing in the waiting room, looking around. "Here's your candidate," says Dom, and he ushers Peter past the young woman and into her office.

The young woman sits down behind her desk and gazes from one to the other. Peter's head bobbles on his neck, Dom still holding him by the arm.

"I'm Suzanne Reeves, one of the HR officers."

"Nice to meet you," says Dom.

She looks over at Peter.

"Howdy," says Peter.

"I had a phone call from Sheila Taylor," she says. "Sheila told me Mr Henderson would like Peter to have a job and asked us to sort out a contract. But that's all I know. So, I'm just a little confused. I mean, what's the job?"

Dom leans forward, looks at the young woman, and claps his hand on Peter's shoulder. "You're not going to believe this Suzanne, but my boy Peter is going to be the new Director of Human Resources. I hear he's really gonna shake things up."

Suzanne's mouth drops open. "What?"

Dom laughs. "Come on, I'm kidding. Just give him a contract for anything. Something basic, though. Peter can start at the bottom."

"Okay," says Suzanne, looking relieved. "I could draw up one of our standard contracts for custodial staff."

Dom looks over at Peter. "How's that sound, Peter?"

"I don't know what that means."

"It's perfect – you're gonna love it," says Dom.

"Okay," says Peter.

Dom looks back to Suzanne. "So, is my boy hired?"

"Yes, you're hired Peter."

"Thanks," says Peter.

CHAPTER 8

Jean-Pierre Lavelle served with *Jeanne d'Arc* for twenty-two years of his naval career. He'd started out as a petty officer and had been promoted up the ranks until he was made ship's captain for the final three years of the carrier's service. When the government retired *Jeanne d'Arc*, he was sixty-seven and he retired with her. He had joked about *going down with his ship* and people laughed when he said that, but there was a sad truth behind the joke. That was four years ago, of course, and this morning he was sleeping off a hangover. He felt himself moving to and fro, and, half-asleep, he had the sensation that he was back at sea.

"Get up, Jean! You won't guess who is on the phone."

Jean-Pierre opens his eyes and sees that his wife is rolling him briskly by the arm.

"What? Leave me to sleep. I am half-dead."

"It's Barnard Roux," she says.

"Barnard? Chief of Staff for the Navy? Why didn't you say so?"

"I just did, Jean!"

Jean-Pierre grunts loudly, hefts his large form out of bed, and walks to the phone in the living room, still in his underpants. "Hello Barnard – Jean-Pierre here."

"Jean-Pierre. It's good to hear your voice. It's been too long. Is retirement suiting you?"

"Not really, sir. But it makes my doctor happy."

Barnard laughs. "Jean-Pierre, I'm going to be brief as I'm meant to be in a meeting. I know this is a sore point with you, but you are aware that we need to find a firm to break down *Jeanne d'Arc* and we'd rather it was done overseas. Secretary of State Dupont called me this morning. Max Henderson of Henderson Nautical Works has expressed interest. He would like a tour of *Jeanne d'Arc*. We thought you would be just the person to show him around."

Jean-Pierre is stunned by the suggestion. He had seen his old ship from the harbour several times but the thought of going back on board was difficult. "I'm not sure, sir. Perhaps one of your ministers would be better, or someone from the naval base. Someone less attached."

"Jean-Pierre, I know you have a lot of feeling for your ship. We will

THE EDGE OF THE WORLD

certainly send a minister, but I'd really like you to lead the tour. Of course we will compensate you for your time, but France needs your service in this regard. We know Max Henderson. His firm has worked on our ships more than once. He's a sentimental fellow. Secretary of State Dupont thinks you are just the person to meet with Max."

An image came into his mind and Jean-Pierre saw the bridge of his old ship clearly, his staff walking around or focusing on computer screens. The room seemed to spin slightly. "One moment, please... sir."

Jean-Pierre places the receiver against his pale belly and gazes out the living room window, filled with a vague sense of hesitancy. He still feels the weight of national duty, but what the hell – he was retired now. He puts the phone back to his ear. "Sir, I need to ask you. These reports about contamination in the press. What's going on?"

"Jean-Pierre, surely you've read the government's position? The reports are nonsense."

"I'm not asking about the government's position, sir – I'm asking you, Barnard."

"I'm telling you, these newspaper reports are total rubbish. Some undergraduate student from the University of Paris-Sud claimed to get into Cherbourg's naval base with a Geiger counter, and this kid goes to the press with a story saying he detected higher than normal levels of radioactivity near *Jeanne d'Arc*. Of course, we do regular testing anyway but we had our best specialists do a thorough assessment and there are *no* leaks. Jean-Pierre – do you honestly think I would send you or anyone onto a ship with nuclear contamination?"

Jean-Pierre felt reassured. He didn't always trust government reports, but he was sure Barnard would not lie.

"The problem," continued Barnard, "is that this story and the student protests are accelerating things. I know you never agreed with the decommissioning of *Jeanne d'Arc*. I was on your side, if you recall. But we are well past that now and we have to find a solution."

Jean-Pierre still did not want this task, but his years of service and deference to the military chain of command got the better of him. Though unconscious of his movements, he stood straight and raised his vision. "Of course I will help, sir."

"Thank you, Jean-Pierre. And don't worry about having to deal with any difficult political questions. Our minister will be well-briefed on all that. Oh, and one other thing. We thought it might be a good idea if you met Max in your captain's uniform. We thought it would give the event some gravitas. I assume you still have your uniform?"

"I do, sir. It's in the closet." Jean-Pierre looks down at his protruding and naked belly. "I don't think the trousers will fit, sir."

The Chief of Staff laughs. "Don't worry – I will send a tailor over."

"Good idea, sir. When is Max Henderson coming?"

"Day after tomorrow. He'll be with you about 4 PM. We'll send a security detail to pick you up at home. Max is coming over on the ferry, so you'll meet him at the crossing point."

Jean-Pierre reflects for a moment. "Sir, would you have any objection if one or two of my old crewmates joined us? I'm thinking of my engineer and aeronautics chief. They may be able to answer any number of questions."

"Yes, yes. Perfect. Max Henderson will love that. Are they retired now?"

"Yes, sir."

"See if you can get them back into their uniforms as well, okay?"

"I'll see what I can do, sir."

"Jean-Pierre – *Jeanne d'Arc* was a great ship, and you were the finest of her captains. There is a place in French history for both of you."

"Yes, sir," replied Jean-Pierre.

Jean-Pierre was pleased with the Navy Chief's words, though he had no idea how true they would become.

CHAPTER 9

Max and Dom stand together on the starboard side of the top deck of a Brittany Ferries' ship called the *Barfleur*. Dom had driven them from Portsmouth to the ferry at Poole. He'd parked his BMW at Poole, and they had walked onto the *Barfleur* together at 2 PM. Dom hands Max a tuna fish and cucumber sandwich he's just purchased from the galley.

"Cheers, Dom."

Dom nods, and they stare together at the port of Cherbourg, inhaling the salt air and listening to the low rumble of the engines and the seagulls crying. The ferry is five hundred metres out and is slowly manoeuvring itself into position for docking.

Max points towards the stern of the ship. "Did I tell you we replaced the rudders on the *Barfleur* a few years ago? We found air bubbles in the metalwork of the original rudders. Had to make new ones for her from scratch."

"No, boss, I didn't know that," says Dom, forcing a smile onto his face. Dom is feeling irritated with Max because they had covered a lot of topics in the car and on the ferry, but Max hadn't told him much about what they were doing. Dom liked knowing what he was walking into and so their discussions about current news, sports and work gossip left him a little cold. Seeing as they were about to arrive at Cherbourg, this really didn't seem like the time to talk about rudders.

"Boss, can we talk more about what we're doing here? I'm just not clear on what the plan is."

"Sure, Dom. The French are going to give us a tour of *Jeanne d'Arc*. This is really an amazing opportunity. Not many civilians have ever been on board."

"You said that, boss, but we turned down the work on this ship, right? I just don't get why we're here."

Max is standing on his toes and gazing into the distance, directly off the starboard side. "I can't see her," says Max.

"What's that, boss?"

"Cherbourg harbour," says Max, "is segregated into commercial and naval." He points straight ahead. Where we're docking – that's all commercial. The ferry, shipping, and pleasure boats." Max points off the starboard side. "There are docking stations over that way for the navy, but I can't see *Jeanne d'Arc.*"

Dom straightens his tie. It doesn't need straightening but it's a gesture he does out of habit to displace his frustration. "But who are we meeting?"

Max pulls a small notepad from his pocket and puts his glasses on. "Captain Jean-Pierre Lavelle, Chief Engineer Alexis Girard, Chief of Aeronautics Hugo Dubois, and some Minister of Naval Communications."

Dom scratches his head. "I don't get it. I thought the ship was decommissioned."

"It was," says Max. "I think they got some of the old crew together. It's a nice idea, don't you think?"

Max is looking at the landing the ferry is heading for. About fifty or so people are standing on the large pier, probably waiting to receive family or friends. Max leans over the railing, removes his glasses, and squints. "Dom, have you got those binoculars?" Dom pulls out a compact set of binoculars from a shoulder bag and hands them to Max, who holds them to his eyes. Max begins to chuckle. "Well, would you look at that!" he says.

He hands the binoculars to Dom. "Focus on the middle of that group of people on the pier, right at the front. There are three officers in full naval dress. Lots of shiny buttons – you can't miss them."

Dom holds the binoculars to his eyes and finds the men easily. They wear blue naval uniforms with rows of gleaming brass buttons up the front, and white caps with gold naval embroidery. They look pretty old, and the one in the middle is very overweight. There are two men and a woman who are clearly flanking the officers. They wear dark suits, sunglasses and earpieces. "Yeah, I see the navy officers. There's a security detail of three with them," says Dom.

"Well, we're visiting a French military shipyard – I don't think that's surprising."

This is a stupid waste of time, Dom thinks. "Boss, I just don't get…"

Max turns and rests a hand against one of Dom's large biceps. "Hey, when's the last time you had a holiday?"

Dom shrugs. "I went to Venice a couple of years ago."

"Dom, just think of this as a little holiday, okay? You're gonna get a tour of the finest nuclear-powered aircraft carrier the French ever built. Enjoy yourself."

Dom sighs heavily. "Okay, boss."

The *Barfleur* begins to reverse and Max realises it's going to take at least twenty minutes for her to dock. "I need to give Hedvika a quick ring," he says. Dom nods and Max steps back a few feet and dials.

"Hello, Max," says Hedvika.

"Hi, Hedvika – is this an okay time to speak?"

"I've stepped out of a meeting, but they can wait."

"Y'know that conversation we had about *Jeanne d'Arc*? Just wondering what you learned?"

There is a pause on the line. "I've done some research, Max. What we're definitely talking about is private ownership of a vessel of war, and this ship isn't a landing craft or something like that. It's very complicated. I've had two law students helping me look into this. The short answer is that it's really a bad idea."

"Well, a lot of great things started out as bad ideas, right?"

Hedvika couldn't think of anything great that started out as a bad idea. "Like what, Max?"

"I don't know – penicillin?"

"Max – that doesn't make any sense."

"Hedvika, I know you. You don't leave any stones unturned – right? So, what have you got?"

Hedvika sighs heavily. "Max, if you want this ship there might be a way, but it involves some very difficult legal manoeuvring. As your lawyer, I might be able to make something work if I bend every legal precedent and make some arguments which probably don't even exist. But, as your friend, I really think this is a terrible idea. What I've discovered is complicated. Can we meet up?"

"Absolutely." The long guttural note of the ferry horn blows.

"Max, where are you?" asks Hedvika.

"I'm taking Dom on a short holiday. The man is a bag of stress. Anyway, you're busy. I'll let you go."

"Alright Max. Take care of yourself, okay?"

"Absolutely. And Hedvika – great work. I really mean that."

"No, Max. It's not great work. It really isn't. Let's speak soon, okay?"

41

CHAPTER 10

Dom leans against a wall a few feet down from the door to the Captain's Cabin. He checks his watch and makes a face – 9:45 PM. A burst of laughter comes from inside the cabin and someone bangs a table with a drinking glass, and someone else starts in on another story. Behind the door, Max and the three officers have been talking and joking for over an hour, and Dom's neck is feeling stiff. This tour of the *Joan of Arc* worries Dom, mainly because he just doesn't understand what Max is doing. These naval officers are all pretty old, maybe even retired, and here they are, all dressed up as if they are part of a veteran's day parade. There is another burst of laughter and something shouted in French, and then the sound of Max laughing.

Dom glances down the ship's corridor and scans the two men and single woman who make up the security detail. They are speaking in French, in low voices, and seem to be keeping an eye on him. Dom closes his eyes and images of the ship's tour come to him. He had to admit, *Joan of Arc* was impressive and in better shape than he'd imagined. Dom had a thing for high-performance cars, but the scale and engineering of a carrier like this was beyond comparison. Images of the tour drift through Dom's mind. They had walked the more than eight hundred feet of the flight deck with Captain Lavelle telling stories about scary landings. When they went down into the flight hangers, it was Hugo Dubois, Chief of Aeronautics, who led the discussion. The jet fighters were gone now, but he painted pictures of them and the pilots in a way that made it surprisingly easy to imagine. Although any nuclear fuel had been removed, it was the two nuclear power plants which really made an impression on Dom. The Chief Engineer, Alexis Girard, had walked them around the power plants and Dom had been impressed by the size and complexity of these engineering monsters. And as the tour had progressed, Max and the three officers fell into this rhythm of enthusiasm and shared affection, like old school friends who had not seen each other for years. Max seemed to respond to each new piece of information with questions which were so astute, you could tell that the officers were deeply impressed with his nautical knowledge. The only one not having fun seemed to be the government minister, who's name

Dom had forgotten.

Shouting comes from beyond the cabin door, and Dom feels a sting of anxiety and leans closer. There follows a howl of laughter coming from all of them and the sound of clinking glasses, and he realises this is a friendly argument. Dom looks down the corridor and can tell that the security detail had taken notice as well, but seemed relaxed. He decides that Max's party is not going to end soon, and he feels a little bored.

He adjusts his tie, walks down the corridor, and looks the security team over, sizing them up. Where they are standing, the passage opens up into a larger space where two other corridors join. One of the men is tall and lanky, the other short and fidgety, and the woman seems distracted and bored. They have taken their earpieces out, which makes sense as they are all standing next to one another.

"So, is it true what they say about French tanks?" says Dom.

"What do they say?" says the tall officer.

Dom offers them a grin. "That they only have one gear – reverse."

The tall officer frowns and the two others look confused. "Is it true what they say about British footballers?" the tall officer says.

"Yeah, what's that?" asks Dom.

"That they only have one gear – shit."

Dom laughs and points a finger at the officer. "Good one."

A burst of laughter is heard from down the hallway and Dom looks back in that direction. He then reaches into his jacket vest pocket and pulls out a deck of cards. "Okay, we got the insults out of the way. It might be a long night. Let's play some cards."

"What can we play?" says the tall man.

"There are four of us. Do you know how to play Euchre?"

"Are you joking for me?" the officer says. "The French invented Euchre. It comes from Alsace."

"Wonderful," says Dom. "Let's play."

The tall officer says something in French to the others and they reply. He then points to the short man and says, "He doesn't know how to play."

"Well, let's teach him."

The tall man seems uncertain and looks towards the Captain's Cabin. "We have to provide security."

Dom smiles broadly and points down the corridor. "Your officers and my boss are going to be drinking and telling stories for hours. The biggest risk they are facing is a hangover. Let's get a table from somewhere and set it up here – we can still keep an ear out for those nutcases."

On the other side of the cabin door, Max sits on a comfortable leather couch next to Alexis Girard, the Chief Engineer. Captain Jean-Pierre Lavelle and Chief of Aeronautics Hugo Dubois sit in armchairs opposite, a polished oak coffee table between them. Jean-Pierre is telling another story about *Jeanne d'Arc* and, for some reason, Max cannot stop smiling. Max glances around the interior of the Captain's Cabin, absorbing the moment. He notices the oak-panelled walls and bookcase, the captain's polished desk, a framed painting of some French admiral he doesn't recognise, and the small kitchen. It's like an expensive metropolitan apartment, except smaller and more… naval.

Engineer Alexis had made the meal himself, a creamy Chicken Dijon. The dinner plates now cleared away, the officers drink red wine and Max has a beer. A series of wine corks are popped and several bottles of cold beer have been plunked down on the table in front of Max without a word said. Max loses track of time, his vision glazes, and he feels a kinship which seems strangely comfortable.

"… you know what the architects didn't consider when they designed *Jeanne d'Arc*?" asks Engineer Alexis.

"Sex," replies Chief of Aeronautics Hugo Dubois. The officers laugh and so does Max, though he isn't sure what he's laughing about.

"What?" says Max.

Jean-Pierre reaches across the table and claps Max on the shoulder. "Yes, seriously," says the Captain. "The bunks are so small that sex is almost impossible. The ship's designers assumed that all the men and women would forget about sex once they went to sea. Very silly, really."

"A big floating university dorm," says Hugo. "That's a carrier at sea. You put fourteen hundred young people in a boat for months on end and they are going to end up having sex all over this ship – supply closets, maintenance spaces… Do you remember that navigation officer?"

Jean-Pierre and Alexis laugh in recognition. "What happened?" asks Max.

"A navigation officer had sex with one of the infirmary nurses in a ventilation junction," says Hugo. "They got locked in there and tried to find their way out through the ship's ventilation system but got hopelessly lost. They ended up banging on the aluminium walls and we had to send a rescue team in to get them." Hugo claps his hands and laughs. "Don't you love it? A navigation officer got lost inside his own ship."

They all laugh and Hugo looks over at Captain Jean-Pierre. "You were a little lax, Captain."

Jean-Pierre raises his wine glass. "Of course I was lax! If you are lazy or make a stupid mistake then you get disciplined, but you can have as much sex as you want on my ship as long as I don't have to watch."

The officers laugh and Max smiles. He likes these men. He likes the stories they tell and how much they know and care about the ship. Hugo's knowledge of carrier jets was extraordinary, and Max had soaked in every word of explanation the aeronautical chief had offered. Even more interesting had been the explanation of the ship's nuclear propulsion systems provided by Alexis, and Max had asked the engineer every question he could think of. It is clear that these three officers have been good friends as well as shipmates. Time slips past, wine and beer go down, and the evening feels easy. Max wonders when the evening will end, and he and Dom will be driven to a nearby hotel, but no one seems in any rush to get off to bed.

Jean-Pierre begins to tell a story about when *Jeanne d'Arc* had been off the coast of Libya supporting a no-fly zone. Max gets a sense of the story – something about the difficulties of landing one of the planes, but his vision is watery and he is aware of this pleasant and unreal sense of the moment. He is up late and drinking onboard a graceful and powerful aircraft carrier with the Captain, the Chief of Aeronautics, and the Chief Engineer. There is seemingly no end to the stories being told or the descriptions of technical facts and engineering processes. And... Max feels happy, and he knows suddenly that this is something he has not felt for a long while.

CHAPTER 11

Prime Minister Margaret Williams squints and tries to follow what the Work & Pensions Secretary is saying. The man seems to be suggesting that they should rename the benefits categories that are in use, but Margaret can't understand why this would make any practical difference. She checks her watch and notices that the Tuesday morning cabinet meeting has been going for almost an hour. Margaret wants to wrap things up, get her weekly meeting with the Queen out of the way, and deal with some really pressing issues. Her gaze softens, the minister's words fade into the background, and she discovers that she is observing the interior of the room. Margaret's twenty-two cabinet ministers are crammed together at the long table with piles of paperwork strewn around them. Like all the rooms at 10 Downing Street, the interior is sumptuous and well-appointed, but it always feels like an uncomfortable dinner party. It occurs to her that the Americans would never put up with a setting like this.

The Northern Ireland and Scottish Secretaries simultaneously begin objecting to the suggestions concerning benefits categories, and Margaret is just about to interrupt them when she notices an aide enter the room and make her way over to the Defence Secretary, Ronald Hudd. This is unusual, so Margaret has to wonder what's going on as she watches the aide whisper into Ronald's ear while handing him a report. Ronald scans the report, and then Margaret makes out the single word which he utters in disbelief. *"What?"* Ronald is normally a pretty cool customer, so when he looks worried, Margaret feels worried.

"Excuse me," said Margaret. She looks over at the Work & Pensions Secretary. "It seems clear that your ideas need consideration. Can you do some further work in the subcommittee and liaise with your colleagues in Northern Ireland, Scotland and Wales, and bring this back." She looks over at her Defence Secretary. "Ronald, is there a problem?"

"Prime Minister," he says, still gazing down at the report. "I've just received some very surprising news. Apparently, *Joan of Arc*, the French nuclear aircraft carrier, is two miles off Portsmouth Harbour."

"Oh," says Margaret. "There's a shipyard at Portsmouth. Are they doing repairs on the ship?"

"No," says Ronald, "that's not possible. *Joan of Arc* was fully decommissioned by the French. There are even reports that she may be contaminated, but the French deny this. It's not possible that *Joan of Arc* would be in one of our shipyards for repairs or upgrades. The French have no interest in recommissioning her. What's more possible is that she's here to be broken down, but that would require British-French liaison and official approval."

Margaret is feeling as perplexed as she is annoyed. She pushes herself out of her chair, places her hands on the table, and looks down at the array of befuddled expressions. "Hold on a moment," says Margaret. "Are you telling me the French didn't communicate anything about this?"

"No, Prime Minister," says Ronald. "This is the first I've heard about it."

Margaret looks over at the Foreign Secretary. "Susan?"

"I've heard nothing from the French about this," says Susan.

"Well, what about our own security agencies?" says Margaret. "How can a French nuclear aircraft carrier wander across the English Channel without us knowing? We've got satellite and radar facilities covering every inch of the Channel."

Ronald gazes down at the report for a moment before responding. "I'm very sorry, Prime Minister. There were a number of large cargo vessels in the channel last night – apparently, we mistook *Joan of Arc* for one of those vessels."

"Alright... never mind," says Margaret. "The shipyard at Portsmouth – what's it called?"

"Henderson Nautical Works," says Ronald. "It's owned by Max Henderson."

"Well," says Margaret, "we can't have nuclear-powered war ships parading into British ports without knowing what the hell is going on. Is this a security risk?"

"I don't know, Prime Minister," says Ronald. "The French are allies, of course, but I need to know more."

"Well," says Margaret, "you're right, we need more information. At best, this is embarrassing."

"Prime Minister," says Ronald, "I think we need to get Secretary of State Philipe Dupont on the phone. He must know what's going on, and he really has some explaining to do."

Margaret turns to the Home Secretary, Jared Philcox. "Jared, this...

ship is now in territorial waters. It's a matter for your office as well. What do you think?"

"I think Ronald is right. Let's get Dupont on the phone. We need to understand what the hell is happening before we can respond."

"Okay," says Margaret. She turns to her administrator. "Make the call, please, and use a secure line."

The administrator begins punching numbers into a conference phone.

"What's this about contamination?" the Environmental Secretary says.

"*Joan of Arc* is a problem for the French," says the Foreign Secretary. "There have been student protests at Cherbourg Harbour and claims of nuclear contamination, but the French authorities strongly dispute this."

"Well, that's just wonderful," says Margaret. The phone can be heard ringing when something occurs to the Prime Minister. "Is the carrier under its own power?" she asks.

"No, no," says Ronald. "She's being pulled over by tugs."

"Hello, Office of the Secretary of State," says a female voice speaking English with a French accent.

"This is UK Prime Minister Margaret Williams. Our cabinet is currently in session and we need to speak with Secretary of State Dupont urgently. It's a matter of national security."

"Oh, I'm sorry, Prime Minister. Mr Dupont is not at work today."

Margaret sighs and grits her teeth. "I wouldn't normally interrupt Mr Dupont, but the matter is time-sensitive and we really need to speak with him."

"Yes, Prime Minister. I will try to reach Mr Dupont. He's... how do you say...? Jouer au golf."

Margaret looks over at her Foreign Secretary and raises both hands.

"He's golfing, Prime Minister," the Foreign Secretary says.

"Delightful," says Margaret, gazing down at the speakerphone. "Yes, can you please connect us to Mr Dupont."

A moment of strained silence passes, and then a cheery French voice comes through. "Hello, Prime Minister – Philipe Dupont here."

"Hello, Secretary of State," says Margaret. "I'm in session with the cabinet and you're on speakerphone. I'm sorry to interrupt your golf session, but I'm afraid it's an urgent matter. I've been informed that *Joan of Arc* is two miles off Portsmouth. We've had no communication from your side. Can you please tell us what's going on?"

"Oh, *Jeanne d'Arc*. Yes, I did hear something about that."

There is a pause and the sound of French birds and a water sprinkler. "Mr Dupont," continues Margaret, "our understanding is that the ship has been decommissioned, so we assume she is not here for repairs or upgrades. We didn't know anything about this. What's going on?"

"Yes, yes, *Jeanne d'Arc*," says Dupont. "As I understand it, Max Henderson got in touch with some of our people last week and expressed interest in visiting the ship, and um… well, Henderson Nautical has done work on several of our ships over the years and Max is apparently quite sentimental about capital ships. Anyway, we were happy to give him a tour of the carrier. As you say, she's decommissioned."

There is a pause on the line, French voices in the background, and the sound of a lawnmower. The Prime Minister raises her hands in mock disbelief and glances around at the faces, which are all turned to her. "Mr Dupont, this is all very interesting but it doesn't explain why a French nuclear carrier is currently heading into Portsmouth harbour."

"Oh, that?" says Dupont. "What they told me was that Max Henderson had expressed personal interest in *Jeanne d'Arc*."

"What?" says Margaret. "How do you mean personal interest?"

There are some French voices in the background shouting. "Prime Minister, I'm very sorry, but there's a party behind us that wants to play through. I'm all teed up. Can I just hit this one shot?"

The Prime Minister exhales painfully and shakes her head. "Of course, Mr Dupont."

A moment later there is the unmistakable swish of a club, the click of metal on ball, and then Dupont's voice. "Merde. Accroché!"

Margaret looks at her Foreign Minister and raises her eyebrows. "I think he hooked it, Prime Minister," she says.

Margaret sighs. "What a shame."

"My apologies, Prime Minister," says Dupont. "Now, where were we?"

"Mr Dupont," says Margaret, irritation in her tone, "we've got a French nuclear aircraft carrier arriving at a British port and we don't know anything about it. What the hell does this have to do with Max Henderson?"

"Ah yes, Max," says Dupont. "As I was saying, Max apparently expressed personal interest in *Jeanne d'Arc*. I understand that Max is very fond of capital ships and he really took an interest in the carrier. You know, we have a number of naval staff here who have a similar feeling. I don't know if you have seen *Jeanne d'Arc*, but she is a very beautiful ship with quite a history. At any rate, I understand that Max has taken personal possession of the carrier."

Margaret gazes at the speakerphone in disbelief. "Are you telling me, Mr Dupont, that you sold a decommissioned nuclear carrier to a British citizen?"

"Oh no, Prime Minister. It wasn't like that."

"Well, exactly how was it then?" says Margaret.

"Um, well… I think we gave it to him."

"You what?" says Margaret.

"You know, on reflection," says Dupont, "I can see how we probably should have discussed this with the British government, but to tell you the truth, I think the Navy just sorted out some paperwork, and…"

"Mr Dupont, you can't just give one of your carriers to a British citizen. Especially one that's… contaminated."

"Prime Minister, please! I can assure you that there is absolutely no contamination. These are ridiculous rumours. And… any nuclear fuel was removed as part of her decommissioning."

"Can she run on… conventional fuel?" asks Margaret.

"Well, yes," says Dupont.

"Well, look, Mr Dupont, the point is we can't have British citizens collecting aircraft carriers. Do you know how serious this is, Mr Dupont? Did it occur to the French that the British government might not want a decommissioned nuclear French carrier? I need to consider scrambling jets and dispatching destroyers, and your carelessness has put us in this position."

"Jets? Destroyers?" says Dupont. "Prime Minister, she's decommissioned… she's like, how would you say? Like war memorabilia. We thought it was lovely that Max took such an interest in French naval history. We saw it as a personal acquisition."

"A personal acquisition?" says Margaret. "Mr Dupont, we need to deal with a developing situation, but our respective governments will need to address this… this… incident."

"An incident?" says Dupont, a note of alarm in his voice.

"Yes, an incident. I think this really is an incident."

"But, Prime Minister…"

"Goodbye, Mr Dupont," says Margaret, signalling her assistant to end the call. The line goes dead and Margaret gazes around the table at her staff. "This is ridiculous. Okay, let's have some discussion. What do we do?"

There is a moment of silence as her cabinet members look at one another. Finally, it's the Culture Secretary who speaks, a grin on his face. "I wonder if the French accept returns?" No one laughs.

"Not a great time for jokes," says Margaret. "Come on – I want some discussion. What are our options?"

CHAPTER 12

I'm working from home when my mobile rings.

"Hello, Liz Burton here."

"Hi Liz, it's John, from the news desk. I know you've done a few pieces on that French aircraft carrier."

"What's happened?"

"There was a message left on our overnight answering machine. I haven't verified anything, but the call was from a crew member of a British fishing trawler off the south coast, and he said this massive aircraft carrier just went right past them. He said it looked like the carrier was heading for Portsmouth. That's Henderson Nautical Works, right?"

"Yeah, that's it. Who's the source?"

"The fisherman didn't give his name. He's probably just one of our readers, I think."

"Was the carrier being towed?"

"Yeah, he said it was being towed by tugs."

"How far off the coast were they when he called?"

"Sorry, Liz, he didn't say. The fisherman just said, *off the south coast and heading for Portsmouth*. But I had the impression they weren't far off."

"Thanks. I'm heading there now."

I throw on a skirt and a blouse that are lying on the floor, grab my ID, and make some cereal and milk which I plan to eat while driving. I think about showering but grab a stick of armpit juice instead. If I break a few traffic laws, I figure I can get to Portsmouth Harbour in maybe one hour forty minutes. As I climb into my Mini Cooper, I recall the brief exchange I'd had with Max Henderson at the gate of the shipyard, and I wonder if other journalists will beat me there.

CHAPTER 13

It's 9:15 AM and, by all appearances, the weekly Henderson Nautical Works staff meeting is proceeding as normal. Max sits at the head of the table, Sheila and Dom to his left, Hedvika his lawyer to his right, and ten board members are spread around the long varnished table. The Works Management Executive is giving an update on how several of the current projects are progressing and seems to be saying something about delays in the delivery of certain nautical parts.

"Sheila," says Max. "Can you remind me to call the wholesalers? I'll chase them about the delay."

"Sure, Max," Sheila replies. She watches Max closely. She is pleased that he is smiling easily and seems happy. Sheila wonders if it has something to do with his visit to France with Dom.

The Director of Project Acquisitions has been eyeing a tray of sugared jam doughnuts which is on a side table. He'd already had two, but there was a whole tray of the powdered things just sitting there. He pushes his plump form from the chair quietly, makes his way to the doughnuts and selects the largest one. Feeling some guilt, he turns and faces the conference table and the long plate glass window which looks down onto the estuary. The doughnut makes it almost to his mouth when he freezes. His eyes open wide and the doughnut hangs motionless in front of his gaping mouth. Sheila is the first to notice that something is wrong. She interrupts the Works Management Executive and looks at the plump man.

"You look like you're having a seizure. What's going on?"

Several eyes look up. The Director of Project Acquisitions raises his non-doughnut-holding hand and points a finger out the window. "I... I... but I thought..."

Most of the execs get up from their chairs and look down into the harbour, Max included.

Max claps his hands together. "Ah-ha, she's here. Look everyone, isn't she a beauty?"

There is a moment of silence, and Hedvika is the first to speak. "Max... what's happened?"

Joan of Arc moves very slowly down the estuary, two tugs pulling her from the front and two more tugs attached to her sides. The conference room windows begin to vibrate very slightly from the deep drone of the tug engines as they pull at the 42,500-ton iron behemoth.

"My god, it's huge," breathes the Head of Finance. She then points out the window. "Look, I think there's someone waving at us." The execs move closer to the window and peer at the carrier, sun glinting off her grey naval paint.

"Where?" asks Max.

"There's some people in uniforms high up on the… what do you call it?"

"Sheila," says Max, "are my binoculars handy?"

Sheila opens a drawer from a nearby bureau and then hands Max a pair of binoculars. Max holds the binoculars to his eyes and squints into the morning sunlight. "Ah, yes. It's Captain Jean-Pierre Lavelle." Max waves vigorously out the window. "There," says Max, "about three-quarters of the way up the main island there's a bridge with an external walkway. The Captain's there… and is that Chief Engineer Alexis Girard as well? Well, this is just splendid."

"But…" the Director of Project Acquisitions says, as he places his jam doughnut back on the plate, "that's *Joan of Arc*. I thought we decided to pass on that project."

"Yes, yes of course we did," said Max. "It's nothing to worry about. *Jeanne d'Arc* is a personal project."

"A what?" asks Sheila.

"Like a hobby," says Max. "We haven't used Bay 4 for ages. I'm just going to tuck *Jeanne d'Arc* away there for a while."

There is a knock at the conference room door and a moment later Sheila's assistant enters. "I'm so sorry to interrupt," the young woman says, her face flushed with concern. "It's just that… the Home Secretary is on the phone and he wants to speak with Mr Henderson. He says it's urgent."

"The Home Secretary?" says the Director of Finance. "As in, Jared Philcox, the Home Secretary?"

"Yes, that's what he said his name was," the young woman replies.

"The Home Secretary?" says Sheila. "Max, is everything okay?"

Max smiles broadly and looks his staff over. "Sheila, everything has never been better." He turns to the young woman. "I'm sure whatever it is can't be that urgent. Can you please tell the Home Secretary I'll give him a jingle just as soon as we finish our meeting?"

Max raises the binoculars to his eyes and gives the naval officers standing on the open-air bridge another vigorous wave. He turns to his staff. "Right then, Captain Lavelle knows where he's going. Let's get on with things."

Max sits down and his executives manage to pull their eyes from the gigantic carrier and slip back into their chairs. "Okay," says Sheila, turning to the Works Management Executive. "You were talking about delays in receiving parts."

The man opens his mouth to speak, but there is another knock on the door. Sheila's assistant enters again, her cheeks ruddy with colour. "I'm very sorry, but the Home Secretary says he's on his way here. He says he's thirty minutes away and that he needs to speak with Mr Henderson immediately on arrival." The young woman lowers her voice before continuing. "He said that he's accompanied by... by a substantial security contingent. I'm sure that's what he said."

The room fills with silence, and then Dom reaches over and places a hand on Max's forearm. "Boss..." Before he can continue, Hedvika interjects. "Max, I really need to talk with you... privately... before they arrive."

Max smiles and opens his arms wide. "Of course." He looks at Sheila. "Sheila, can you carry on, please? I'm just going to have a word with Hedvika and Dom."

They reach the office and Max sits down, Hedvika and Dom settling into chairs in front of his large polished oak desk.

"Max," says Hedvika, glancing at her watch. "We don't have much time until the Home Secretary and god knows what army are going to show up. When we met last week and you were talking about your... interest in *Joan of Arc*, the whole thing seemed so impossible, and I thought maybe you'd had a few beers and... I just never thought... Max, how did this happen?"

Max smiles broadly, his face beaming. "I'll tell you what happened, Hedvika. You go through your whole life and they tell you what you're supposed to do and what you're not supposed to do. You worry about whether you're gonna be in trouble, and you worry about... everything... and you're hardly even aware of what's going on. And then one day you wake up, and you just think to yourself, wouldn't it be great to have an aircraft carrier?"

Hedvika squints. "Are you sure that's how it happens?"

Max looks at Dom. "Am I right, Dom?"

"Sure, boss."

Hedvika sighs and frowns at Dom. "Honestly, Dom."

"What?" says Dom. "I think maybe the boss is right. Y'know, people are always fucking with you. So he wants a big boat? Why can't he have a big boat?"

"Because," says Hedvika, "no one is supposed to have a big… a nuclear-powered warship, because…" Hedvika looks at her watch again. "Right, let's do this another way. Max, I gather you have somehow come into possession of this ship. I can't begin to imagine how this happened, but please tell me you signed a contract of some sort."

"Of course I did." Max opens his desk drawer and pulls out a single sheet of paper which he hands to Hedvika.

Hedvika takes the sheet of paper, a mild look of disgust on her face as if Max had just handed her a turd. "This is it?"

"Yup."

Hedvika puts her glasses on and reads aloud.

In Expression of Sincerest Gratitude from the People of France to Maxwell Henderson

Dear Mr Henderson,

The People of France wish to express gratitude for naval shipyard services you have provided to the sea-going forces of our beloved country over these past three decades.

In recognition of naval workmanship of the highest rank, it is with a deep sense of appreciation that we bestow upon yourself the French National Order of Merit.

Hedvika looks up from the letter. "They gave you a medal?"

Max opens his desk drawer and pulls out a gleaming medal. He pins the medal to the lapel of his jacket and smiles. Hedvika and Dom lean forward to inspect it. Hanging from a royal blue ribbon is an impressive medal, encrusted with blue and crystal gemstones. "Pretty nice, huh?" says Max. "You know, I've never had a medal before. Not even when I was in school."

Hedvika sighs heavily and continues to read.

We also note your deep affection for and request to refurbish the illustrious ship Jeanne d'Arc (decommissioned). It is with sincerest thanks and recognition for services to the

Nation of France that we make a gift of Jeanne d'Arc to your person.
Your signature below recognises your receipt of Jeanne d'Arc, and permanent
acceptance/ownership and responsibility for the ship.

With the highest respect, and on behalf of the People of France,

Barnard Roux
Naval Chief of Staff

Max Henderson

Hedvika notes that Max has signed the document below Barnard's signature. "Max, I honestly don't know what to say. This isn't anything like a contract. A contract stipulates responsibilities for two parties. This is basically a letter from the French outlining that they made a gift of the ship to you, and that you were super-happy to accept the gift."

"Well, yes," says Max.

"Well... no, Max. I mean, no, as in... this is bad."

The sound of several cars can be heard just beyond Max's third-floor window, engines heavy and well-tuned. Dom jumps up from his seat and looks out the window, Hedvika joining him. Three large black vans with tinted windows pull up on the other side of the security gate. A dozen or more men and women in black uniforms and flak jackets jump from the back of the vans and fan out, taking up posts.

"Those guns look horrible," says Hedvika. "Why do they need them?"

"Those are Diemaco C7s," says Dom. "It's a standard assault rifle used by special forces."

"Dom, I don't care what they're called. Why do they have guns?"

"They're just setting up a perimeter before the Home Secretary and his staff arrive." Dom looks over at Max. "Boss, I don't know much about this legal stuff. I should probably go downstairs and speak with our security at the gate, and I should be there when the Home Secretary arrives. And I might need to make a couple of calls."

"Well, yeah," says Hedvika. "I mean, this is worrying – should we be evacuating the worksite?"

"I'm thinking not," says Dom. "I don't think they're gonna act like a bunch of stormtroopers. They don't want this to be the headliner on the Six O'Clock News. Besides, there's a French carrier which is probably docking now and apparently they just found out. They already look like a bunch of jack-asses."

Despite her best efforts, Hedvika isn't able to hide a smile.

"Okay, Dom," says Max. "Look, I just don't want anybody getting upset about this." Dom nods, pushes his large form from the chair, and exits the office.

"Max, I hope Dom knows what he's doing. You know I worry about that guy."

"Dom? Dom's fine."

"Max, there are people with guns just the other side of the gate. You know I was involved with background checks when we hired Dom all those years ago. We've talked about this. He was London mafia."

Max smiles. "Hedvika, we've all done some very stupid things when we were younger, right?"

"Well, no, actually. I didn't do very stupid things when I was younger. Did you?"

"Um, not really," says Max. "But Dom is smart... and I trust him."

"What does he mean, he has to make a couple of phone calls? He's always saying he has to make a couple of phone calls?"

Max laughs. "I don't know. I've never asked."

"I need to think," says Hedvika, gazing at the letter. "Maybe this isn't too bad. At least we have documentation that the French gave you the carrier as a gift. This should at least deflect some responsibility."

"So... I might be able to keep *Jeanne d'Arc?*"

Hedvika laughs. "I doubt that, Max. Look, right now my priority is to keep you from being taken into custody."

Max smiles, reaches across the desk and takes Hedvika's hand in his. "I'm sorry for upsetting everyone. I'm sorry for putting you in this position. You don't have to be here when they arrive. You can stay out of this. Let's say you didn't know anything about it."

"No, Max. The Home Secretary will be bringing more than a bunch of guys with guns. He'll be arriving with a small army of the best government solicitors. I'll be here when they arrive, it's just that... what is it you want me to do?"

The sound of more approaching cars drifts up from below.

Max sighs deeply and stares down at the oak varnished desk for a moment. When he raises his head, his expression is sad and serious. "Hedvika, you know I'm a private person."

"Yes, I know, Max."

"Well, I think I have been having some difficulties lately. And... I

58

don't know, when I saw *Jeanne d'Arc* in that staff meeting and learned that she was going to be destroyed, I just… It's odd and maybe it's selfish, but I… wanted her. This doesn't make sense, does it?"

Hedvika squeezes his hand. "Not to me, Max, but it seems to makes sense to you." She shakes her head. "Well, sometimes corporate legal work isn't very exciting. This is going to be different."

Max laughs. "When we spoke on the phone, you said you discovered some legal arguments?"

There is a knock on the door and then Sheila's head appears, concern written on her face. "The Home Secretary and his… associates… are here."

"Thanks, Sheila," says Max. "Are they in the waiting room?"

"No, Max. I don't think it's a waiting room type of situation. I think they're coming straight to your office."

"Sheila," says Hedvika. "In the top left-hand drawer of my desk is a file labelled *Jeanne d'Arc*. Can you get it for me?"

Sheila's nods and closes the door.

Hedvika turns to Max, a look of urgency on her face. "Okay, Max, I've had a couple of law students working on this *Jeanne d'Arc* thing, and we all sat down and talked it through a couple of days ago. I could find only one conceivable legal position and some very weird precedents. If you want this ship, I can try. But we are in bizarro town, legally speaking."

Loud and hurried footsteps can be heard coming down the hallway. "Max, there's no time to talk this through – we're just going to have to go with it. If you really need to speak, that's fine. But perhaps let me speak on your behalf."

"Absolutely," says Max.

Sheila enters and hands the file to Hedvika. She glances at Max, a concerned expression on her face, and then exits the office.

There is an immediate knock on the door, and then Dom sticks his head through and raises his eyebrows. "Mr Henderson, Home Secretary Jared Philcox and some of his staff would like to see you."

"Yes, of course, Dom. Show them in," says Max.

Dom enters, folds his hands, and takes up a post against the wall nearest the door. Five men and a woman enter. Hedvika scans them and clocks their roles immediately. The older, short and balding man with wisps of grey hair, a blue suit and red tie is Jared Philcox. Hedvika recognises the Home Secretary from TV news appearances and *Today in Parliament*. A middle-aged woman wears a tailored purple suit and carries a stylish briefcase. Government solicitor #1. The remaining guy is overweight, bald, wears a grey suit and blue tie, and carries a bulkier briefcase. Government solicitor #2. Three men in matching dark blue suits wear earpieces, so they are obviously security forces. Hedvika is relieved they are not holding guns, though she imagines they are wearing them under their jackets.

"Mr Henderson," says the older man, "I'm Home Secretary, Jared Philcox." He doesn't extend his hand, but Max stands up and offers his, which Philcox shakes with an air of reluctance.

"Max Henderson." Max looks around the office and there is some uncertainty about seating because there are only four chairs in front of Max's desk. "I can ask for some more chairs," says Max.

"It's not necessary," says Philcox. He glances at his security team and they take standing positions against the walls. Philcox and his two solicitors sit down. Hedvika takes the remaining chair and pulls it around to the side of Max's desk.

"So, Mr Philcox," says Max. "It's quite an honour to have a visit from the Home Secretary. To what do we owe the pleasure?"

"Owe the pleasure?" says Philcox. "Mr Henderson, I'm here because there is a 42,500-ton French nuclear aircraft carrier which entered UK territorial waters and is presently docking at your facility, and the British government was never consulted."

"Ah, yes," says Max thoughtfully. "*Jeanne d'Arc.*"

"Yes, precisely. *Jeanne d'Arc.* I want to know what it's doing at Henderson Nautical Works."

"Mr Home Secretary," says Hedvika. "I'm Hedvika Zavatsky. I'm…" Hedvika almost says *I'm Henderson Nautical Works legal representative*, but changes her mind. "I'm Mr Henderson's personal solicitor. I think I can offer an explanation."

Philcox shifts two dark and beady eyes onto Hedvika. "Fine. Let's have it."

"As you may be aware, Mr Henderson and his company have provided many years of valuable marine work for many of the French Navy's ships. Recently, Mr Henderson was invited to France. While there, he was awarded the…" Hedvika picks up the document off Max's desk and glances at it before continuing. "…The French National Order of Merit."

Hedvika turns to look at Max, and everyone in the room follows her gaze. Max sits up straighter and pushes out his chest, his medal prominent and gleaming in the fluorescent glow of the office lights. Hedvika turns to Philcox and his solicitors before continuing. "It's no secret that Mr Henderson has an affection for historically important ships, and the French made a personal gift of *Jeanne d'Arc* to Mr Henderson."

The solicitor in the purple suit interrupts. "Do you have any documentary evidence for what you are suggesting?"

"Of course," says Hedvika, handing Barnard Roux's letter to the solicitor. Philcox and his two solicitors huddle over the letter, their lips moving silently as they digest this strange meal.

A moment later Philcox shakes his head and laughs. "This must be a joke. Even if the letter is legitimate, a British citizen cannot accept such a... gift. There's clearly been a misunderstanding."

"I don't believe there's been a misunderstanding," says Hedvika. "The documentation plainly indicates that a senior representative of the French Government has gifted *Jeanne d'Arc* to Mr Henderson."

"Ms Zavatsky," says the chubby and bald solicitor, pulling a stack of documents out of his briefcase and placing them on his lap. "The legal basis for the French gifting a nuclear carrier to a British citizen is highly doubtful, but it's not the main issue. Even if we entertain the notion of this... gift, there is no legal basis for private possession of a capital ship of war."

"Really?" says Hedvika. "I'm not aware of any laws or legal precedent which specifically prohibits my client's ownership of an aircraft carrier."

The chubby solicitor breaks into a smile and then laughs. "Are you serious? *Jeanne d'Arc* is not a pleasure boat. It was designed and constructed as a weapon. The Firearms Directive makes it quite clear what sort of weapons a UK citizen can and cannot own. For goodness sake, our citizens can't own semi-automatic weapons, rockets or mortars, so I'd think a nuclear aircraft carrier is out of the question."

"Well, that's just the point, isn't it?" says Hedvika. "There's nothing in the European Firearms Directive which specifically prohibits ownership of a carrier."

"Of course there isn't," says the chubby solicitor. "As you well know, laws are interpreted and cannot provide for every circumstance. When the Directive was drafted, I doubt anyone imagined somebody would be mad enough to acquire a nuclear aircraft carrier, but there isn't a UK judge alive who would listen to such an absurd argument."

"Well, perhaps the issue needs to be put before the courts," says Hedvika.

"Nonsense," says Philcox. "This isn't a joke. That... ship is going back to France."

Dom notices several voices beyond the window, as if a crowd is beginning to form. He quietly drifts over to the window and looks down. Sure enough, just beyond the gates and the perimeter of security forces, he can see about twenty-five people. A few carry video cameras, so he imagines this is a mix of reporters and curious individuals. The word is getting out.

"More to the point," says the solicitor in the purple suit, "is that a UK citizen cannot form or hold a standing army or militia. That is the prerogative of the State."

"Really?" says Hedvika. "Just a minute." She rifles through some paperwork in her file, and then scans some handwritten notes. The voices from beyond the gate grow louder, and two of the Home Office security team join Dom at the window and look down. Max looks between Hedvika, the solicitors and Philcox, a concerned expression forming on his face.

"Are you referring to the Militia Act?" asks Hedvika.

The solicitor looks uncertain. "Well, yes, of course. The Militia Act, for starters."

"Okay," says Hedvika. "If you want law which covers standing armies and militias, we pretty much have to rely on the Militia Act… of 1661, don't we? And, yes, the Act prohibits private citizens from forming standing armies, but it also says that the right to form an army or militia belongs exclusively to *the King*, so I don't think that's going to help very much, is it? And besides, that law was…"

"Okay, that's enough," barks Philcox. "I'm not here to have a legal debate about weapons or militias. Let's get to the point. As Home Office Secretary, my job is to determine whether there are threats to the safety of the people of Britain. As far as I'm concerned, private ownership of a nuclear aircraft carrier by a UK citizen represents an unacceptable threat. And that… is a decision which my office can make with approval from the cabinet." Philcox stands up, places his palms firmly on the desk, and glares down at Max before continuing. "Are there any aircraft on that carrier?"

"Ah, no, I don't think so," says Max.

"Let me be clear," continues Philcox. "I will be advising the cabinet of my views. You can be sure that the ship will be secured under Home Office authority in very short order. I expect your full co-operation, Mr Henderson. Is that understood?"

Max looks down at his desk and rubs his mouth hard with a hand. Silence hangs heavy in the room. A moment later Max looks up, a note of resignation around his eyes. "Mr Home Secretary…" he begins.

"Max," says Hedvika suddenly. She stands up and looks down at the Home Secretary. Philcox stands up straight and locks eyes with Hedvika but has to crane his neck as Hedvika is four inches taller than him. "Mr Home Secretary, there are relevant circumstances which I have not as yet made clear. You should be aware that any seizure of the ship will be an infringement on the sovereignty of…" For a moment, Hedvika appears to lose her way, and then finds her words. "… The sovereignty of… *Jeanne d'Arc.*"

"Ms Zavatsky," says Philcox, exhaling painfully. "I do not have a great deal of time and I am losing my patience. What… are you talking about?"

Hedvika takes a breath and blows it out slowly. She sits down again. "Shall we sit down Mr Home Secretary? I don't want this discussion to be adversarial." Philcox makes a face, shakes his head, and takes his seat with reluctance.

Hedvika pulls a sheet of paper out of her file, which she scans, and then looks up. "Consistent with the 1933 Montevideo Convention on the Rights and Duties of States, we assert that Jeanne d'Arc is a sovereign state and, as such, entitled to the rights of all sovereign states."

"What?" says Philcox. He looks from one of his solicitors to the other.

The solicitor in the purple suit laughs. "Ms Zavatsky, it's a ship. It's not a country. I really think you are clutching at straws."

Hedvika sneaks a glance at Max, who is smiling at her with a mix of wonder and amusement, which she takes as encouragement. "On the contrary," says Hedvika. "We are entirely serious. The Montevideo Convention stipulates that a nation needs to meet four criteria in order to exist – a permanent population, a defined territory, a government, and the capacity to enter into relations with other states. I'm not authorised to provide all the details at the moment, but we believe *Jeanne d'Arc* can meet all such criteria."

"Ms Zavatsky," says the overweight solicitor. "As it happens, I specialise in international law. You've clearly done a bit of homework, but you're not making sense. The Montevideo Convention is hardly the accepted legal standard for the acceptance of any new state. The international standard is the Constitutive Theory of Statehood. And, as you may know, that standard stipulates that the existence of a state requires international recognition by other established states. Essentially, a process facilitated through the United Nations. I don't suppose *Jeanne d'Arc* is recognised by other states?" The solicitor laughs, rolls of fat threatening to pop the buttons on his shirt.

"Do you know what's interesting about the Constitutive Theory of Statehood?" asks Hedvika. "It's a *theory*. It's an idea. States cite it when it suits them, other states rely on the Montevideo Convention. It's really a matter of taste. The Montevideo Convention doesn't require recognition by other states."

The solicitor shakes his head. "There is no precedent for the legitimate establishment of an independent state in the absence of recognition by the international community."

"But there is precedent," says Hedvika. "The Principality of Sealand was founded right off the British coast in 1967."

"That's a joke country. It's just an old gun platform left over from the War. No one takes it seriously."

"What about the nation of Christiania," says Hedvika, "established in 1971?"

Philcox raises his hands and stares at his solicitor. "This is a waste of time. What the hell is she talking about?"

"She's talking about so-called micronations," the solicitor replies. "Christiania is basically a drug slum. A bunch of squatters occupied a disused army barracks in Copenhagen, fenced the place in and declared sovereignty. That's Christiania. It's nonsense."

"Christiania has a population of over one thousand," says Hedvika.

"Sure," says the solicitor. "A thousand homeless potheads. It's not a country. You're missing the point – you can't be a sovereign territory without international recognition."

"But getting recognition is a process," says Hedvika. "There are many territories with legitimate claims to statehood which have not as yet been formally recognised. Somaliland, Abkhazia, Northern Cyprus. It takes time. Thailand isn't even recognised by the UN."

"That's because Thailand hasn't bothered to ask for recognition," says the solicitor. "It's beside the point."

"What the hell are we talking about?" shouts Philcox. "It's a bloody boat! It's not a country."

"Mr Home Secretary," says Hedvika. "It's our view that *Jeanne d'Arc* is a sovereign state and entitled to... independent rule."

"Really?" says Philcox. "Are you aware that your sovereign state just sailed right down the Solent Estuary? As far as I recall, I think that's UK territorial waters."

"I do apologise, Mr Home Secretary," says Hedvika. "It's been a very hectic time for *Jeanne d'Arc*. It's a regrettable oversight and I can assure you that we are addressing the problem."

"No," says Philcox. "You won't be addressing the problem. The problem is going to be addressed by the Home Office." Philcox stands up and looks at his solicitors, who stand as well. "I'll be advising the cabinet in short order, and you can expect that the British Government will be securing the carrier imminently. Then, we will sort this out with the French. As I say, we expect your full co-operation."

Philcox takes a step towards the door. "With all due respect, Mr Home Secretary," says Hedvika. There is a cold edge to Hedvika's voice which causes Philcox to turn and stare at her. "There is something else you should be aware of."

Philcox blows out a breath in obvious exasperation. "And what might that be, Ms Zavatsky?"

"While we are citing the Montevideo Convention of 1933, *Jeanne d'Arc* does take the issue of international recognition seriously. That's why, this morning, we have written to the General Secretary of the United Nations, in petition for membership of the UN."

Philcox gazes at Hedvika and then shakes his head. "Oh, for god's sake," he says. He turns and follows a security agent out the door, his solicitors trailing behind him.

When the last security detachment exits and closes the door, Dom grins broadly at Hedvika and shakes his head. Hedvika blows a large breath out and looks at Max. "Jesus, Max. What have we got ourselves into?"

"You were incredible, Hedvika," says Max. "Where did you get all of that?"

"Well, like I said, after we spoke I spent some time with a couple of students, looking at the problem. It was an interesting thought experiment. It was *supposed* to be an interesting thought experiment."

With Philcox and his solicitors gone, the noise from beyond the gate is more apparent. Dom returns to the window and looks down. "There's a lot of people out there now," he says.

Max turns to Hedvika. "You wrote a letter to the General Secretary of the UN?"

Hedvika laughs. "Are you kidding, Max? I just found out about all of this. When was I supposed to write a letter?"

CHAPTER 14

Hedvika had spent most of the morning researching the legal quagmire she had fallen into and speaking with a couple of close colleagues she had studied law with, people she could trust to keep a secret. But she really needs to see Max for an update. She knocks on Sheila's door and then enters. Sheila is on the phone, so Hedvika sits down.

"That's all I can tell you... no, I can't provide you with any information about that... I can't comment on that either... I don't know if Mr Henderson will be making any public statements... I'm sorry, but I really have to go now...." Sheila hangs up and looks at Hedvika. The phone rings again immediately.

Sheila groans. "I'm not answering it. In fact, I think I am just going to stop answering the phone altogether."

"Who's been calling?" asks Hedvika.

"Mainly reporters. But a few people who are just nosey. There was a guy who said he belonged to an aircraft carrier club and he wanted to know if he and his mates could have a tour."

"Do you know where Max is?"

"He's on that bloody boat of his, isn't he?" says Sheila.

"Okay. I need to see him. Will I even know how to find him?"

"Dom is down by the security gate. I'd get him to walk you over to the boat."

"Thanks, Sheila." Hedvika is about to leave, but there is something in Sheila's expression which stops her. "What is it, Sheila?"

"Can I talk to you... privately?" says Sheila.

"Of course."

Sheila gets up and closes her office door, returns to her seat, and turns the answering machine on. "I've known Max for more than thirty years. I've worked with him closely, day in and day out. I'm really worried about him. He puts on a brave face, but I see more than others. For a long while now he's been getting... I don't know how to describe it. There's this sadness in him, you know? Most people don't see it, but I do. And this business with the aircraft carrier isn't right. He trusts your judgement, Hedvika. Can't you tell him to stop this nonsense?"

"Sheila, believe me, I've advised Max all the way along that getting involved with this boat thing isn't a good idea. I've told him that you really do not want to get on the wrong side of the government."

"But this is suicidal," says Sheila. "I just have this terrible feeling that it's going to end badly and that Max is going to get hurt. Max depends on you, Hedvika. Can't you just tell him that you won't support it? That you won't help him with something so... destructive?"

Hedvika sighs and looks down at her hands for a moment before looking back at Sheila. "I've thought about that. It's just that... Sheila, I'm going to tell you something in confidence, alright?"

"Of course," says Sheila.

"Many years ago, when I was newer to Henderson Nautical, I went through a very bad time. Everyone knows now that I'm a lesbian, and that I've been with Gloria for years. But when I started at Henderson Nautical, I felt I had to keep all of that a secret. I was younger and there were men here, some of them executives, some of them managers, and they... It was subtle at first. They would ask me out and I would make excuses, but they didn't like hearing *No*. It got worse. There was a lot of sexual innuendo and they would touch me a lot. I had only moved over from the Czech Republic recently, and it's confusing when you are in a new country, with a new job, and you don't really know how things are done. Some of the men started talking about how I must be a lesbian and of course they were right, but I didn't want anyone to know. I couldn't sleep. I was getting sick. One day I went to Max and tried to resign. He didn't want me to leave and he kept asking me to tell him what was wrong. I broke down and I told him everything..."

Hedvika pauses for a moment, her heart pounding, the old feelings running through her body. "What happened?" Sheila whispered.

Max picked up the phone and called Dom. Ten minutes later Dom is escorting these six guys into Max's office. They are all standing there with Dom against the door. Max stands up and I just sit there, staring at the floor. The expression on Max's face – I'd never seen him look like that. He really tore into those guys. It was a long time ago and I can't remember exactly what he said, but Max was shouting and getting right in their faces. He grabbed one or two of them by their jackets and pushed them against the wall. He threatened to fire all of them if they ever touched me or spoke to me with anything but respect." Hedvika releases a nervous laugh, recalling more. "I think Dom even threatened to personally beat the shit out of them as well. It was really scary."

"Oh my god, Hedvika. I'm so sorry. I had no idea that was going on."

"It's alright. Overnight, those guys became perfect gentlemen. It was like they were scared of making even the slightest mistake. They're all gone now, anyway. Moved onto other jobs over the years. I'm not sure why I'm telling you all this."

Hedvika pauses to collect her thoughts. "It's not just what Max did for me concerning those guys, but that was important in a way which is hard to explain. I think the way Max stood up to those guys was one of the things which gave me the courage to come out about who I am. I don't know what Max is going through at the moment, but there are times when I thought I was cracking up, and I find it hard not to help Max now, even with this."

Sheila comes around from her desk and gives Hedvika a hug. "Can you just keep an eye on him, Hedvika?"

"I will. You too, okay?"

Hedvika finds Dom standing next to the security hut by the entrance, sucking on an E-cig and scanning the reporters and crowd on the other side of the fence. Three other members of Dom's security team are standing around as well. The entrance through the gate is closed, which is unusual during working hours. Hedvika stands next to him.

"Everything alright?"

"I guess." Hedvika scans the people on the other side of the fence. There seems to be perhaps a hundred of them, many with cameras, some holding microphones. "They're like a bunch of squirrels," says Dom. "They keep asking questions and sticking their microphones at us, and we keep not answering them. They've calmed down a bit, but they're just standing out there. I don't know what they're waiting for."

"Dom, can you take me to see Max?"

"Sure."

Dom leads Hedvika along the perimeter fence and a male reporter thrusts a mic in her direction, another man behind him holding a shoulder camera. "Are you Hedvika Zavatsky? Ms Zavatsky, can you tell us what *Joan of Arc* is doing here?"

"I'm sorry, I can't comment at this time."

"But Ms Zavatsky…"

Dom and Hedvika quicken their pace, and then Dom leads Hedvika through a labyrinth of work yards and workshops.

"I like how you handled those bean counters this morning," says Dom.

"That just bought us some time. And I honestly don't know what we're doing. Look, Dom, you know Max better than any of us. Is he… okay?"

"Define okay."

"Come on, Dom. Okay, as in… not going a bit nuts. This… boat obsession isn't… normal."

Dom stops and looks at Hedvika. His gaze is easy and he smiles, but Hedvika has this awareness of the enormous size and strength of Dom. She experiences this often with Dom, and it gives her this unnatural mix of reassurance and unease. "To tell you the truth, Hedvika, Max isn't really saying much about what's going on with him. But I just think the boss needs to do whatever the boss needs to do. What the fuck is normal, anyway? I've known lots of normal people, living normal lives, every day the same, following the rules. Then one day they top themselves and everyone is confused and shocked, and then a week later no one gives a shit anymore."

Hedvika sighs. "I care about what happens to Max, you know that, but I have to look after the whole organisation as well."

"The organisation will be fine. People want their boats built and fixed, right? Besides, what is it they say? All publicity is good publicity."

"I doubt that."

"Come on," says Dom, and he walks Hedvika through another workshop. Eventually, they enter shed four. In all her years of working at Henderson Nautical, Hedvika can't recall if she'd ever been in this shed. They had entered a normal-looking door and found themselves standing on a walkway about fifty metres above the ground. Hedvika involuntarily stops and stares. They are essentially standing in a colossal aluminium shed. The enormous door at the far end of the shed opens to the estuary, but it is closed now and halogen lighting fills the interior, giving the place a strange glow. *Jeanne d'Arc* floats peacefully in the shed bay.

"My god," breathes Hedvika.

"Looks even bigger when its inside, doesn't it?" says Dom. "Max said that if she was ten feet longer, they wouldn't have been able to close the shed door. By the way, I should warn you – he's probably hanging out with his new French mates."

"Who are these people, Dom? And why are they here?"

"The ship's Captain is Jean-Pierre Lavelle. He was the actual Captain of *Joan of Arc* before she was decommissioned. He's the one with the captain's hat – gold scrolly bits on it. Then there's Alexis Girard, Chief

Engineer. The other one is Hugo Dubois, Chief of Aeronautics. I think they are old shipmates of the captain's. In fact, all three of them are old farts. I don't know how they got tangled up in all of this, but I think they're here to run the ship."

"What do you mean, run the ship?" asks Hedvika. "I thought Max was just interested in refurbishing it."

"Shit. I don't know what's going on, Hedvika. Come on, I'll take you to Max."

Dom leads Hedvika down steps to the concrete base at the bottom of the bay, and then over a walkway which allows them to board the carrier. They walk through the ship, down labyrinthine corridors of grey paint and up more sets of stairs than Hedvika thought possible. Eventually they come to a door which Dom knocks on.

"Enter," says a French voice.

As they walk into the room, Hedvika has a sudden realisation. She recalls the photograph Max had shown her of the ship's bridge, and she knows that's just where they are. She scans the room, taking in sophisticated-looking computer panels, big leather chairs, dozens of handles and buttons, and the windows which form a seamless surround. She recalls how this place reminded her of the Starship Enterprise.

"Ah, Hedvika," says Max, "I'm so glad you're here. I want you to meet *Jeanne d'Arc*'s crew."

Max proceeds to introduce her to his three crew members. Max and his crew are all drinking coffee, the Captain and Max standing, the other two sitting in a couple of the big chairs. Hedvika shakes hands and tries to seem affable, though this takes some effort.

"Hedvika," says Max, "is the smartest solicitor in the British Isles." The three shipmates nod approval. "Hedvika," continues Max, "let me get you a coffee."

"No thank you, Max. To be honest, we need to speak. We need to update our... situation."

"Of course, of course," says Max. "Jean-Pierre, Alexis, and Hugo are part of the project. It's fine to speak with them as well."

Hedvika glances at Dom and then scans the three men, who all seem to share the same benign smile. Captain Jean-Pierre raises his cup and nods. "We are at your service Hedvika," he says.

"Okay, fine," says Hedvika. She looks at Jean-Pierre, wondering how you are supposed to address a ship's captain. She decides she doesn't care. "Captain Jean-Pierre, I appreciate I don't know you and I don't wish to be impolite, but we don't really have a lot of time. I just don't understand... look, what exactly is your role here?"

"Well, Max has taken me on as ship's Captain. So, doing that, I guess."

"Yes, I understand," says Hedvika. "But why? I mean, why are you doing this?"

Jean-Pierre takes a thoughtful sip of coffee. "Well, I suppose when they decommissioned Jeanne d'Arc, the navy decommissioned me as well. I tried joining a bridge club. That's wasn't too bad, but my wife wanted us to go to American country and western line dancing. Have you ever seen a group of older French men line dancing and wearing cowboy hats? It's dreadful."

Hedvika looks over at Alexis and Hugo. "And what's your excuse?"

Alexis points at Jean-Pierre, smiling. "He's the Captain, right? I'm following orders."

Hedvika notices that Max is wearing some sort of naval cap, blue with a gold emblem of leaves. "Why have you got a cap, Max?"

"I'm a petty officer now. A Major, in fact."

"Congratulations," says Hedvika. "Look, I'm just really concerned. I'm trying to understand our legal situation, which is one thing, but at any moment we could have some sort of naval or military forces arrive, and then what do we do? I can't even imagine what might show up?" She looks at Jean-Pierre. "Do you know?"

"There are three British naval vessels which arrived about an hour ago," says the Captain. "A couple of destroyers and a carrier. They've taken up a position about five miles off the coast."

"What? How do you know?" asks Hedvika.

Jean-Pierre waves his pint of beer at the computer banks in the room. "*Jeanne d'Arc* may be decommissioned, but her systems work if you turn them on. There might be a submarine out there as well, but we can't tell from here. This is a very odd situation, so it's really hard to know what to expect. If they get serious, on water it will be destroyers, a carrier of their own, and maybe a sub. On land, I'd think they'd use special forces. They wouldn't want to trust this situation to regular army, so probably SAS."

Hedvika frowns. "Well, that's just great." She scans the four men and wonders why they are still smiling.

"Okay," continues Hedvika, "so a bunch of British naval and special forces could show up at any moment. You see, the thing is, you guys don't seem to be... how would you put it? You don't seem to be on much of a war footing."

Jean-Pierre laughs and raises his cup. "Hedvika, this is our war footing."

"You're kidding," says Hedvika.

"Not at all," says the Captain. "The plan is very simple. If any military forces of any sort show up, we surrender immediately."

"You do?"

"Yes, of course," says the Captain.

"Alright," says Hedvika. "I guess that makes sense." She looks back at Max, who she realises is wearing the same amused smile as his new shipmates. She is feeling irritated at all of them. "Max, you know something? I've spent the last few hours trying to figure out if the government has a legal basis for arresting you and your mates, or for confiscating your boat."

"And what have you discovered?" asks Max.

She sighs. "Nothing that's very clear, which is why I suspect those destroyers and god knows what else are leaving us alone for the moment. Those government solicitors we met earlier are probably scratching their heads over Section 19 of the 1984 Police and Criminal Evidence Act."

"What's that?" asks Max.

"Under the Act, the police or other authorities actually have some wide-ranging powers to seize property they believe is relevant to an investigation. But in order to seize property, like maybe an aircraft carrier, they have to convince a judge that a crime has been committed. They might be having a hard time figuring out what crime you've committed Max. If you haven't committed a crime, seizing your boat might itself be illegal."

Max waves his cup at his shipmates. "Didn't I tell you – the smartest solicitor in the British Isles."

"That's brilliant," says Hugo.

"Really impressive," says Alexis.

"No, boys," says Hedvika, "it's really not. Look, I'm describing the law, but this is the government we're talking about. They're going to do whatever they want – believe me. Like the Home Secretary said, they might just declare you and your boat to be a national security threat. If that's the case, you can throw Section 19 in the toilet."

"I must tell you, Hedvika," says Hugo, "Max told us what you said about *Jeanne d'Arc* being sovereign territory. That was very amusing."

"Yes, amusing," says Hedvika. "That's a good word for it." Hedvika gazes out the bridge windows at the fluorescent glow of the aluminium walls, and then looks at Max. "The thing is Max – what do you want me to do?"

"I want you to stop working and let me get you a cup of coffee. We need your charming company."

Hedvika smiles, despite herself. "No, thank you. I really don't think my company will help your party."

"Then knock off early, go home and have a glass of wine, and spend some time with Gloria. Tell her about how you stuck it to those government solicitors." Max smiles and waves his cup at the room. "And tell her about the impossible people you have to work with, especially Captain Jean-Pierre."

"Me?" says Jean-Pierre, a feigned look of hurt on his face.

Hedvika smiles despite herself and looks over at Dom, who is wearing a big grin. "Dom, you'd better help me find my way out of this tin can."

CHAPTER 15

Max picks up his phone and taps in Sheila's number.

"Hi, Max," he hears her say.

"The sun is setting in forty-five minutes."

"I'll get the key," says Sheila. "Do you have the cooler?"

"Of course."

A few minutes later, Sheila arrives at Max's office door. She and Max walk down the stairs together silently, along a walkway separating two work sheds, and then enter shed three which at 7 PM is empty of any staff. Max hits the lights and they ascend a flight of stairs which takes them to the top of the shed. There, they face a door, and Sheila puts the key into the lock and turns it. She opens the door onto a balcony which sits five stories above the ground and looks over Portsmouth Harbour. Max picks up a couple of cushions from just inside the door and arranges them on two comfortable deck chairs. Sheila closes the door and sits down. Max opens the cooler, places a wine and beer glass onto a table between the chairs, and then lays out a selection of cheeses and crackers. He pours white wine and a pale ale into the glasses and drops into his own chair.

They sit together, the air still and warm against skin, sipping their drinks. The sun melts into the sea, casting hues of red and orange against wisps of cloud and the ripples of waves on the harbour. Gazing across the estuary water, they can see Spinnaker Tower, the masts of the tall ships *HMS Warrior* and *HMS Victory*, and the glittering city skyline with countless windows winking in the setting sun.

They are silent for a while, long enough for the sun to dip over the horizon and spit out hues of lavender and magenta. "Did you know," says Sheila, "that you can watch the Big Bang on your television set. The cosmic background radiation can be seen in the black and white fuzz when a station isn't tuned in properly."

Max takes a sip of his pale ale and nods. "I love it when you say things like that, Sheila."

CHAPTER 16

Hedvika takes a sip of coffee from her travel mug as she works her way through Portsmouth's morning traffic. She really doesn't want to listen to the news but forces herself to turn on BBC Radio 4. The host appears to be interviewing someone

"... *but the real question is, what's it doing here in Britain?*"

"*Well, let me say this, John. There is a deafening silence coming from the government, the French, and Henderson Nautical Works. The blindingly obvious question is this: if there's nothing illegitimate about Joan of Arc being in Portsmouth Harbour, then why won't someone explain what's going on? The only comment you get from government ministers is that they're looking into what may have been a procedural or communications oversight. That says something and nothing.*"

"*And what about statements to the effect that Max Henderson is now the owner of the nuclear carrier?*"

"*Well, that's harder to say. There are a couple of reports that have suggested that, but the idea seems preposterous and so far the sources of the information are unnamed, so I think we need to wait on that one...*"

Hedvika's car phone rings and she sees it's Dom calling. She feels sure this is not good news. "Hi, Dom. What's the good news?"

"Yeah," says Dom. "I'll see if I can think of any, but right now I've got a bit of a situation." Hedvika can hear Max's wife shouting in Spanish in the background.

"What's happening?"

"Well, a lot. I arrived to pick up Max about twenty minutes ago. There's a big group of reporters in his front garden. Unpleasant bastards. I had to push my way into the house and one fucker tried to follow me inside."

"Dom, you didn't do anything..."

"The reporter? I think he tripped and fell into a bush."

"Oh god!" says Hedvika.

"That's not all. Violeta is hysterical. She's screaming at Max in some disgusting mix of English and Spanish and she's giving me a headache. I'm keeping quiet but I'm pretty close to shoving a sock in her mouth. And we're watching TV. It's all over the news."

"I know. I've got Radio 4 on."

"There's more good news," says Dom. "That Home Secretary called and left a message on Max's phone. It's pretty much an ultimatum, saying Max needs to make a decision this morning." Hedvika goes quiet, her mind calculating.

"Hedvika, what should I do? I can probably get Max to my car, but if those reporters fuck with me on the way…"

"No, don't do that, Dom. Look, I'm only five minutes from Max's. I'll come straight there. The reporters and Violeta are the least of our problems. I need to hear that phone message as soon as I arrive."

"Okay. I'll keep an eye out for your car. You're gonna need help getting in here."

Dom hangs up and stares at Max and Violeta. Max is at the kitchen table, trying to drink his coffee. Violeta is in her bathrobe, her hair tied up in a towel. She is standing over Max, her face flush, shouting. "Hombre estúpido! Is true." She turns on a bare heel and marches over to the kitchen sink, places her face in her hands and begins to sob angrily.

Dom sits down next to Max, who looks a little pale. Dom leans into his ear. "I could lock her in the garage, boss. Do you want me to lock her in the garage?"

Max smiles. "She'll be alright, Dom. She just needs some time to calm down."

Dom wanted to say *She will never be alright, boss*, but held his tongue.

"What'd Hedvika say?" asks Max.

"She's coming straight here. She wants to listen to the message from the Home Secretary. In fact, I need to watch out for her."

A moment later, Hedvika pulls up on the street in front of Max's because there are too many vehicles and reporters in Max's driveway. A couple of staff pick cameras off the ground and walk towards her car, and she checks to make sure the doors are locked. Hedvika hears several raised voices, and she can now see Dom walking swiftly towards her, ignoring reporter's questions. They seem to be letting him pass without problems, but follow behind him, and she wonders if this has something to do with the reporter who… fell into the bush.

She opens the car door just as Dom arrives. Hedvika feels Dom's hand around her upper arm and watches him slam her car door shut. She locks the car with her key fob and then feels herself being walked briskly through a sea of microphones, faces, and shouted questions.

"Ms Zavatsky, does Max Henderson own Jeanne d'Arc now?"

"Ms Zavatsky, are there warplanes or operable guns on Jeanne d'Arc?"

"Ms Zavatsky, do you know what the UK government is planning to do now?"

Microphones are being thrust at her and the journalists are jostling with each other. She can see Dom pushing journalists and camera crews as they make their way to the door, and his grip is almost painfully tight on her arm as she feels herself pulled forward. She watches Dom working, a little scared about whether they will get to the door of the house, but more afraid of what Dom might do if the news crews don't let them through. A moment later they are at the door. Dom knocks loudly and the door flies inward, revealing Max. Several cries of *"Mr Henderson!"* can be heard. Dom's hand grips tighter still and she feels herself being lifted over the door sill and plunked down on the entrance flooring. The door slams and they are safe on the other side.

"Fucking animals," spits out Dom.

Hedvika rubs her arm and makes a face. "Sorry Hedvika – you okay?"

"A little sore, but I'm fine. Thank you, Dom."

Max looks a little stunned as he gazes at Hedvika. "That was awful. I'm sorry you had to go through that, sweetheart."

Hedvika looks at Max and Dom. "Guys, I'm fine. I want to hear that message from the Home Secretary."

They follow Max into the kitchen and are immediately faced with a tear-stained Violeta. "Este es terrible," she says, speaking at Hedvika. "Qué dicen estas personas sobre mí?"

"Don't worry, Violeta," says Hedvika. "They're not saying anything about you. They're talking about Max."

"No entiendo," says Violeta, confusion on her face.

"No están interesados en ti," says Hedvika. "No te preocupes. Por qué no te cambias?"

"Ok, gracias," says Violeta. She turns and goes upstairs.

"Wow," says Dom. "I've been trying to get rid of her all morning. How the hell did you do that?"

"I said she should probably get dressed."

"Oh," says Max. "Does she need to get dressed for some reason?"

"No reason at all," says Hedvika. "Max, can you play the Home Secretary's message?" Hedvika notices the TV is on in the next room, and she can see a reporter standing on Max's lawn but can't quite hear what she is saying.

Max begins poking at his phone. "When was the message left?" asks Hedvika.

"Late yesterday evening, but I just listened to it this morning."

'Mr Henderson, this is Jared Philcox, Home Secretary. The issue of Jeanne d'Arc's presence at your facility has been discussed by the cabinet. The view of the Prime Minister and cabinet is that the transportation of Jeanne d'Arc occurred without government approval, and we are exploring whether a crime has been committed. It's also the view that the carrier poses serious risks to national security. Our view is that the British authorities should take Jeanne d'Arc into our possession until such time a decision can be made about its future. However, in the interest of public safety, I am strongly advising that you simply hand over Jeanne d'Arc to the government and make a public acknowledgement that the normal means of communications and procedures were overlooked. Our communications minister can help draft a statement for you. Please contact my office immediately. If we do not hear from you by 11 AM tomorrow, we will need to initiate seizure of the carrier. Thank you.'

"What do you think, Hedvika?" asks Max. "Should we do what they say?"

"It's an interesting play," says Hedvika. "Philcox is sounding tough and seems to be giving you an ultimatum, but they clearly do not want to show up at Henderson Nautical Works with any sort of force. They'd much rather put you in front of a microphone, Max, and get you to say, *Oops, I made a mistake.*"

"So, what do you think?" asks Max.

"I think it's a bad idea to screw with the government, Max."

"Right," says Max, gazing down at the kitchen floor.

Hedvika sighs. "But I guess it really just depends on how important this boat thing is to you. I mean, I don't really get it myself, but everyone is different. Let me think for a moment."

Hedvika paces through the kitchen a few times, her heels clicking on the ceramic flooring. "Okay, I can see three options. Option one: call Philcox and tell him you want to do it his way. They can prepare a statement for you, you make a public address and read it out, the government takes your boat. When it's in their possession they will work with the French and it's very doubtful you will ever see it again, but I think you will not be in much trouble because of your co-operation. The government will work the *'misunderstanding'* angle and, if you go along with that, there shouldn't be much fuss. Option two: we do nothing, but I don't actually think Philcox is bluffing. The longer you have the ship, the more stupid they look, so they will probably come and seize it tomorrow. It's hard to say what charges the government will bring, but they will probably think of something, and I'm going to have a job keeping you out of trouble, or even keeping you out of prison. Option three…"

Hedvika gazes at Max for a moment. "You know," she says, "I think it's probably just two options."

Max smiles. "Hedvika?"

Hedvika shakes her head and exhales loudly. "Okay, Max. Look, option three isn't such a hot idea – but I'm your solicitor, so you deserve to have them all." She pauses, reflecting while staring at the floor. "Max, do you play poker?"

"Just a few times with Dom. But Dom's the poker player."

"Okay, I play a bit of poker," says Hedvika. "When it's your turn to bet, you've got three choices, really. One, you can fold. Throw in your cards. Its low risk but you're out of the game. Two, you can match the current bet. There's some risk, you give them the initiative, but you stay in the game. Three, you can raise the bet. Giving Philcox the boat and making a public statement is basically folding. Waiting is the equivalent of matching the bet. You're just watching to see what they're going to do. Option three is raising the bet. But in this situation there's very little time, so if you're going to raise the bet, I think you're going to have to shove a lot of chips on the table."

Dom is smiling. "I like option three already."

"I don't," says Hedvika.

"So, come on," says Dom. "How do we go all-in?"

Hedvika sighs heavily and looks at Max. "You make a public statement, Max, and you do it quickly. But the statement isn't something the Government Communications Director prepares. It's your statement."

"But… what do I say?" asks Max.

Hedvika smiles and laughs. "Max, my advice is that you do not go with option three. But if you're going to make a statement, and if you want even a slim chance of keeping that ship, you're going to have to say more than *the French gave it to me*. I think you are going to have to talk about the sovereignty of *Jeanne d'Arc*."

"Will that work?" asks Max.

"I doubt it," says Hedvika, shaking her head and raising her hands in the air. "Sovereignty is an absurd argument but this is an absurd situation so it's really all I've got."

Max places a hand to his chin, lost in thought for a moment. "I can talk about that," he says. "But you know, I think there are a couple of other things I might want to say."

"I like option three," says Dom.

"Arrggghhh," says Hedvika, glaring at Dom. "Can you let me talk to Max, okay?" She looks back at Max. "Look, you're taking the biggest risk of all with option three. It's really hard to predict where this will go, but I'm sure of one thing: the more you piss off and embarrass the government, the harder it's going to be for me to keep you out of prison."

Max thinks for a moment, turns and walks to a window that has the shutters drawn. Max stares at the shutters, deep in thought. He speaks, but almost as if he is talking to himself. "There are all sorts of prisons, aren't there?"

Hedvika starts to respond, but something on the TV draws her attention. She jabs Dom in the arm and points to the images. They watch film footage of the front step of Max's house and see Dom literally lift a journalist off the ground and then throw him six feet through the air and into a bush. Journalists and film crews begin shouting and gesturing. Hedvika sighs. "Fell into a bush? Really, Dom?"

"Well, the camera angle makes it look a little different."

"Dom, don't you think the legal issues I'm dealing with are complicated enough?"

"I'm sorry, Hedvika. That guy just really pissed me off."

Hedvika shakes her head. "Never mind. We'll deal with it if we have to. I guess that guy was trying to enter the house. At least you didn't shoot him."

Max opens the shutters and gazes out at his front lawn, scanning the journalists and news crews. Voices are raised suddenly, and Hedvika, Dom, and Max watch the journalists pushing forward. Max appears to scan the reporters, seeming to look for someone or something.

"Hey, Max," Dom calls. "Hedvika thinks I handled that reporter pretty good on account of not shooting him."

"Yeah," says Max, his voice dream-like. "Good job."

Dom looks at Hedvika. "The boss is happy, right?

Hedvika rolls her eyes.

"There she is," Max says, pointing out the window.

"There's who?" asks Hedvika.

Max walks over to them and pulls his wallet out, fishing a business card from it. "My reporter," he says. He reads the card. "Liz Burton."

Hedvika looks a little confused. "Liz Burton?" she asks.

"If I'm making a statement, we'll need a reporter, right?" Max looks at Dom. "Can you get Liz in here?"

CHAPTER 17

It's 10:15 AM and Prime Minister Margaret Williams is sitting at a polished cherrywood table in her office at Number 10. She takes a sip of her coffee and gazes across the small table at Home Secretary Jared Philcox and Defence Secretary Ronald Hudd. Ronald is giving them technical information about *Jeanne d'Arc*. Margaret decides that this is a relative waste of time. If there's one thing she has learned as a politician, it's that if you want to understand a situation you need to know who you are dealing with. It's people who matter.

"Excuse me, Ronald, but what do we know about Max Henderson?" she asks.

Ronald opens a manila file and scans some text. "MI5 put together a brief report yesterday," says Ronald. "Henderson is fifty-eight years old and a successful businessman. He started his own shipyard nearly thirty years ago at a time when every shipyard in Britain was closing. He's married to a Spanish woman named Violeta who was a well-known international classical singer many years ago. They have a son, Peter, who seems to be a heroin addict. Aside from developing a shipyard, Henderson has lived a remarkably ordinary life. No trouble with the law. No affiliation with any radical organisations. The only red flag I can see is his head of security, a guy named Dominic Delfino. He's had links with London mafia and a criminal history for assault, money laundering, and racketeering, but from what we can tell he's kept his nose clean for several years now. It looks like he managed to leave the life."

"Alright," says Margaret. "But are we sure Henderson isn't some crack-pot? Are you certain he's not tied into any cults or groups with extreme ideologies?"

Roland lowers his voice. "Henderson might be a crack-pot, but I've had an off-the-record conversation with GCHQ. There's nothing in Henderson's digital footprint which suggest links to any radical ideology."

"Okay," says Margaret. "But what's all this nonsense about the ship somehow being sovereign?"

"Our solicitors tell us this is a very obscure legal point," says Philcox, "but apparently it's not totally crazy. We checked with the UN this

81

morning and they have no record of Henderson petitioning them for statehood. But who knows? The petition could be in the mail or sitting on someone's desk in New York City."

"Well, it sounds absurd to me," says Margaret. "Anyway, it's irrelevant because we are going to take possession of that carrier before any of that drivel gets off the ground. What I need to know is… what the hell actually happened? Do we know more from the French?"

"I've had a further phone call with Secretary of State Dupont," says Ronald. "Dupont says there was authorisation for awarding Henderson the French National Order of Merit for his maritime building and repair work to the French Navy. He thinks there was some miscommunication and the Naval Chief of Staff, Barnard Roux, accidentally gave Henderson the carrier as well."

"You're joking," says Margaret.

"Dupont says he's looking into it, but he thinks there was a big mix-up with paperwork."

"A mix-up with paperwork?" says Margaret.

Ronald sighs. "Dupont thinks that the carrier was supposed to be handed over to Henderson Nautical Works in order that it could be broken down as part of its decommissioning process, and somehow this got mixed up with the National Order of Merit award. Rather than commissioning Henderson to break the ship down, they accidentally gave the ship to Henderson instead, thinking it was a gift somehow connected to the National Order of Merit."

Margaret gazes at Ronald, her mouth hanging open. "How the hell do you accidentally give away a nuclear aircraft carrier?"

"I don't know, Prime Minister," says Ronald. "The French are either being cute with us, or this was a genuine balls-up."

Margaret stands up and walks to the window. She turns and looks back at Philcox and Hudd. "You know what?" she says, "I'll bet there's someone in France who likes old nuclear reactors. We've got a few of those lying around. Why don't we drop one off? I'll tell you what, we'll decommission it first."

Philcox and Hudd smile. "And is that damn thing contaminated?" says Margaret.

"No," says Ronald. "I've had strong reassurances from the French on that score."

"Well," says Margaret. "This is ridiculous. Let's keep things simple. We need to go and get the ship, secure it at our Plymouth naval base, and then we give the damn thing back to the French."

"I agree, Prime Minister," says Jared. "But I'd rather Henderson just handed over the ship, and it would be better if the French and Mr Henderson can offer some explanation. I'd rather the French look like idiots. I've left a phone message with Henderson yesterday evening telling him to hand over the ship, but I said we are going to have to act quickly if he doesn't."

"Good," says Margaret. "I want this sorted out today, before it gets deeper into the news cycle."

There is a knock on the office door and the Prime Minister's Personal Assistant enters the room. "I'm very sorry to interrupt, Prime Minister," the young man says, "but there's been a development concerning that aircraft carrier. There's a report which is just about to air. I think you might want to turn the TV on. BBC 1."

Margaret thanks her PA, and Home Office Secretary Philcox turns a TV on which is in the corner of the office. Images are replaying of Dom throwing the reporter into the bush, complimented by a voice-over. *"Once again, the man who assaulted the BBC reporter is Dominic Delfino, who heads up security for Max Henderson... oh, okay. I've just been told that we are ready to go to a live interview between Britain Today's Liz Burton and Max Henderson."*

"Who is Liz Burton?" the Prime Minister asks.

"Never heard of her," says Philcox.

They find themselves looking at a scene of Max's living room, Max and Liz sitting opposite each other in front of a fireplace. There is a pause as Max is getting some help from an assistant who is attaching a microphone to his jacket.

Margaret leans closer to the TV and squints. "What's that cap Henderson's got on his head?"

"It appears to be a French naval cap," says Defence Secretary Hudd. "I think the insignia would make him a petty officer, but I'm not an expert on French naval rankings."

Margaret points at the TV. "And that medal on his lapel. Is that the... what was it?"

"Yes," says Philcox. "That's the French National Order of Merit."

Margaret shakes her head. "Nutter. Complete nutter. That's what we're dealing with."

"Okay? Can we get started?" says Liz to whoever is holding the camera.

Liz looks directly into the camera. "Good morning, Britain. I'm Liz

Burton, and I'm here in Portsmouth with Max Henderson, who is the owner of Henderson Nautical Works, one of Britain's largest remaining shipyards. Mr Henderson has been good enough to grant Britain Today an exclusive interview." Liz turns to Max. "Thank you, Mr Henderson, for inviting us into your home."

"I'm happy to have you, and please call me Max. Everyone does."

"Thank you. Max, the British public were pretty surprised when a gigantic French nuclear aircraft carrier, *Jeanne d'Arc*, arrived at your naval shipyard here in Portsmouth yesterday. But we understand that the Home Secretary was dispatched to Henderson Nautical Works as well, and arrived with several heavily-armed security forces. This has led to a lot of speculation. Can you help us understand what happened?"

"Of course, Liz. I've been in the shipbuilding and repair business for many years, but ships have always been about more than money. I have a real fondness for ships, especially the great capital ships. In many ways, I sometimes think that the history of the great capital ships for the past five hundred years has been the history of the Western world." Max pauses and reflects for a moment. "You know, life is a funny thing. I never imagined two weeks ago that *Jeanne d'Arc* would be here in Portsmouth. We had a staff meeting, and I learned that the French wanted to break her down."

"Break her down?" asks Liz.

"Yes," says Max. "That's literally pulling a ship into pieces and then disposing of those pieces, or maybe reusing what you can. But it means the end of any ship. I just felt bad about that. *Jeanne d'Arc* is such a beautiful and powerful ship, with a distinguished service record. She's not old, either. Just needs a bit of care, really."

"But I'm not sure how *Jeanne d'Arc* ended up with you?"

"Oh, that? Well, the French awarded me with the National Order of Merit for services to their navy, which I thought was very nice of them."

Liz leans forward and points. "Is that the award, Max?"

Max looks down at the gleaming blue and crystal gemstones at the end of the blue ribbon. "Yes, it is, Liz. I suppose it's a little ostentatious to wear it, but I thought maybe that was okay for an interview."

"Of course, that's fine. And you were saying... about the ship?"

"Oh, yes. So, while Dom and I were in Cherbourg for the medal award, we were given a wonderful tour of *Jeanne d'Arc*. I wasn't hinting, mind you, but I must have let slip how much I admired this fantastic ship. And wouldn't you know it, they gave me *Jeanne d'Arc* as well."

Liz pauses, rather stunned by the revelation. "But, Max, doesn't that seem a bit extraordinary. Why would the French give you an aircraft carrier?"

"Well, Liz, the French can be a very generous people, you know. The Statue of Liberty was no small feat of engineering. They gave that to the people of America as a gift. Incredibly generous."

Margaret glances across the table at Jared and Ronald. "I don't like the feel of this."

"Why's that?" asks Jared.

Margaret frowns. "He's... likeable."

"He sounds like a naïve idiot to me," says Ronald.

"Yes, but a likeable one," says Margaret.

"Okay," says Liz. "But by all accounts the UK government isn't happy about these developments. The day *Jeanne d'Arc* arrived, we understand that The Home Secretary was dispatched to Henderson Nautical Works. As I said, there were several heavily-armed security forces present. It looked like this was some sort of stand-off. A lot of people thought things might even turn violent."

"Oh no" says Max. "It was nothing like that. The Home Secretary and his advisors were a little concerned, I suppose, but we had a good visit with them."

Margaret glances at Jared. "It was nothing like a good visit," snaps Jared.

"But the security forces... the guns?"

"Perfectly fine, Liz, no problems. They just wanted to understand what I was up to with *Jeanne d'Arc*, which does seem reasonable."

"And I guess that's really the main question, isn't it? I mean, that's what people want to know. What are you doing with a French nuclear aircraft carrier? Are you going to refurbish it? Is it going to be open for tours? Will it be equipped with fighter jets?"

Max rubs his mouth with a hand, reflecting. "Can I have just a moment please, Liz?"

"Of course."

Max looks down at his hands, gathering his thoughts. The brim of his blue naval cap covers most of his face, the gleaming bronze cap insignia glinting in the lights of the camera. A moment later he clears his throat and looks up.

"You know, Liz, I love this country of ours and its history. Of course, Britain has taken a few bad steps over the years, but on the whole I think we tried to do the right things for the world and for our own people. Britain, as much or more than any country, helped to bring liberty and democracy to so many people – not to mention cricket, football, and golf, though I think the Scots really get credit for golf. Anyway, we made some mistakes. The Industrial Revolution was an extraordinary accomplishment, though we didn't treat our workers well. But Britain learned, and through the horror of two world wars, we helped save millions from tyranny. We handed over the lands of a once sprawling empire to its citizens, and we became more compassionate and humble along the way. We gave our people the NHS so that the sick and mentally ill would know they would be cared for, and we did that at a time when our country was completely broke. We helped build the League of Nations and then the United Nations, doing what we could to create decency and peace... but something has gone wrong, Liz. Where is the compassion? You walk the streets of any British town or city and you see so many unwell homeless people living in fear and squalor. The NHS isn't working any more, massive corporations no longer pay tax, and our politicians seem so focused on insulting one another... I don't know how they get anything done."

"Do you see Britain as having had some golden age?" asks Liz.

Max sighs. "Well, I think that's a complicated question. Let's think about the Empire, and, for example, what happened in India. I mean, we shot an awful lot of those poor fellows before we left, and that really wasn't okay. On the other hand, we really cared about them too, and gave them so much – the railways, the rule of law, geographical surveys, a census, vaccinations and medical care. We caused a lot of trouble around the world, but I think we had a vision, and in our own way, we cared about people and human progress. Today, I see a level of cynicism and self-interest which really upsets me. We can't even figure out how to look after our own people. And it's not just Britain. Almost all of the Western nations are putting up walls, looking inward, allowing vast corporations to run everything..."

Max seems to lose his train of thought and stares into space.

"He's rambling," says Jared.

"Shhhh," says Margaret.

"Max," says Liz, "you have some strong views... which I think some people might agree with... but I don't understand how this relates to *Jeanne d'Arc*?"

"Oh, yes," says Max. "*Jeanne d'Arc* is a beautiful and powerful ship.

I'm going to refurbish her – restore her. But I want *Jeanne d'Arc* to be for people who really feel like they don't belong. For people who know they have something to give, but maybe they feel forgotten… ignored. People who are… I can't think of the right word…"

"Alienated?" suggests Liz

"Yes, that's a good word. Alienated. *Jeanne d'Arc* will be more than just a ship. We are making a petition to the United Nations for…" Max glances down at some paperwork and then looks back at the camera. "Under the 1933 Montevideo Convention on the Rights and Duties of States, *Jeanne d'Arc* is petitioning for sovereign statehood."

A look of confusion passes over Liz's face. "Sovereign statehood? Are you suggesting that you want *Jeanne d'Arc* to be… like… its own country?"

"Well," says Max, "we actually feel that under the rules of the 1933 Montevideo Convention, *Jeanne d'Arc is* sovereign now, but we want to do things the right way, so that's why we're petitioning the UN."

"And… you want this state… or country… of *Jeanne d'Arc*… to be a place for people who are… alienated?"

"Well… sure," says Max. "Like any sovereign state, *Jeanne d'Arc* will have citizens. In fact, we need citizens because that's one of the requirements of the 1933 Montevideo Convention."

Liz looks a bit stunned and at a loss for words. A few moments pass before she seems to find her way. "Max, I think a lot of people have a particular idea of what a country is. Most people don't really imagine a ship can be a country."

"You know, Liz, I'm having to learn a lot about this myself. But you would be surprised at the places that claim sovereign statehood. Some of them are pretty weird."

"Okay, Max," says Liz. "But if you think *Jeanne d'Arc* is already a sovereign state, doesn't it seem a little odd that you're in Portsmouth estuary."

"Well, yes, that's true, but things have just developed so quickly."

Liz places a finger against an earpiece and then looks at the camera. "Well, we need to go back to our news desk in a moment." She turns and faces Max. "If I may say, I think what you are suggesting is going to raise a lot of questions, but you certainly are expressing some heartfelt ideals."

The station switches to another presenter and Philcox hits the mute button. Margaret looks across the table at her Home and Defence Secretaries, her vision glazed. A single word drops from her mouth. "Shit."

CHAPTER 18

Max steps off the aluminium bridge and onto *Jeanne d'Arc*. He pauses, this morning's events passing through his mind. After the interview with Liz Burton, many of the reporters did some short on-air filming in front of his house and then left, heading back to their offices to write copy. Dom, Hedvika, and Max drove to Henderson Nautical and Max tried to get some work done in his office, but it wasn't easy. Max's staff looked at him with strange, questioning eyes, and Sheila and her office staff had to field a lot of inquisitive phone calls. Max felt bad and wondered why he hadn't imagined this sort of reaction.

Max hears a clanging sound of metal on metal and wonders what it is. He walks down steps to the first level beneath the deck and follows the noise, making his way through various holds and hangers for about five minutes. Eventually, he walks into an empty fighter jet hanger, and sees Captain Jean-Pierre. The Captain is on his knees, hitting something with a large hammer.

Max watches for a moment until Jean-Pierre notices him and pushes himself to his feet. Max stands straight, raises his chin, and offers a salute.

"Captain Lavelle. Do you need assistance?"

Jean-Pierre smiles broadly. "As you were, Petty Officer Henderson." Max makes a display of relaxing his posture. "I must teach you how to salute properly some time, Max."

"Yes sir, Captain. What are you working on?" asks Max.

It's one of the systems for lifting the plans from the hanger up to the flight deck, but the lift is stuck. There's a small bit of twisted metal which is catching."

"I didn't know the captain made repairs."

"I wasn't always a captain. I was in engineering to begin with. If I see something that's broken, I like to see if I can fix it. It's an old habit. What brings you down to *Jeanne d'Arc*?"

"I need to get away from the office."

"I saw your interview," says Jean-Pierre. "Hugo showed me on YouTube. Are things a bit fraught?"

"Yeah. It's difficult to get any work done."

Jean-Pierre nods. "You know, you need someplace on *Jeanne d'Arc* that can really be your own. There's the Captain's Cabin…"

"I wouldn't dream of it," says Max. "The Captain's Cabin belongs to you."

"That's very nice, Max, but you're paying for Hugo, Alexis and myself to stay at the Holiday Inn."

Max straightens himself once more. "These are strange times, Captain, but the chain of command must be respected."

"Well, there is the Executive Cabin, which I think might suit you well. It's a cabin which was always reserved for high-ranking visiting officers. Let me show you."

Max follows the Captain through the naval grey corridors, which all seem to look the same, up and down stairwells, and at one point through the ship's mess hall. Jean-Pierre stops there and gets a six-pack of beer from a refrigerator and some bread and cheese before carrying on. Eventually, they stand in front of a door with a copper nameplate reading *Cabine Executive*. They enter, the Captain flips a light switch, and Max takes in what appears to be a slightly smaller version of the Captain's Cabin, but, with all the same comforts – plush leather armchairs and a couch, a coffee table, small dining table, a desk for writing, a compact kitchenette, and a comfortable single bed in the corner. There is a large painting of *Jeanne d'Arc*, steaming in a heavy seas, her flight deck filled with jet fighters. One wall of the cabin contains a series of porthole windows which let in the eerie glow of Bay 4's florescent lighting.

"What do you think?"

Max feels a strange emotion and he looks away from Jean-Pierre for a moment, needing to conceal his reaction. "It's too good for a Petty Officer, I'm sure. But, yes, this will work really well."

Jean-Pierre nods, opens a cupboard, and pulls out a pint glass. He opens a beer and pours it, looks over at Max, and waves at the couch. "Have a seat, Max."

Max sits on the couch, unsure of what is happening. He watches Jean-Pierre cut slices of bread and cheese, and then put the cheese and pint of beer on the table in front of him.

"I imagine you need to be alone… to think," says Jean-Pierre.

"Thank you, Captain."

"Call me if you need anything else."

After the Captain leaves, Max sips on his beer, chews slowly on crusty bread and cheese, and stares into space. Unmarked time slips past and Max realises at one point that *he* isn't really thinking at all, but instead watching images of the past two days play out in front of him, as unreal to him as if he were watching a film. The images seem too strange to be a real part of his life, but the fact that he is sitting in the Executive Cabin of a nuclear-powered aircraft carrier is an affecting reminder that this *is* real.

His phone rings. "Hi, Dom."

"Hi, boss. Just wondering if I can catch up with you about a couple of things."

Max looks at his empty glass and realises that he wants to show Dom his new cabin. "It's after 5 PM, Dom. Come and have a drink with me. I'm on *Jeanne d'Arc* in what's called the Executive Cabin."

"Be over in a minute," says Dom. "Just keep your phone on."

Max hangs up. He doesn't know how he does it, but Dom can locate him through his phone signal. Max pours two beers, cuts more cheese and bread, and sinks back into the couch. It isn't long before Dom knocks on the door and makes himself comfortable opposite Max in a plush leather armchair.

Dom smiles broadly at Max, looking around the room. "And people wonder why you want your own aircraft carrier."

"Cheers, Dom. Jean-Pierre picked it out for me. Have a beer. How's Hedvika doing with all of this? I've put a lot on her plate."

"She's alright, boss. I saw her a couple of hours ago. I think she's working on that UN petition."

"Dom, do you think I'm losing my mind?"

"Nah. Look at you. You're drinking beer and relaxing on your nuclear aircraft carrier. You're alright." Dom takes a swig on his pint.

"But people think I'm crazy, right?"

"I don't know boss – I'm not taking any polls."

Max takes a sip of beer and finds himself thinking about his son. "How's Peter getting on?"

Dom laughs. "Peter has been at work for three days now. Have a look at this." Dom reaches into a bag and pulls out a laptop. He opens the laptop, sits next to Max on the leather couch, and switches the computer on. "One of our security guys sent me an email with a clip from one of our CCTV cameras. Your son is the star."

"Oh god, what happened?"

Dom opens an email, clicks a link, and a video begins to run. Max sees his son in one of Henderson Nautical Works' warehouses, wearing standard green janitorial overalls and leaning against a broom. Suddenly,

Peter drops the broom and begins to run for the entrance of the warehouse. A young man appears at the bottom of the screen and runs after Peter. Just as Peter is about to reach the warehouse door, he is tackled from behind by the other man. The other man is tall, lean, and well-muscled. He pulls Peter to his feet and leads him by his arm out of sight of the camera. There is some shouting, but Max can't make out what is being said.

"What the hell just happened?" asks Max.

"That was Peter trying to do a runner."

"Who's the guy who tackled him?"

"That's Robert. He had a try out for the England National Rugby team some years ago. Didn't make the squad and doesn't play professionally anymore. But he can still move pretty good. He normally works in ship maintenance. Painting hulls, mostly. I put him on my security team."

"And his job is... what?"

"He keeps an eye on Peter," says Dom.

Max laughs. "So this guy's job is tackling Peter if he tries to run off?"

"Pretty much, boss."

Max shakes his head. "Jesus. What about after work hours?"

"Peter is staying with a friend of mine for now," says Dom. "He's in an apartment over in Somerstown."

"Somerstown? That's a pretty rough area. This friend of yours – will he keep Peter safe?"

Dom grins. "I've known this guy since I was a kid. If Peter doesn't behave himself, my friend will probably thump him. Like you said, boss, rehab doesn't work."

"Alright. Thanks. Let's call this *Dom's very intense rehab programme*. If it works, I think you deserve a Nobel Prize."

"Boss, I need to talk to you about something. I think we need to hire a few more security staff."

"For Peter?" asks Max.

"Well, probably," says Dom. "But that's not what I'm thinking about. People are still showing up. There's a big crowd of them outside the gate right now.

"Reporters?" asks Max.

"Maybe, but it seems different. There is music and people holding placards – people are singing. They seem like an odd mix and I really don't know what they're doing. I just think we need a few more staff to make sure the site is secure."

"Yeah, that's fine, Dom. Do what you need to."

Dom takes a swig of his pint. "Boss – the thing is, a lot of people saw your interview. I checked an hour ago and more than 135,000 have watched it on YouTube."

Max sighs and finishes the last of his pint. Dom follows suit and downs his. "Boss, we need to be a bit more thoughtful about your security. You're a little bit of a celebrity now."

"Bugger that," says Max.

"I mean it, boss – you should have a look at this crowd."

"Okay, let's go have a look."

They stand up. Dom looks around the Executive Cabin and then touches Max's arm. "Actually, boss, I think having this cabin is a good idea. You need a place where you can disappear if you want to. Maybe you shouldn't tell people about it – I mean, aside from Sheila and Hedvika."

They walk for the door. "Dom, I think all of this is hard on Sheila and Hedvika. I want to do something for them."

"Okay, boss."

"Something nice. Hedvika told me she's shopping for a car. Something sporty, she said."

"I'll look into it, boss."

Max and Dom navigate their way off the ship and eventually enter Max's office. When they arrive, they see Hedvika sitting in front of Max's desk, looking at her phone. They had been aware of noise from the crowd outside the gates of Henderson Nautical as they walked over, and they can hear it now through the window.

Hedvika looks up. "Max, do you know what's going on?"

"I try not to. It gives me headaches."

"Max, you're all over the internet. Twitter, Facebook, YouTube – all the major news outlets. You're... what do they say... trending."

"That's impossible, Hedvika. I'm middle-aged and I wear trousers which I'm told are too short. It won't catch on."

"Max! Please be serious."

"Hedvika, I take things every bit as seriously as the universe does."

Hedvika groans, but Max detects a smile his lawyer is trying to conceal.

The noise from outside the window hits a new pitch and they can hear singing. Hedvika stands up and walks to the window, Max and Dom joining her. They can see a crowd of perhaps one hundred and twenty people standing just beyond Henderson Nautical's entrance gate. Someone has been leading the crowd in chanting slogans and now many of them are trying to sing the U2 song *Pride*, but they seem to be getting a lot of the words wrong. The crowd of people are facing them and some are holding up handmade signs. Max scans the signs:

PEOPLE POWER
THE CORPORATE PIGS ARE RUNNING
JEANNE D'ARC IS A NATION OF LOVE

There are a few signs which read *THE MAX FACTOR IS HERE!*

Max looks at Hedvika. "What do they mean by the Max Factor?"

"You're the Max Factor," she says. "A factor is something you have to consider, right?"

There is a collection of pallets by the gate and they watch as a few people make four piles of them, joined together. This forms something resembling a small stage. Two people are then helped up onto this impromptu stage by others, and they stand there, facing the audience. They seem like a strange couple. One of them is a very tall guy – skinny, long hair, a scraggly beard, maybe in his late thirties. He's holding a megaphone. Standing next to the man is a short and very overweight woman with purple hair, about the same age. She looks very unsteady on the pallet stage and waves her arms, as if trying to keep her balance. The singing of *Pride* seems to peter out, possibly because the crowd is now really making a mess of the words, and possibly in anticipation that the guy with the megaphone might say something.

The skinny guy raises the megaphone to his lips and waits for a moment, and the noise from the crowd dies down. "You're here – I'm here – because we heard a message of hope..." He pauses and a few people clap tentatively. "And we heard that message of hope from Max Henderson, a man who spent his life building ships, a man who has become so sickened by what he sees that he has decided to build a nation... for people who a broken society forgot, for people like you and me..." There is more clapping and a few people cheer and whistle. "You don't hear too much about arks these days. It's just a metaphor, but Noah built an ark in order that humanity could begin again... and now, maybe for the second time in history, humanity needs an ark... and, let me tell you, she's arrived... *Jeanne d'Arc!*" There is more cheering and a smattering of clapping. "But the government is coming for Max... you can be sure of it. They're coming. They want to shut Max up, shut him down. But let me tell you something – when the government comes for Max… they're coming for you… they're coming for me… they're coming for everybody! Are we going to let them come for Max?" A handful of people shout *"NO!"*. "You listened to the news… you know that some people are saying Max is crazy, right? Well, guess what? They said that Jesus was crazy, that Gandhi was crazy, that Martin Luther King was crazy. And why? Because they all said we needed kindness and compassion. Well, maybe the world is ready for a little bit of Max's crazy!" The crowd cheers and claps, and there is a growing confidence now in their shared response.

Some vehicles pull up – a rusty van with a sunrise painted on the side and a couple of old cars. People pile out of the van and cars. "There's more coming," says Hedvika.

Max nods and gets two beers out of his office fridge. "Do you want a drink, Hedvika?"

Hedvika shakes her head. "No, I've got work to get to." She looks over at Dom. "Keep a close eye on Max, okay?"

"I always do," says Dom.

"I know, Dom, but this is different. That guy just compared Max to Jesus, Gandhi, and Martin Luther King. That's nice, but if I recall they shot all of those guys."

"I'll be fine, Hedvika," says Max.

Hedvika leaves, and Max goes to the window and hands Dom a beer and a glass. They watch as the skinny guy continues bellowing into his megaphone, and occasionally the obese short girl standing next to him punches the air with a chubby fist for effect. They remind Max of Laurel and Hardy.

"What do you think?" asks Max.

"Well, that skinny guy seems to think that what you're doing is pretty important."

Max nods and takes a long swig on his pint. "You like fast cars with big engines, right Dom?"

"Sure, boss."

"You got a collection, haven't you?"

"I wouldn't call it a collection. But yeah, I've got a few muscle cars tucked away in a garage. I like to take 'em out for a drive, clean 'em, give 'em a wax. Keeps me out of trouble, right?"

"I bet shopping for a jet aeroplane would be fun?"

"I suppose so, boss. I don't really know anything about planes, though."

"That's alright," says Max. "We know someone who does."

"You mean Hugo Dubois?"

Max takes a large swig on his pint and gazes at Dom, his eyes glassy with the drinking he'd been doing. Max jerks his thumb at the window again. "I'd like to talk with that guy."

They look down at this odd spectacle. The guy is still shouting into the megaphone and he's quite animated now. The pallet platform isn't very stable, so when the guy gets especially dynamic the overweight girl standing next to him has to grab his arm so as not to fall off.

"You want me to bring the guy to you, boss?"

"Yeah. Why don't you wait until he finishes his speech and then say I'd like to meet him."

"You want me to bring the fat bird too?"

"Sure," says Max. "Why not?"

CHAPTER 19

Prime Minister Margaret Wilson sits at her desk at Number 10, gazing into space. It's 5:30 PM and she is annoyed that she is still working. She had considered calling an extra-special cabinet meeting to discuss *Joan of Arc* but decided not to, in large part because she was hoping this situation would not develop into anything remotely extra special. The problem is that the media seem to love the story, and her aides are having a hard time sticking to *'the Prime Minister is looking into the situation'*. She decided that if she doesn't act or make a public statement tomorrow, the rumours and conjectures will only grow.

Margaret's intercom comes to life and she hears her PA's voice. "Prime Minister, Home Secretary Jared Philcox, Defence Secretary Ronald Hudd and Secretary for Digital, Culture, Media and Sport, Sarah Keeling, are here."

"That's fine," says Margaret. "Show them in, please." Margaret is surprised that Sarah is here as well, but she imagines there must be a reason.

A moment later, her staff walk through the door and sit together around her oval office table. "Good evening, Prime Minister," says Sarah. "I hope you don't mind me joining. Jared thought it might be helpful."

"Absolutely fine," says Margaret, looking at her PA who is still standing in the doorway. "Can you bring us tea, please?"

"Yes, Prime Minister."

"Right," says Margaret. "It's late. Let's get straight to it. Can I have an update?"

"The situation is well contained," says Ronald. "We have two destroyers, *HMS Northumberland* and *HMS Dauntless*, one carrier, *HMS Prince of Wales*, and our nuclear submarine, *HMS Vanguard*, all situated five miles off the Portsmouth coast."

"How does that help?" says Margaret. "I want the damn thing gone, not blockaded."

"Prime Minister, we need to be prepared for every eventuality. This is a capital ship of war which is sitting in one of our ports and it's not under our control."

"Okay, fine," says Margaret, looking at Jared Philcox. "What are we hearing from Henderson?"

"Well, I'm afraid Henderson isn't returning my phone calls," says Jared.

"Wonderful," says Margaret. "What else?"

"We have eight MI5 operatives," says Ronald, "who are situated in the crowd at Henderson Nautical. I'm getting reports at thirty-minute intervals."

Margaret sighs. "What crowd?"

"There is a crowd of people," says Ronald, "that have gathered just outside the gates of Henderson Nautical Works. We're estimating there are between four hundred and fifty and five hundred people."

Margaret squints. "Why? What are they doing there?"

"Prime Minister," says Home Secretary Philcox. "We've been looking at *Jeanne d'Arc* as a security issue and of course that makes sense, but I've asked Sarah here because I think we now need to look at this as a public relations issue as well. Sarah has been exploring this angle. Sarah?"

Sarah Keeling opens her laptop and turns it on. "Prime Minister," she says, "people started turning up at Henderson Nautical Works following Henderson's interview, and the crowd seems to be growing in size. I've been trying to develop a profile on just who they are and what they're doing there. The MI5 operatives have been mixing with the crowd and speaking to some of them. There are also news reporters in the crowd, and they've done some interviews which have aired. People seem to be there for a variety of reasons."

Sarah faces her laptop in the direction of the others. "This is a BBC interview which aired about an hour ago. It gives us a starting point in understanding this phenomenon."

She plays the video. A female journalist is standing in the crowd and speaking. *"I'm standing just outside the gates at Henderson Nautical Works, where a crowd of people have gathered. You can see behind me that there's quite a large number of people here now. There's someone making a speech and you can see that a number of people have made placards and there are others playing music and singing. There're some vendors over there selling food and beer. There seems to be something of a party atmosphere and I'm seeing a number of families here with children too".* The reporter takes a couple of steps and stands next to a woman and two of her children. *"Hello there. I understand you have come here earlier today with your family. Where have you come from?"*

"My husband and I and our two children came down from London this morning. My husband is over there, getting some beer."

"Right. And why have you come here today?"

"Well, we saw Max Henderson on TV doing that interview, and we just thought, y'know, that's great, you know, the things he was saying. And we heard that other people were coming here too. So we said, let's go and see what's happening." The woman looks down at one of her children. *"Jennifer, don't hit your brother",* she says. The woman looks back at the camera.

"So, there's a lot of people here", says the interviewer. *"Does anyone seem to be organising this?"*

"I don't know. I think people just started showing up. I think it's great. My husband and I wanted to bring our kids too because we wanted them to see what you can do through social action. I think it's a good experience for them."

"Thanks for your time."

The interviewer takes a few steps away and is suddenly hit in the arm by a Frisbee. *"Oops. What's that?"* She bends down and picks the Frisbee up and hands it to a young guy who jogs up to her. *"Sorry",* he says.

"That's okay", says the interviewer. The interviewer then walks several feet over to a man who is placing t-shirts onto hangers in front of his truck. *"I want to have a word with one of the vendors as well".* She points her microphone at the vendor selling t-shirts. *"Hello sir, I'm with the BBC, do you mind if I ask you a few questions?"*

"Sure."

"Where have you come from today?"

"Oh, we live right here in Portsmouth."

"Uh-huh. And what are you selling?"

The man holds up one of his t-shirts, which displays a picture of an aircraft carrier and the words **The Max Factor is Here!**

"Wow, you sure got those t-shirts together quickly", says the reporter.

"Yeah, well, we got a shop in town. Mostly we sell novelties to people on holiday, but we do t-shirts as well, so it wasn't difficult."

"And do you think they'll sell?"

"I sold two of 'em and I ain't even got my stall set up properly."

"Well, good luck to you and thank you for your time, sir."

The reporter walks a few feet and stands near a middle-aged man and woman who appear to be smoking pot. *"Hello there, I'm with the BBC, I'm just trying to understand what brings people here today – can I have a word with you?"*

"Um... okay", says the woman.

"Have you travelled far to get here today?"

"We come up from Southampton in the van with the dogs this morning", says the woman.

"And why did you want to make the trip?"

"Because the government doesn't give a shit about regular people", says the woman. *"It's all about special interest groups and kick-backs. We heard Max on TV and we come down here to protest."*

"And what's your view, sir?" the reporter says, pointing the mic in the direction of the man. He takes a hit on what is clearly a large doobie and blows out smoke. *"I love that Max has got a nuclear aircraft carrier. I think everyone should probably have a nuclear aircraft carrier or something like that. Some people think he shouldn't be allowed to have one, but I think it's great. We're thinking about becoming citizens of Jeanne d'Arc."*

"Really?"

"Yeah. I mean, we don't know what it all involves, but we're thinking about it."

The Communications Secretary pauses the video and looks at Margaret. "There's more I could show you, but I think that clip is a fair representation of the sort of people who are there."

"Alright," says Margaret. "So there's people who have gone down to Portsmouth to throw Frisbees, sell t-shirts, and get stoned. I don't see how this changes things. We can't have private ownership of nuclear aircraft carriers, so the ship needs to be seized."

Sarah and Jared exchange glances. "Prime Minister," says Sarah, "as Jared said, I think we need to consider the public relations consequences if we go in there with security forces. We've done some polling on Max Henderson and…"

"What?" says Margaret. "We're polling this guy?"

"Yes, Prime Minister. We really felt we needed to gauge public opinion. It's just a preliminary poll, but sixty-nine per cent of people approve of what Henderson is doing."

Margaret stands up from the table and walks to the office window. She looks out at the London Street, shakes her head, and then turns to look at her colleagues. "Sixty-nine per cent? What the hell? My approval rating has been stuck in the forties for months."

"The polling on Henderson does seem strange," says Sarah, "but we've managed to do some follow-up interviews and a few focus groups, and I've talked through the data with my team. It seems that a fair number of British people see Max Henderson as some sort of anti-hero."

"Anti-hero?" says Margaret. "What does that even mean?"

"Well," says Sarah, "it's sort of like a heroic figure, but one that's unconventional, one that doesn't fit the stereotype of a traditional heroic figure."

"Ridiculous," says Margaret. "Don't the British people understand that this guy is playing around with a nuclear-powered warship and endangering national security?"

"I think people do have a vague idea of that," says Home Secretary Philcox. "Personally, I think Henderson is a fruitcake who has no business owning a capital ship of war. But – and I think it needs saying Prime Minister – the public perception of the Government is not positive at the moment. People think private interest groups have too much influence and that we aren't getting things done. So along comes this guy with a nuclear carrier who throws out a few glib comments about how we're all supposed to be nicer to one another, and…" Jared seems to lose his thread of thought and looks over at Sarah for help.

"People like him, Prime Minister," says Sarah. "That's the issue."

Margaret laughs. "So you're telling me that we shouldn't take possession of that damn ship because some people like Max Henderson. And why is this my problem? Where are the French in all of this? It's their balls-up. Why aren't they acknowledging what happened and taking their damn boat back?"

"I've had a further conversation with Secretary of State Philipe Dupont this morning," says Jared. "Dupont says they are discussing the matter, but he's suggesting they are likely to have legal difficulties getting the ship back from Henderson."

"What sort of legal difficulties?" says Margaret.

"Well, Dupont pointed out that they signed a document formally gifting the ship to Henderson. The document is apparently binding under French law, so they may not have legal grounds to force Henderson to return the boat."

Margaret stares at her Home Secretary. "Well, this is just fantastic. Henderson isn't returning our phone calls, the French don't accept returns, and we're not supposed to seize the boat because people think Henderson is an anti-hero, whatever the hell that means."

Margaret paces back to the window again and reflects. A full minute passes before she turns around and faces her staff. "I appreciate your views, but the fact is that this absurd scenario represents a threat to national security and is making the government look weak and indecisive. I want us to seize that boat." Margaret looks at her Defence Secretary. "Ronald?"

Ronald opens his mouth to speak, but Home Secretary Philcox jumps in. "Prime Minister, Ronald has prepared a plan of assault and seizure of the ship and Max Henderson which is no doubt competent, but there's another element I'm afraid we have to consider."

Jared turns his laptop so Margaret can get a good look at it before continuing. "I'm sure Sarah's profile of that crowd is quite accurate," says Jared, "but there's a certain element which we need to take into account if we really are going to make an assault. There is a man and woman who have been standing on a pallet stage and making speeches much of today."

"What's a pallet stage?" asks Margaret.

"It's not important, Prime Minister. It's just an impromptu stage that got made out of some pallets which were lying around."

Jared points at the laptop screen which displays the image of the pallet stage, on top of which stands a tall skinny guy and an obese short woman."

"Who are these two?" asks Margaret. "They remind me of Laurel and Hardy."

"The skinny fellow is named Winston Godfred. He's the one making speeches. The content is mostly left-wing socialism and it's not overly flattering of the Government. Winston is thirty-eight, comes from a wealthy family, and has a mental health history. He's been a psychiatric inpatient on three occasions and has attempted suicide at least twice. He's been diagnosed with mania, personality disorder, and half a dozen other problems. He's actually got a Ph.D. in history from Oxford, but he's been fired from two university teaching posts, including one at Oxford. He's not an idiot, but he's definitely got issues."

"Is he coordinating this crowd?" asks Margaret.

"Not especially Prime Minister. But I'm not sure Winston Godfred is our biggest worry. We think he's a well-meaning guy who has problems. The one who worries me is the individual standing next to him," says Jared, pointing to the purple-haired woman. "She's well known to MI5. GCHQ also have her on their radar. Her birth name is Laura Beech, but she legally changed her name some years ago to Sunrise70. She's been arrested eight times over the past ten years, normally for disturbing the peace, but she's done prison time for destruction of property and assault on police officers. She's been connected to a couple of far-left socialist groups at one time or another, but she's a bit of a single operation. You can't predict where she will turn up. She hasn't been making speeches — she's just standing on the stage with Winston Godfred."

"Why does she call herself Sunrise70?"

"We're not entirely sure, Prime Minister," says Jared. "One of the agents at MI5 suggested that 1970 was the year that students protesting the Vietnam War at Kent State University were shot by the National Guard. That's her sort of protest."

"What's the connection between Winston and Sunrise70?" asks Margaret.

"We can't find an obvious connection, but it's possible they know one another. It's also possible they met when they showed up at Henderson Nautical Works. But what I want to emphasise, Prime Minister, is that Winston Godfred has been making rather maniacal speeches all day. As Sarah pointed out, there are people throwing Frisbees around, listening to music, and smoking pot. But there are a fair few people who are listening to Godfred. If we go in with security forces, even at night, I just think we need to consider that particular element. And, wherever Sunrise70 turns up, there tends to be problems and arrests."

Margaret stands up and walks to the window, looks down into the street, and gives herself a minute to sift through this information. A moment later she turns and faces her Secretaries. "Oh, Christ!" she says.

"What's that, Prime Minister?" says Jared.

"Waco, Texas," says Margaret. "That's what you're worried about, isn't it, Jared?"

Jared sighs. "I wasn't going to mention Waco specifically, Prime Minister. Waco was different in many ways, but it certainly went through my mind. This situation is unprecedented and has developed quickly, so it's difficult to predict how people on site will react if we make an assault. To be honest, it's difficult to predict where any of this is going. The interest in this story may gain momentum in some way, or maybe something else interesting will pop up in the news cycle and distract everyone. But what worries me right now, Prime Minister, is this – if we make an assault on Henderson Nautical and there's even one fatality, it could have serious political consequences."

"Can't we just make the assault from the estuary and avoid the crowd?" says Margaret.

"We've considered that, Prime Minister," says Ronald. "Unfortunately, the doors to the shed are closed and locked. We could blow them open from the exterior, but you would still risk injuring or killing people. We think the assault needs to be coordinated from the sea and the land."

Margaret turns and again looks down into the street. Words slip from her mouth, almost as if she is speaking to herself. "What the hell are you doing, Henderson?"

CHAPTER 20

Dom opens the door to Max's office and shows Winston Godfred and Sunrise70 in. Max stands up and extends a hand across his desk.

"Hello, I'm Max Henderson."

Winston shakes his hand, his eyes lighting up. "I'm Winston Godfred. Mr Henderson – what an extraordinary honour to meet you in person."

"Please, call me Max."

Max extends his hand to the woman. "Hello," says Max.

The woman takes his hand briefly, her eyes shifting about the room. "Sunrise70."

Max is confused. "What's that?"

"That's her name," says Winston.

"Oh," says Max. "Nice to meet you, Sunrise70. Won't you both have a seat please?"

Everyone sits down, Dom taking a seat in a corner on Max's side of the desk. A moment later, Sheila walks in with a tray of tea and biscuits which she places on Max's desk. After sorting out everyone's tea, Sheila makes an exit, closing the door. Max takes a closer look at his guests. Winston wears khaki trousers and an army-issue olive green shirt, but there is a three-inch strip of bright red material which has been hand-sewn around the forearm area. He is beaming with childlike enthusiasm through long hair and a scraggly beard. He looks like he needs to see a dentist. Sunrise70 stares blankly at Max. Her purple hair is shaved very short, which seems to accentuate her pudgy features, and there is something not right about her face. It takes Max a moment to figure it out – her eyebrows are missing.

"So, then," says Max, "you've met Dom?"

"Yes, yes," says Winston, waving at Dom.

"I've asked to see you," says Max, "because we couldn't help but overhear some of what you have been saying Winston. You seem rather... engaged."

"Mr Henderson... I mean Max," says Winston. "When I saw you on television, I got on a bus and came straight here. It was like you were speaking directly to me. You have a vision, Max, and I felt that vision. I knew immediately that I had to come here and help you in any way I could. Just let me know how I can help, Max."

Max laughs and looks over at Dom. "Well, that's enthusiasm." Dom grins.

"So, what brings you here, Sunrise?" asks Max.

"It's Sunrise70."

"Oh yes," says Max. "What brings you here, Sunrise70?"

The large woman looks down and shakes her head, and for a moment it seems like she isn't going to respond. But then she says, under her breath, "You're shaking shit up."

Max waits a moment, wondering if she has more to say. He looks back to Winston. "So, how do you two know each other?"

"We just met," says Winston. "I was making a speech and I saw Sunrise70 dragging these pallets around. I didn't know what she was doing, but then at one point I understood she was making a stage. I assumed she was going to use the stage for making a speech herself, but she comes over to me, points to the stage and says, *"That's for you"*. She said, *"Get up there – the people will be able to see and hear you better"*. I thought that was very nice of her, so I said, *"Come and stand up there with me"*, and she did."

Max nods. "Alright."

"Max," says Winston, "this is all about *Jeanne d'Arc*, isn't it? *Jeanne d'Arc* is the new world, a chance to begin again. Like you said on TV, a place for forgotten people. Please let me help you. I'm happy to accept any role. Just let me know what you want me to do. I'll sweep the floors and do the washing up if that's what you need."

Max smiles. "Winston, I'm going to need more from you than that. The government wants to take *Jeanne d'Arc* away from us. If we are going to be able to make a proper petition to the UN for sovereign statehood, she's going to have to look an awful lot more like an independent state. I need citizens and every other feature of a fully functioning nation-state. Everything."

Winston takes a deep breath and blows it out slowly. He then places both hands across his chest. "Max," he says, his voice filling with emotion, "it would be the greatest honour of my life to play this role. Ever since I saw your interview, I've been reading about the 1933 Montevideo Convention and studying other micronations when I have time. When can I start?"

"Right now." Max looks over at Dom. "Dom, can you sort out a workspace for Winston on *Jeanne d'Arc*? He needs a large room where he can work, and a cabin to sleep in if he needs it."

"Sure, boss."

"Now, Sunrise70," says Max, "do you want to be involved?"

"Fuck, yes," she says.

"Good," says Max. "I want you to be Winston's assistant."

Sunrise70 nods her head slowly.

"Right. If you'll have a seat back in the waiting room, Dom will be with you in a moment."

They stand up and Winston pumps Max's hand. "Thank you, Max. Really... thank you."

"That's fine, Winston."

Dom closes the door after them and sits down in front of Max's desk. Max opens his arms. "What do you think, Dom?"

"I don't know boss. I haven't been able to do any background checks."

"Okay... okay. But what do you think?"

"Well, that Winston character seems like he'll be a good soldier. Sunrise... I can't even bring myself to say her name because it's so stupid. I don't think she's gonna be anybody's assistant."

Max nods his head. "Alright. Well, can you get them sorted out, and let's see what they can do."

"You got it, boss."

Max walks to the window and looks out at the crowd beyond Henderson Nautical Works' metal gate. He notices several tents he hadn't seen before and a number of camper vans, some of which have opened awnings. Some kids are playing tag, a woman is playing guitar, and a handful of people are singing along with her.

Max waves his hand at the crowd. "This is just so... surprising. They're not leaving."

"Yeah, it's unexpected, I guess," says Dom.

"What have they got to eat?"

"I don't know. Maybe they brought food. There was a vendor selling food earlier, but I think he's gone for the day."

"I didn't expect people to come here."

"I know, boss."

Max looks at these people, thinking. "Let's get a food truck, Dom. Have it parked right down there."

"Alright," says Dom. "I can arrange it. What sort of food?"

"I don't know. Something for breakfast, lunch, and dinner. And something to drink. Tea, coffee, juice — that sort of thing. Bill my personal account."

"You got it, boss."

CHAPTER 21

Max sits in a corner seat of Portsmouth's *Brewhouse and Kitchen*, checks his watch, and notices that it's just after 7 PM. He isn't sure if meeting up with Peter at a brewpub is the best idea, but Max decided that keeping things as normal as possible might work best. Plus, Dom had reported that Peter was getting on with his janitorial job and hadn't attempted to run off over the past couple of days. The pub served a gorgeously hopped in-house IPA and pale ale and displayed an antique wooden model of the *Cutty Sark*, so there was that too.

Max takes a sip of his IPA and then waves at Peter, who is walking through the front door. Walking beside Peter is a six-foot-five man with broad shoulders and a square jaw. Anyone noticing their entrance would assume these were two mates out for a drink, rather than a heroin addict in the early days of recovery and his 'handler'.

The big man offers his hand to Max. "How're you doing, Mr Henderson? I'm Robert."

"Good to meet you, Robert," says Max, shaking his hand. "Thank you for looking after my son."

"That's fine, Mr Henderson. I'm just gonna have a seat at another table – give you and Peter a chance to catch up."

Max hands him a twenty. "Get yourself a drink and something to eat, Robert."

"Thank you, sir," says Robert, heading off to the bar.

Peter drops down into a seat and grins broadly. "Hey, Dad."

Max inspects Peter closely, and then places a hand against his son's clean-shaven face. Max can see that his son is still underweight, but Peter's chiselled good looks are evident again. "Those cuts and bruises are healing up, Peter. You're looking better."

"Thanks, Dad."

Max motions to a passing waitress. "You want something to eat? You want a drink?"

"I already ate," says Peter. "I'll have a coke, though."

"One coke, please," Max says to the waitress.

Max looks back to his son. "How's the job going?"

"It's good," says Peter.

"What have they got you doing?"

"Sweeping the floors. Mopping. Picking up garbage."

Max nods and then points to Robert, who is collecting his drink and making his way to a table by the door. "The situation with that guy must seem a little strange. I think it's sort of like Dom's rehabilitation programme."

Peter smiles. "When you're an addict, nothing is strange. It's alright. It's better than normal rehab."

Max and Peter gaze at each other for a moment. "So, do you think you're gonna make it?" asks Max.

"I hope so," says Peter. "But I don't know. When the withdrawal is over and I'm not using I always think I'm never gonna use again. This is the time when I'm confident. But then I always blow it."

"Well, this time can be different, right?"

Peter shrugs. "I hope so, Dad."

Max reaches out, takes his son's long, bony hand, and squeezes it between his fingers. "Is there anything else I can do?"

Peter thinks for a moment, smiles, and then jerks a thumb in the direction of his 'handler'. "Give Robert a gun. If there's a day when he can't catch me, have him shoot me instead."

Max grimaces. "That's not funny, Peter."

Peter laughs. "It's a joke, Dad."

Max steers his Audi A8 along Fawcett Road, images of Peter drifting through his head. He recalls giving Peter a hug fifteen minutes ago and turning him over to the retired rugby player. The whole situation seemed strangely normal, and he hoped it would stay that way. Max realises suddenly that he is driving home. Of course he is heading home – why wouldn't he be heading home? That made sense, and yet Max didn't know if he wanted to go home. Home meant seeing Violeta if she was in. Home meant being alone if Violeta wasn't in. He checked his watch: 8:35 PM. He rings Dom.

"Hi, boss. What's up?"

"Just checking in. Can I buy you a drink? I'm not far away."

"Wish I could, boss. I'm hosting poker at my place tonight." Max hears some laughter in the background.

"Okay," says Max. "No problem. Another time."

There is a pause on the line. "Boss, come on over. Sit in on a few hands. You got money to lose, right?"

"Nah. You guys have fun."

There is another pause on the line. "You gonna be okay, boss?"

"Stop worrying, Dom. I'm fine. Enjoy your poker. I'll see you tomorrow."

"Alright. Take it easy, okay?"

"Yeah, yeah," says Max. Max hangs up and continues to steer his car towards home, not knowing what else to do.

Ten minutes later he pulls his car into the garage, kills the engine, and stares into space. He feels the ache of something dark and nameless, right in the middle of his chest. It's not exactly painful. It's heavy and feels less like something and more like an absence. He'd felt this many times before and had once asked Dr Anoop about it. Dr Anoop had asked him to point to where he felt the sensation and Max had pointed. Dr Anoop said *"That's your solar plexus"*, and then reminded him that he had done a cardiogram not too long ago and that Max was fine.

"Sod it," Max says, shaking his head forcefully. He didn't know what a solar plexus was but when he felt like this he understood that he had *to move*, that he had to do something. He jumps from the car and walks through the garage door and into his kitchen. He hears singing coming from upstairs… Violeta singing. Max pulls a beer from the fridge, pours it too quickly into a pint glass, kills nearly half the glass in three large mouthfuls, and belches. He makes his way up the stairs, walks silently down the hallway, and then stands just outside the bathroom. The door is open and Violeta is naked, facing away from him, shower steam still hanging in the air, water droplets clinging to her skin. Violeta sings Rachmaninoff's Zdes' khorosho, the sad notes rising and falling, every moment hinting at completion but just missing, and then the cycle beginning again, perhaps with something new to consider, but, however beautiful, never releasing the tension. Max remembers that the song will finish but will never release the tension, and he recalls that this is what made that song so perfect and awful.

Violeta raises and extends her arms as she sings. His wife is not just singing – she is performing. He wonders which performance. Images come to Max and he can see Violeta on stage at the Wiener Konzerthaus Haus in Vienna. She is accompanied by two trumpets and piano, and the small ensemble is conducted by a tall man who moves his baton and body with the rising and falling of the notes. Max is three rows back, right in the middle seat, the audience captivated and utterly silent.

Violeta finally raises one naked arm, water droplets falling to the bathroom floor. She allows her hand to dip forward, her other hand resting on her heart, and the last note trails off into silence. The bathroom is quiet but Max can hear the thunder of the Viennese crowd as they leap to their feet, clap loudly, and shout brava! Violeta stands tall, raises her right arm, acknowledges the crowd and no doubt smiles brightly. Violeta freezes, then turns suddenly and stares at Max, the memory for both of them broken.

"Max," she shouts, "what are you doing there?"

"I was just... I was listening."

Violeta grabs at a large plush towel and wraps it around her body, irritation written on her face. "You are like... espionaje. Furtivo."

"I'm sorry, Violeta. I can't remember those words."

"You are a spy," she spits at him. "A sneak."

"I was remembering when you sang that song in Vienna."

"I sang in Vienna many times," says Violeta. "Many halls."

"Yes, but you know the one I mean. The Wiener Konzerthaus. The architecture was art nouveau. It was... I think twenty-five, maybe twenty-six years ago. Do you remember?"

Violeta smiles, despite herself. "They gave me so many bouquets of flowers that night I needed three stagehands to help me carry them to the car."

"I know. I carried the flowers too. We stayed that night at the Grand Hotel Wien. Do you remember?"

Violeta nods. "It was down the street from the Vienna State Opera House."

"That's right," says Max, and images of the sex he and Violeta had that night come into his head, the memory strangely vivid. The warmth and softness of her skin under his hands. He remembers entering Violeta. He was really hard and it seemed that he had completely filled her, and he recalls the way she had moaned. "And there was a couple getting married we met at breakfast," says Max. "Their florist had botched everything, and you gave them all your flowers to use for their wedding. We couldn't take the flowers on the plane anyway. Do you remember?"

Violeta offers a small nod. "I remember the performance. The rest... un poco. It was a long time ago."

Max takes two tentative steps, now standing just inside the bathroom. He raises one hand, wondering if he will touch her face. "In our room at Grand Hotel Wien they had silk sheets. Do you remember?"

Violeta's expression hardens. "I'm going out, Max. I have to get dressed."

"Violeta…" says Max.

"You're going to make me late."

Max turns quickly, makes his way down the stairs, and a moment later finds himself standing in the middle of the kitchen. His heart is thudding against his ribs and his body goes into motion, hands moving without thought. He pulls six bottles of pale ale out of the refrigerator, grabs two freezer packs from the freezer, and puts everything plus a bag of crisps and a pint glass into a carrier bag. He takes the bag up to his office on the third floor, his movements mechanical. Max pours one of the pale ales into his pint, pops the glass onto his desk, turns his computer on, and places the remaining five beers on the floor of his office. He places the two freezer packs between the beers on the floor, then throws a towel over the beers to keep them chilled.

The melody of Rachmaninov's Zdes' khorosho plays on in his head. He doesn't want to hear it anymore, but the tune had taken root now and he remembers more. Zdes' khorosho was set to words by a Russian poet whose name Max has forgotten, but what he recalls is that it tells the story of an ethereal paradise in the distance, an earthly idyll, but it is also about the reminiscence of loss, and the yearning to recapture an old emotion.

Max hears Violeta begin to hum to herself, so he plays music from an alt-country playlist through his computer speakers. He takes a long swig of beer and decides to do something he hasn't been able to get around to – researching arms fairs. He is about to open an internet browser when he remembers that a couple of weeks ago Dom had installed a VPN onto his computer and made Max promise that he would use it. Dom had explained that when Max activates the VPN software, all of his internet traffic gets routed through a different server, which makes him anonymous. Dom had told him that the government might be monitoring his internet use. Max chooses a server in the Netherlands and activates the VPN. Thirty seconds later, the VPN confirms that his IP address had been changed and his traffic is now anonymous.

Max takes a large swig from his pint, opens his browser, and types in *Arms Fairs*. Forty-five minutes drift past as Max listens to music, drinks quickly, and reads through several websites. Max is stunned at what he discovers. For one thing, there aren't just one or two military arms fairs. Across the world, there are nearly a hundred major arms fairs every year. Many countries host one or maybe two, but Britain and America lead the pack, hosting five and nine respectively. And pretty much every country gets an invitation, even if you have a civil war going or are using child soldiers. And then Max comes across a contradiction which is so absurd he laughs and accidentally spits beer at his computer monitor: the five permanent members of the UN Security Council – the US, Britain, France, China, and Russia – are responsible for manufacturing seventy per cent of all the weapons arming the rest of the world. More like an *insecurity* council, thinks Max. At one point, Max uses Google Images to get an idea of what an arms fair actually looks like. The range of weapons he sees is huge and menacing, but what really gets to Max is the images of businesspeople handling all of this deadly stuff. There was something very weird about photos of men in expensive suits or robes and turbans sitting in a tank or looking down the sight of an anti-aircraft gun.

The experience leaves Max feeling oddly disoriented. It's the sheen of normality which covers everything. The utter legality of everything that's happening is just... weird. If you sell some pot in Britain, you can be arrested. But if you sell land mines, vicious assault rifles, or Apache attack helicopters... that's perfectly fine. Max pours the last of his pint down his neck. He closes his internet browser, stares into space, and feels the weight of his own contradictory behaviour. The moral indignation he feels suddenly bumps up against something else. What was *he* doing researching arms fairs anyway? When decommissioned, *Jeanne d'Arc* had been stripped down and now looks a bit like a floating platform rather than the grand ship she really is. One thing Max's research had told him was that most of what he needed to fit her out – the fighter planes, the deck guns, and more – it was all there at these arms fairs. His ship could be made whole again.

Max hears the front door close and looks out his office window. He pours another pint, his fifth of the evening, and watches Violeta walk to a blue sports car. Violeta laughs and waves at whoever is sitting behind tinted windows. She opens the door and gets in, and the car backs out of the driveway and then accelerates down the street. Max wonders vaguely at how no one opens car doors for women anymore.

The alcohol is warming Max's head and he has a vague sensation of knowing he's in trouble and not caring. Max closes his internet browser and opens up his email. The language for his email log-in is in Dutch which reminds him he has activated the VPN. When he tries to log in, he gets a security message from his email provider. This had happened before and Dom had explained how to get around the problem, but Max couldn't recall what he'd said. Max couldn't be bothered. He turns off the VPN software and logs directly into his email. There are a few messages related to work and a couple of automated emails from Amazon and eBay.

Max takes a long drag on his pint and squints at another email, his eyes now watery with the drinking. The email is from someone named *Lonely Girl* and has a subject line which reads *Hi I'm Candi Let's Talk*. Max knows it's some sort of spam. He's had messages like this before and had never opened one. Max guesses most people get this sort of spam, maybe even women. He should probably delete it, but for some reason he just stares at those words. Without seeming to make a decision, he clicks on the email. He wonders if his computer will crash or his virus protection software will launch into action, but all that happens is that the email opens. He sees text and a photo of a thin woman smiling at him, maybe in her late thirties.

Hi sweetheart, I'm lonely tonight and I just need someone to talk to, unless maybe we want more. If you need someone to talk to as well, please get in touch. Just click on the link below, and we can video chat. You don't need a credit card and it doesn't cost anything. Huge cuddles. Candi.

Even though Max's brain has been marinating in beer for the last few hours, he knows he shouldn't open that link. The problem is, he doesn't really know what else to do. He could keep drinking but then maybe he would need to get out of the house, and he had a vague image of standing on the bridge and then those police officers. There are people he can call, but he is too drunk for that, and would they even want to hear from him? He doesn't want to ruin Dom's poker game. He looks at the photo of the woman more closely. She is pretty but looks like life has been hard on her. Maybe this is a real woman, after all.

He doubts anything will happen if he clicks on the link anyway, except maybe he'll get sent to some porn site. Max pauses the music he's been listening to, runs his hand through his greying hair, and clicks the link. He takes a swig of beer as the link buffers, and a moment later the image of the woman he'd seen in the photo comes into view. There is rock music playing in the background and she is in her bedroom, which looks quite plain.

The woman smiles and runs her hand through hair dyed a shade of pink-red. "Hi, sweetheart. How are you? I'm Candi." Her accent is cockney British.

"Um… hi, I'm Max."

"I'm glad you got in touch, Max," says the woman. "I was sort of going out of my mind wondering what to do with myself."

"Yeah. Me too," says Max. He feels a little stupid saying this.

The woman arches her back and puts her arms behind her head, her breasts pushing against the thin material of her t-shirt. "What you been doing today, Max?"

"Just been at work. I'm home now. Been doing some research on the computer for a personal project."

"Stressful day, Max?"

"Yeah… it's been stressful, I guess."

A Siamese cat appears from somewhere, stretches, and then sits on the woman's lap. Candi smiles and looks down at her cat and then back to Max. "So, Max, do you want to pet my pussy?"

Max knew the joke. It was an urban legend, a routine Zsa Zsa Gabor probably did on the Johnny Carson show but which would never have made it past the censors. Max smiles and says the line that Carson had reportedly delivered so many years ago. "Sure, but you'll have to remove that damn cat from your lap."

The woman laughs as if Max had delivered that line for the first time ever. "You're very funny, Max. Handsome too. You don't often get a handsome man *and* a sense of humour."

Max feels like he needs to explain that the joke isn't his, but he just watches her. The woman pours white wine into a nearly empty glass and then holds the glass up. "What are you drinking, Max?"

"It's a pale ale."

Cheers," she says, and Max hears a *clinking* sound as she taps her wine glass on the monitor at her end.

"Cheers," says Max, clinking his own pint glass against his monitor.

Candi puts her wine glass back on the table and offers Max a mischievous grin. She pulls her t-shirt over her head and drops it on the floor. Max is stunned, his mouth dropping open in disbelief as he gazes at this woman who is sitting there in her bra.

Candi is laughing. "Max, the look on your face – it's priceless."

Max smiles. "Sorry."

Candi effects a coy expression. "I'm normally shy about this sort of thing, but life is just too short," she says. "And besides, I like you, Max. You seem like the sort of guy a girl can just have fun with, y'know?"

Max's eyes are watery from the booze and he wipes them with a hand. "Sure," he says.

Candi unclasps the front of her bra, holds the clips together, and then gives Max the sort of smile which suggests they are sharing in a private misdeed. She removes her bra and drops it on the floor behind her.

Candi offers a school-girl frown and looks down at her breasts. "I don't really like my boobs that much."

Max completely disagrees.

"What do you think Max?"

"I completely disagree," he says.

Candi laughs loudly and her boobs bob and shake with her laughter. This seems all very strange to Max, but, on the other hand, what does he know about what people get up to on the internet? He wonders if maybe Candi is just some lonely woman, maybe even someone whose life is as messed up as his. Maybe people did this sort of thing all the time. Max feels his dick twitch and begin to fill with blood.

Candi takes a sip of wine. "Max, you're a nice-looking man. I hope you don't mind me saying that."

Max did not mind at all.

"Max, can you take off your shirt for me?"

This surprises Max. But she'd taken off her bra. Maybe this is the sort of thing she likes. "Okay," says Max. He unties his tie, folds it, and places it on his desk. Max unbuttons his blue Oxford shirt and drops it on the floor in the manner Candi had done with her clothes. Max involuntarily tightens his muscles, feeling self-conscious. Candi smiles and moves one of her hands to her lap, but Max can't see that far down on his monitor.

"You... are... fit, Max," says Candi.

"Uh-huh," says Max, his brain apparently unable to produce anything more than these two dim-witted syllables.

Candi gives him that mischievous and coy grin he was getting familiar with. She stands up and backs away from her monitor so that Max can see everything from her head to her knees. She's wearing a bright pink skirt. Candi pulls her skirt up to her waist, revealing white G-string panties. She is thin, and Max sees two hip bones jutting out at him. His dick throbs again and an erection is now pointing downwards into his trousers and feeling pretty uncomfortable. He is speechless, struck dumb by the strangeness of the moment.

Candi steps out of her pink skirt, places a hand on a sharp hip bone and smiles at Max. "Do you want me to take my panties off, Max?"

"Uh-huh," he says.

Candi removes her panties and *pings* them towards the monitor, slingshot style. She laughs and stands in front of Max, clean-shaven, smiling. The erection in Max's trousers is now getting positively painful, and he has to shove a hand into his pants and make an adjustment.

"Max," says Candi. "I'm getting pretty hot. Are you hard?"

"Uh-huh."

"Can I see your cock?" Candi says, placing a hand between her legs.

Max feels his heart thudding against his chest. His mind makes a few clumsy calculations. The idea of being naked scares him, but she is completely naked and she really seems to want to see him. She hadn't wanted a credit card or anything like that. Max grabs his pint, takes a long swig, stands up, takes his belt off, and then drops his trousers to the floor. Without any thought, he pulls his briefs down to his knees and his erection pops out.

"Wow. That's amazing Max," says Candi. "I want to see all of you. Take your trousers off and stand back from your computer."

Max does as he is told and a moment later is standing about six feet from his computer, naked except for a pair of blue socks. "Oh god, Max," says Candi, "you're getting me so hot. Turn to the side and look at me so I can really see your cock."

Max does as she asks, pulling the muscles of his stomach in. A moment later Candi steps forward and leans over her computer, and then Max hears a *click,* and he feels confused. The expression on Candi's face is suddenly one of concentration and she is looking at her computer rather than him.

A moment later Candi sits down at her computer and looks directly at him. "Max," she says, her tone flat, "you should probably check your emails." Her image disappears and Max's house suddenly feels very quiet.

"What?" says Max to an empty room. He stumbles forward, gazes at his monitor, and finds himself looking at the webpage with the link he'd activated. He closes the page, feeling confused and scared. What had he done? Max looks down at himself and sees that his erection has gone mostly flaccid. He pulls his briefs on and realises he needs to take a piss. The walls seem unsteady on the way to and from the toilet, and Max realises he is drunker than he thought.

Max sits in front of his computer and opens up his emails, hoping that all of this has been some pointless joke. The top email is from *Lonely Girl* and the subject line reads **DON'T IGNORE**. Max wonders if he should show this to Dom before he opens it, but he doesn't want to disturb Dom now. Max takes a sip of beer and double clicks on the email.

Dear Max Henderson, please have a look at the attached photo. You need to transfer £10,000 to account number 08678455 sort code 20-88-62 within 7 days. If you do not, I will sell the attached photo to tabloid news agencies and give them a very interesting story about the photo. You are a successful person Max. You don't want the business community, the British public, and your family to know what you get up to. Don't be stupid Max. Make the transfer.

Max opens the attached photo, and there he is, his erection on display. And the expression on his face makes him look every bit the idiot he feels himself to be.

CHAPTER 22

Max wakes up, and his surroundings immediately feel strange. He looks around the room and remembers that he is in a hotel in Cairo. Early morning sunlight fills the air-conditioned room. Max rolls onto his back, gazes at the stucco ceiling, and allows images of the previous day to run through his mind. He recalls Dom picking him up, his three French shipmates already in the back seat of the BMW SUV. He remembers the drive to London Heathrow, Jean-Pierre, Alexis, and Hugo telling stories and cracking jokes. Dom and the Frenchmen traded national insults in good humour and argued about history for most of the trip and Max tried to join in where he could, but he felt a little overwhelmed by what he had put in motion. Max checks his watch – 7:20 AM.

There's a knock on his door, and then Dom's voice. "Boss, you up yet?"

Max gets out of bed, wearing his briefs and a t-shirt. He lets Dom in and then sits back down on the bed. Dom is wearing khaki cargo shorts, closed-toed sandals, a light beige summer jacket over a blue cotton shirt, and his sunglasses atop his jet black hair which has been combed back.

"Sorry about the state of this hotel, boss. It's a dump, isn't it?"

"Nah, it's alright, Dom."

"I think they over-sold it when they came up with the name of this place."

Max laughs, remembering they were staying at a place called *Magnificent Hotel*. To add insult to injury, 'Magnificent Hotel' was spelt out in enormous bright letters stuck to the front of the building.

"I'm dying for a cup of strong coffee," says Dom. "Shall we see if we can find something?"

Max nods, puts on a pair of shorts and a short-sleeved shirt, and then walks with Dom down to the reception area. There is a bar and restaurant adjacent to reception, but with signs saying *Closed*. Dom walks up to the reception desk and smiles at the olive-skinned man and a woman wearing a headscarf. "Any chance we can get a couple of strong coffees around here?"

"I am sorry, sir, the kitchen does not open for thirty minutes," the man says.

Dom opens his wallet and holds out four hundred Egyptian pounds. "You fellas must have some access to the kitchen. How about doing us a favour?"

The man grins, looks around, and takes the money. He says something in Arabic to the woman and stands up. "Back home in Britain," says Dom, "that's about ten pounds for a cup of coffee. So I need real coffee. Not instant. And strong. One black, and one with a bit of milk."

"Yes, sir, I understand." The man disappears into a back room and five minutes later returns with two large steaming cups which he places on the desk. Dom sniffs the black coffee, winks, and hands the man another one hundred Egyptian pounds. "Thank you, sir," the man says. "You can use the dining rooms. Don't worry that it says closed."

Dom smiles and leads Max to a table by a window. They sit and look out the window, noticing the morning traffic and bright sunshine which is having a difficult time penetrating the smoggy Cairo air. Max takes a sip of coffee, a bitter and bright flavour with subtle hints of citrus and rich chocolate. "Now that's a ten-pound cup of coffee Dom."

Dom takes a sip and nods in agreement. "You think things taste better sometimes just because you're somewhere new?" says Dom.

"Maybe," says Max. "You got enough walking around money?" *Walking around money* is Max's term for the one thousand pounds a month that he transfers into Dom's account for any incidentals, like bribes for good coffee. Max had noticed that at the end of the month Dom would transfer back any money which hadn't been used. He'd never asked Dom to do that, and this was just one of those reasons why he trusted him.

"Sure, it's plenty," says Dom.

"Can I ask you something?" says Max. "Why did we come to Egypt? One of the world's biggest arms fairs is right in London."

"Because, boss, British security forces are probably keeping a close watch on you. MI5, GCHQ, and who knows who else. Hedvika's biggest worry is that they are going to eventually think up some reason to arrest you, and going shopping at an arms fair in London will just make things a lot easier for them. To be honest, I was worried you were gonna be stopped at Heathrow. When you said you wanted to do a little shopping for *Joan of Arc*, I talked to Hugo and Alexis, and I said I wanted something which was outside Britain and a little more under the radar. They gave me a list of fairs – one in Tunisia, one in Jordan, one in Lebanon, and here. I chose the Egypt Defence Expo because it was the first one on the calendar. Plus, Egypt was part of the Empire, right? I figure the Egyptians are still a little bit pissed off, so maybe they will be less likely to co-operate with the British government if it comes to that."

Max nods, taking another sip of coffee. "Makes sense."

Dom gazes down into the Cairo morning haze of sand and honking horns, and takes a sip of coffee, deciding how to frame a question. "Boss, um, what are we doing here exactly? I mean, going to a weapons fair? This really doesn't seem like your scene. It's just... a little out of character."

Max smiles. "I know, it must seem odd. It's that... *Jeanne d'Arc* is a beautiful capital ship. You should see some of the photos of her when she was fully fitted out. When a navy decommissions a great ship, unfortunately the ship gets stripped of a lot of what makes her what she is. *Jeanne d'Arc* is a little... naked at the moment. She just doesn't look right. She needs a bit of restoration to put her back together."

"But how do you know what to buy?" asks Dom.

"I have a few ideas, but I've left a lot of that to the Captain and his mates. I think they've drawn up a shopping list of sorts."

Dom and Max look out the window and drink coffee for a while, watching noisy Cairo fly past at a pace that makes London seem sedate by comparison. Max likes how he and Dom can talk when there is something to say, and be quiet and think when there isn't. It sure makes everything easier. But there is something Max needs to say, and now is as good a time as he's likely to get. "Dom, I've got a little problem I need to talk over."

Dom puts his cup down, folds his hands, and nods. "Sure, boss." Max sighs, looks around the empty dining room, and talks through what happened three nights previously with Candi, or whoever the hell she is. Max doesn't leave out any details as he imagines Dom probably needs to have a good understanding of his situation. Dom listens closely, nodding now and again, and Max finds it curious that Dom doesn't look surprised at the strange events he's describing.

"Well, it's a honeytrap, isn't it?" Dom says eventually.

"A honeytrap?"

"Sure," says Dom. "Honeytraps are probably associated with the sort of clandestine spy stuff that happened during the Cold War. You know, attractive Soviet women developing sexual relationships with Western military men or politicians. Then there's some drunken pillow-talk and information gets fed back to Soviet authorities. But honeytraps have been around for very long time, and used for different reasons – sometimes for information, sometimes for blackmail." Dom points a finger at Max and offers him a friendly smile. "This Candi – she got you, boss."

Max shakes his head. "I feel like such an idiot."

"Aw, don't worry about it boss. It happens. You're not the first one. What she did is just a modern slant on the honeytrap, and it's a clever one."

"You've heard about… women doing this sort of thing on the internet?"

"Sure boss, I've heard about it. But it's not just women. It's as common for men to scam people in this way too."

"She wants me to pay her within four days. It's not really a lot of money. Should I pay her?"

"Absolutely not, boss. You pay her once and that won't be the end of it. When she's broke and wants more money, she'll be back."

"But, what if… she's serious about… you know…"

"Leave it with me and don't worry about that," says Dom. "I know a guy. He's gonna need to have a close look at your computer so we can track down this Candi. But we'll find her, and then I'll have a word with her, and then you won't have a problem anymore."

"You're not gonna hurt her, are you?"

"No, no, nothing like that, boss. I'm just gonna straighten her out."

Max looks out the window, takes another sip of coffee, and then looks back at Dom. "You know what really bothers me about this, Dom? I mean… it's feeling stupid about what happened. That's true. But I just can't believe that she did this, ya know? I mean, I have this feeling that maybe she's not really a bad person. Maybe there are reasons."

Dom laughs. "Boss, there's a reason alright. She's probably too lazy or stupid to work an honest job and she wants your money. She's a hustler. When I was growing up, everyone was hustling. I was a hustler too. There's no great mystery here."

"I don't know, Dom, maybe you're right. I know what she did was wrong, but I just sort of saw something in her too, some kind of potential. I mean, to be able to use the internet like that… " Max looks out the window and then back at Dom. "Look, when you have your talk with Candi, or whoever she is, I want to be there too. Okay?"

Dom frowns. "I don't know, boss. Maybe you should just leave this to me. Keep your hands clean."

"No. When you find her, I want to have a word with her as well. I want to hear her explain things."

Dom nods. "Okay, you got it, boss."

Dom takes the last sip of his coffee and pulls his mobile out of his pocket. "Right, let's get the frogs out of bed."

Max and Dom sit in the back of a cab which is working its way through the traffic of New Cairo, a metropolitan suburb of Cairo itself. Trailing behind them in another cab is 'the French Navy', Dom's collective term for Jean-Pierre, Alexis, and Hugo. Dom leans over and talks into Max's ear. "Boss, there are a few things we need to watch out for. Some of these events have protesters and art activists, and that means there will be news crews. We want to avoid anything like that. If you get spotted by reporters, you're gonna be a bigger story than whatever else is happening."

Max nods and Dom reaches into a duffle bag. He pulls out a straw hat with a large brim. "Can you wear this, boss? If we see any reporters at all, look at the ground as you walk."

Max smiles and accepts the hat.

Their cab pulls up at the entrance to the Egypt International Exhibition Centre. Max and Dom climb out, Dom pays the driver, and a moment later the French Navy arrives in a second cab. Dom was pleased they all had the sense to dress in casual civilian clothing rather than the naval uniforms they wore on board *Jeanne d'Arc*. Alexis smiles and pats Dom on the arm. "Egypt, eh? One of yours, I think. Why did you ever let this one go?"

Dom doesn't laugh but instead leans into the three Frenchmen. "Listen, guys, let's have a drink later and laugh things up then. Right now, we keep it low-key. I don't want any unnecessary attention, okay?"

"Sorry," says Alexis, realising his error.

"Let's keep together," says Dom. "Don't talk to any reporters if they approach you, and if there are any signs of trouble, tell me. I'd suggest we do what we need to and get out of here." Dom looks over at Max. "The hat, boss."

Max puts his floppy-brimmed straw hat on and Dom takes the lead as they walk into more than 40,000 square metres of air-conditioned exhibition space. They are greeted at a desk by pretty, uniformed Egyptian women wearing attractive headscarves. They each accept a map and a list of the exhibitions, and Max turns to Captain Jean-Pierre. "So, where do we go?"

"This way," says the Captain, and he leads them down one of the corridors created by long rows of exhibits.

Max looks closely at the exhibits and people as they walk along, and he is struck by the strangeness of this place. It's like a separate and temporary world created in the desert, and he notices things you could never see anywhere else. There are groups of wealthy sheikhs in white robes and traditional headdress speaking very quietly to one another as they walk past. He sees a Western businessman handling and discussing a deadly-looking assault rifle. There is a woman in a traditional black robe and hijab who is trying out a shoulder-mounted rocket launcher. A group of olive-skinned men wearing military uniforms covered in medals are standing next to an enormous tank, one of them getting some help as he climbs through the main hatch. Western pop music echoes as it bounces off the walls. There are signs and slogans all over the exhibition space, some of which try to stick together the idea of *peace* and *military power*, which seems a little disingenuous. Max is struck by a thought. As long as you have money, there is no discrimination here. It literally doesn't matter who you are – African, Middle Eastern, Western, male, female, religious fundamentalist nutcase, secular nutcase, liberal democrat, dictator – anyone with money is a welcome member of this very weird club.

Captain Jean-Pierre stops walking and studies his map of the exhibition. He taps the map with a finger and looks at them. "I know where to go."

CHAPTER 23

I'm sitting in the waiting room at Henderson Nautical. Sheila, Max's PA, walks in and hands me a cup of tea.

"Do you want to hear something funny, Liz?" she asks.

"Sure," I say.

"Max refers to you as *"Liz Burton, our journalist"*. This morning he said, *"Sheila, can you give Liz, our journalist, a call and ask her if she can come and see me this afternoon?"* "

I laugh. "Well, that's okay with me. Do you know why Max wants to meet with me today?"

"I have some idea, but I'll let Max explain things."

She walks to the door, but then turns and looks at me. "When you write about Max, can you remember something? He's not crazy, like some people are saying."

I nod my head. "Sheila, you've known Max longer than anyone here, right? I'd really value having some time to speak with you. Could we talk, maybe over a lunch break?"

"I'm happy to talk, Liz, but we won't get through lunch without being interrupted. Better to do it after work."

"Great – I'll give you a call."

Sheila heads back to her office, and I get my notepad out of my workbag and review what I've prepared. The thing is, even though I've organised a list of questions, there's only one question that really needs asking – exactly what are you planning on doing with *Jeanne d'Arc*? Reporters have to develop some sort of relationship with the people they interview, and that can mean having some patience and tact. But at this point, I don't know how much time I'm going to have with Max, so I resolve to make sure I get to this question.

A few minutes later, Dominic Delfino appears in the doorway. He greets me, shakes my hand, and tells me that Max wants to meet with me on *Jeanne d'Arc*. This is fantastic luck, and I walk with Dominic through a few work sheds and an open section of the yard.

We exit one of the work sheds and I can see people on the other side of Henderson Nautical's gates. "Dominic," I say.

He smiles at me. "You can call me Dom."

"Okay, Dom – are there still quite a few people outside the gates?"

"There seems to be. Some have left, but others have arrived. I counted about thirty tents and another twenty camper vans this morning."

"Why do you think they stay?" I had spent time speaking with a number of those people, but I was curious to hear what Dom thought.

"I'm not sure, exactly. Some of them are probably angry at their life circumstances. I imagine some of them might be homeless or semi-homeless. But I've seen other people who look very middle-class. There're a few people sleeping in tatty sleeping bags with the stuffing falling out, but others have really nice camper vans. Some people seem needy, but for others maybe it's ideological."

I nod. Dom is smart and his assessment of the people on the other side of the gate matches my own view. "Do you think these people want to become citizens of *Jeanne d'Arc*?"

"I'm not sure," he says. "Maybe."

Dom walks me into a vast work shed and I find myself looking at *Jeanne d'Arc* from a high platform. I am stunned by the size and appearance of the ship. There are things I want to say, but it feels wrong to speak. It's like when I was a kid and my parents would take me to this huge and very old church. If I said anything when we walked in, they would shush me, and you learned that if you spoke at all, it had to be in whispers.

Dom checks his watch. "We're a little early for the meeting." He looks over at me, thoughtful. "I remember meeting you when you were waiting at the gate of Henderson Nautical. You knew something was up with Max and this ship before I did, maybe even before Max himself knew. You must have a pretty good nose for this stuff."

I smile. It's a nice compliment. "Do you mind if I ask you a question?"

"I'm single, but I think it's a little unprofessional for you to want to know about that sort of thing."

I laugh. "That's not what I was going to ask. What I'm curious about is Max's interest in creating a nation and these citizens. Is it just about finding a way to keep the ship, or is there more to it?"

Dom stares out into Bay 4 and thinks for a moment. "I'm not sure, but it probably is about looking after these people and creating something. The boss… well, he seems to love just about everybody, and he seems to see the good in pretty much everyone too."

"And you don't see things the same way."

Dom laughs. "Not really. I grew up on the streets of South London.

Where I come from its best to assume that everyone is on the take until proven otherwise."

"Do you have a sense of where things are headed?"

He looks at me for a moment. "Not really. Liz, I like you and Max seems to like you and my gut feeling is that you're a genuine person, but my job is to protect the boss, okay? You understand what I'm saying."

"I do, Dom."

He checks his watch again. "Okay – we can get going."

A few minutes later I'm following Dom through the innards of *Jeanne d'Arc*, down corridors painted in grey, through elliptical hatches, and eventually we come to a varnished door with a copper plate which reads *Cabine Executive*. Dom knocks on the door, and a moment later Max opens it.

"Ah, Liz Burton," Max says, extending his hand. "So good of you to make the trip at such short notice. Won't you please come in." He's wearing the same naval cap and French Order of Merit Medal I'd seen at the TV interview.

Max shakes my hand warmly, his face beaming. He shows me into quite a lavish cabin. Everything is fine varnished wood, shining brass or steel, deep leather chairs, graceful naval portraits, and plush throw rugs. His solicitor, Hedvika Zavatsky, stands up and extends her hand. "Hi, Liz," she says. "It's been less than two weeks since we met at the TV interview you did with Max, but it feels much longer."

Her hand is warm in mine, and I feel a shiver of anxiety pass through me. I'm a bit overweight and on the short side, and I always seem to feel intimidated by very beautiful women like Hedvika. "Yes, a lot has happened," I say.

"Please have a seat, Liz," says Max, pointing to one of the deep leather chairs. "Can I get you something to drink?"

I notice Max is drinking a beer and Hedvika a glass of white wine. "I'm fine, thank you," I say.

This feels surreal – the four of us are sitting in these deep leather chairs and I'm looking at an original painting of what I'm guessing is a French Admiral.

"So then," says Max, "you must be wondering why I wanted you to come down from London today?"

"I suppose I am."

"In a moment," says Max, "you're going to meet a couple of people – Winston Godfred and Sunrise70. They were among the first to show up at Henderson Nautical when word got out. If *Jeanne d'Arc* is going to have sovereignty, someone needs to coordinate all of that. I've put Winston in charge and I've asked Sunrise70 to help him. Winston seems very passionate about what's happening, which is curious, but I like his enthusiasm. I haven't quite figured Sunrise70 out. She's quiet and seems a little angry."

"Liz," says Hedvika, "I don't want to interfere in your job, but can I ask – does your paper have an agenda for this story?"

"Oh, come now, Hedvika," says Max.

"Max," she says, "I just think it needs asking."

I take a sip of wine and look at Hedvika. "No one is telling me how to write this story. I just want people to know the truth."

"Good," says Max. "Now, let's go see what sort of progress Winston is making. Apparently, he's got people helping him – some sort of working group. I think Winston and that side-kick of his have got volunteers from that crowd outside to help them. They're meeting now."

Max and Hedvika put their drinks down and we follow Max out of the cabin. He leads us through several glossy grey corridors and more hatches than I can count, and I'm amazed that anyone can remember how to get from one place to another in this labyrinth. Eventually we arrive at a metal door with a plaque which reads *Salle de Réunion 1*. Max raises his hand as if to knock on the door, and then looks back at the three of us. He smiles broadly and raises his eyebrows. "Behind this door," he says, "we may witness something quite special." I notice for the first time something wild in his eyes, and I can't be sure if he is being ironic or very serious. He reminds me suddenly of that Willy Wonka character from the original movie, and I feel a bit worried for reasons which are not clear.

He knocks on the door, a voice tells us to come in, and we all follow Max into a fairly large conference room. There are porthole windows along one side, beyond which I can see the green aluminium walls of the work shed. About twenty people sit around a table, and it's clear that their conversation has stopped for us. There is a tall skinny man sitting at the head of the table, wearing khaki trousers and an olive army-issue shirt with a hand-sewn band of red material around the arm. He pushes himself up from his chair, stands straight at attention, and smiles broadly through long hair, unfortunate teeth, and a scrappy beard. The man begins to make a bad show of saluting and then thinks better of it. "Major Max Henderson," he says, "is on the bridge. I mean ... in the conference room. Anyways, he's here, everyone."

Max waves a hand. "Hello everyone. You're having a meeting and I don't want us to interrupt what I'm sure is fine work." Max briefly introduces Dom and Hedvika to the group, before saying, "And this is Liz Burton – she's an honest journalist who is going to help our story get told. Maybe you saw her when I did that interview on TV. Now the four of us are just going to take some seats and we'll try not to interfere." People nod and seem to accept us, except for one woman sitting at the foot of the table opposite Winston. She has a tattoo of the sun on the side of her neck… and she's giving me a hard and uncomfortable stare. This, I think, is Sunrise70.

"Of course, of course," says Winston. "Everybody act normal."

We sit down in the few remaining seats and I glance around the table, noting that most of them have hand-made nameplates in front of them with their first names and some title. I catch titles such as *Commissioner for Passports, Minister of Propaganda, Director of Games and Recreation, Secretary General for Citizenry.* The titles seem a little random and hastily concocted, and the people around the table strike me as a dissonant group. Like the crowd outside, some look very middle class, others like they may have been sleeping rough.

I slip my notepad and pen from my purse and place it in front of me. "Okay, we were talking about citizenry," says Winston. "Sally?"

A woman sitting behind the *Secretary General for Citizenry* nameplate addresses the room. "We're up to one thousand two hundred and sixteen people who have expressed interest in becoming citizens of *Jeanne d'Arc*."

Winston beams and looks over at Max, who returns his smile. "That's great," says Winston. "How did you do it?"

"Well," the woman says, "I just hung a notice up in front of Henderson Nautical Works asking people to sign up if they're interested. Some people signed up on the spot and gave us an email or home address. Others signed up through a Facebook page I created. Of course, we don't know how many will actually apply for citizenship when we give them the chance. There's also something I don't understand. If UK citizens want to become citizens of *Jeanne d'Arc*, will they have to give up their UK passports?"

Winston looks over at Hedvika. "Well, we've got a solicitor here. Any ideas, Hedvika?"

"Under *normal* circumstances," says Hedvika, "if a UK national is granted citizenship by another country, they don't have to give up their

UK passport. But there isn't anything normal about our circumstances, so I have no idea how the Government will react to us."

"Wonderful," says Winston. I have to hide a smile because it's not clear what Winston seems to think is wonderful. "Okay," continues Winston, "so how do we actually make them citizens?"

"Well," says Sally, "I researched the citizenship application forms for Britain and the US, changed some of the wording, and printed *Jeanne d'Arc* and an image of our ship at the top."

Sally hands around copies of her form and everyone spends a few minutes reading through it. Winston looks a bit concerned. "Sally, I love what you're doing here, love it. But it seems a tad officious, y'know? There're questions on here about criminal history, education, employment, current nationality, marriage, history of residence. It's sort of like a beauty contest, y'know? How about if we just ask them their name, some contact information, and whether they want to be a citizen of *Jeanne d'Arc*?"

There is a moment of silence and then a man across from me says, "What if we end up with a bunch of dickheads?"

Winston frowns. "Brian, that's not cool, okay?" Winston looks over at Max. "What do you think, Max?"

"I like your view, Winston. No bureaucratic nonsense. But shouldn't people agree to certain principles? Something like the rule of law?"

"Absolutely," says Winston, pointing to a woman who has a nameplate reading *Secretary for Harmonious Relations*. "Mary's working on that."

Max smiles and points at the woman. "I love your title, sweetheart."

"Thanks," she says, smiling. "I made it up."

"Outstanding," says Max.

Max looks around the room and claps his hands. "Y'know, I just think you're really amazing people for being here and wanting to help. I just want to say that."

There are smiles all around the room. "Okay, enough of me," says Max. "Winston, carry on."

"Okay, how about we go with the simplified citizen application form, but at the bottom we ask that they try their best to follow the principles established for *Jeanne d'Arc*. Mary, when we figure out what that is, we can just attach it to the application form. All agreed?"

Everyone raises their hand except for Sunrise70, who looks around the table for a moment. She frowns, and then slowly raises her hand.

"Okay," says Max, "but there's something else to consider. When we grant people citizenship, we'll want to be able to get them on board. When *Jeanne d'Arc* was operational she had accommodation for as many as thirteen hundred sailors, so our country has room for a fair number of citizens. But we need to be able to support our citizens, y'know? It needs to be a nice place." Max looks over at Winston. "Can we get some people to look at the accommodation? We're going to need bedding, and we'll need to get the kitchen stocked up with food and supplies. Talk to Captain Jean-Pierre Lavelle. He should know what we need, and send the bill to me, okay?"

The meeting goes on in this sort of fashion and the rate at which they appear to be throwing together a country is astounding. They discuss the need for a national anthem and the *Minister of Culture and Arts*, a middle-aged man named Ed, puts forward a Mariah Carey song called *We Belong Together*. It's pointed out that this song is copyrighted and so they can't use it. Ed then suggests another Mariah Carey song called *Always Be My Baby*, and he needs to be told that it doesn't matter which Mariah Carey song he chooses, they are all copyrighted. Ed looks crestfallen and seems to be out of ideas. I can't imagine how he was made *Minister of Culture and Arts*. An older woman with the title *Director of National Intelligence* speaks next. Her title strikes me as a little heavy-handed, but by this point I am pretty sure people have just chosen or made up their own titles. At any rate, she suggests that they ask someone named Busker Barbara, a woman who we were told is currently sleeping off a hangover in her tent, to write a national anthem.

This idea meets with general approval and Winston moves the meeting on to the issue of passports. A mock-up of a passport is handed around which has been created by *The Commissioner of Passports*. It looks like a standard passport with a photo and basic identification information, but on the cover it reads *Jeanne d'Arc*, has a silhouette image of the carrier, and the word *Passport*. No one seems to want to issue passport numbers and I'm getting the sense there is a general feeling of anarchy amongst this group of Ministers and Secretaries and Commissioners and Directors. However, Hedvika points out that if two people have the same name, things will get confusing without numbers, so the group relents, but only after agreeing that all citizens can choose their own passport numbers.

There is a discussion about establishing a form of currency and a suggestion that a new currency could be called *'the arc'*, as in, *'here's your ice-cream sir, that will be two arcs please'*. For reasons which don't seem clear, this leads to a discussion about Leninism vs Trotskyism and, for reasons which are even less clear, this leads to a decision that *Jeanne d'Arc* citizens can just use whatever currency they like, traded for goods at present currency exchange values. Winston points out that currency has led to an awful lot of exploitation and that perhaps we were doing the world a favour by not creating any more of it, and this seems to meet with general approval.

I look down at my notepad and realise I haven't written a thing, but I think it's all moving too quickly for that. I find myself thinking about American history and it occurs to me that those guys more or less threw that country together just in time for a Revolutionary War. Thomas Jefferson knocked up that Declaration of Independence in a couple of weeks, and he was drunk every day. And, if I remember my history correctly, somebody ran to Betsy Ross's house and got her to sew together an American Flag in one afternoon.

I notice Winston raises his hand like some schoolboy, and I think that someone needs to explain to him that he is facilitating the meeting. Nobody calls on him but he eventually introduces the topic of a national flag, which is weird as this is just what I had been thinking about. "Now, I hope nobody minds," says Winston, "but I've taken the liberty of having a go at a flag. I appreciate that nationalism and patriotism is a terrible idea, so of course it's perfectly fine for anyone to burn our flag if they want to." He looks over at the Secretary for Harmonious Relations. "Maybe flag burning can go in the rule of law document." She nods and Winston looks over at Hedvika. "I'm thinking that having a flag might help us with the application to the United Nations for statehood, right?"

Hedvika smiles and shrugs. "Well, it probably can't hurt."

"Wonderful," says Winston. He pulls a white pillowcase out of a canvas bag. "Now, this is just a basic knock-up, just to get an idea."

He holds out his flag for us, an apprehensive expression forming on his face. The background is a sea of blue and in the centre is a large pink heart-shaped image. In the middle of the heart is an image of a white dove. "So," says Winston, "the heart of course symbolises love, and I think most people associate a dove with peace. What do you think?"

Everyone gazes at the flag for a moment and then we can all hear a loud sigh of exasperation which comes from Sunrise70. Although she'd not said anything thus far, I'd been very aware of her presence throughout the meeting, mainly because she had been doing a lot of eye-rolling and sighing along the way. I notice for the first time that her title is *Minister of Defence.*

"Is everything okay, Sunrise70?" asks Winston.

"Look," says the woman, holding her hands out. "If that's our flag, people are gonna think we're a bunch of tits." She folds her arms, frowns, and looks around the table. Nobody seems to know what to say, and Winston suddenly looks panicked.

"But... I just thought," says Winston, "... I thought that symbols of peace and love express what *Jeanne d'Arc* was... I thought that..." Winston looks down and I can see a sheen of scarlet crawling up his neck and I wonder if he is going to have a panic attack, or if he might have to leave the room. Oh god – I wonder if he might cry, and I am really hoping that he doesn't. Winston folds his flag and puts it into his bag. "I just..." says Winston, but he is now out of words, and stares at the table. Max stands up and walks over to Winston and puts a hand on his shoulder. "Winston, have a seat, if you like."

Winston nods and sits down. Max looks down the table at Sunrise70. "Have you got a different idea for a flag?" says Max, his voice neutral but steady.

Sunrise70 gazes at Max for a moment and then nods her stocky head slowly. "Come to think of it, I do have an idea. I drew a promotional picture for this band a few years ago. They didn't use the picture, but I think it will do nicely for our flag."

She gets up and tears off a large piece of paper from a flip chart which is in the corner, sits down, and begins to draw forcefully. I glance over at Winston and notice this look in his eyes I saw once when I interviewed people who had been passengers on a train that had just derailed. A few minutes later Sunrise70 holds up her drawing for us to see. It's a damn good drawing and I wonder if she is an artist. I can see a man and a women standing in front of what looks like a municipal building. They raise their right fists high in the air and the municipal building seems to be in flames.

"Now that's a flag with some balls," says Sunrise70.

I look around the table and notice a mix of amused smiles and confused expressions. *The Director of Games and Recreation* finally breaks the silence. "But... did those people set the building on fire?"

"Who can say?" says Sunrise70. "Maybe there's some ambiguity here – maybe they did it, maybe they didn't. So, what do you think? You like my flag?"

Winston glances anxiously around the table but seems to have lost his capacity for speech. A few moments of silence pass and then Max says, "Okay, has anyone else got any other ideas for a flag?"

There's a lot of looking around the table and at some point it seems clear that no further ideas are forthcoming. Max looks at Winston and then studies Sunrise70 for a moment. "I like the emphasis on peace and love, Winston, but Sunrise70 wants to depict strength in some way. Our situation is complicated, people are complicated. Maybe we need peace, love and strength in some way. Winston and Sunrise70, I'd like you two to meet up and sort out a compromise. No, not a compromise, but something better. Something more than the sum of the parts."

"Okay, Max," says Winston, and I notice Sunrise70 nodding. Max then looks around the table before addressing everyone. "Let me say this. I trust all of you to put the nation-state of *Jeanne d'Arc* together. You're doing fantastic work in challenging circumstances, but there's a lot to do." Max looks over at his solicitor. "Hedvika, can you remind us – that 1933 Convention said we needed four things to claim sovereignty as a nation-state, right?"

"Yes, that's right," says Hedvika. "The 1933 Montevideo Convention on the Rights and Duties of States outlines four legal standards for evaluating an entity's claim to statehood. You need to have a permanent population, a defined territory, the capacity to enter into relations with other states, and a government."

"A government?" says the Commissioner for Passports. "What sort of government?"

Max smiles and gives Winston's shoulders a rub, sort of like a coach might massage his boxer's shoulders at ringside. "That's for all of you to figure out. Now look, I've put Winston in charge here, but he is really going to need your support. It's lunch time, right? Let's order pizza in. Figure out what you want and give Sheila a ring."

Then Max does something odd. He looks around the table, but makes eye contact with each person. It's strangely intimate. And then Max lifts his hands from Winston's shoulders and says, "As Stanley Fitzpatrick once said – if you can agree on your pizza order, you gotta be able to create a sovereign nation-state."

This produces smiles all around the table, and then Max nods at Hedvika and Dom and points to the door. They get up and follow Max out of the room and I walk after them. Max and Dom are walking ahead of us, discussing something. Hedvika's impressive high heels have slowed her down on the metal stairs leading up and out of the work shed, so I walk with her. As we exit the shed, Hedvika looks at me.

"So that meeting was a real *disasterpiece*, right?"

"Disasterpiece?" I ask, confused.

"Yes," says Hedvika, "as in... not a masterpiece."

"Oh," I say. "Well, I suppose there were some difficulties."

Hedvika rolls her eyes. We've reached the edge of a parking lot, a natural spot where we would separate, she to her office, me to my car. "Well, you've got your story, right?" There's an edge in her tone, and she's clearly not happy.

"I suppose so," I say. "I'll need to give this some thought. By the way, who is Stanley Fitzpatrick?"

She laughs. "Max just makes that stuff up." Hedvika gazes at me for a moment before continuing. "Look, there's something you should know about Max. He's not like most people. He just seems to see the good in everyone. It's part of why I love Max, but he's... not always very realistic."

"And you don't see things like Max does," I say.

Hedvika laughs. "Are you kidding? I lived most of my life in the Czech Republic, a country misfortunate enough to be stuck between Germany and Russia. I wish I could see people the way Max does, but it's not possible."

She offers me her hand, smiles sadly, and shakes her head. "Goodbye Liz," she says, and then walks in the direction of the office block.

I climb into my Mini Cooper, close the door, and grab my Dictaphone from my bag. I don't want to lose any of the detail of what just happened, so I dictate a stream of images and dialogue, capturing my experience – descriptions of *Jeanne d'Arc*, visual images of the people around the table, the weird collection of titles, the fraught exchange between Winston and Sunrise70, everything I can remember. My heart is pumping and I imagine presenting the finished story to my editor. This is an exclusive, and there is no way this is going to be anything but the lead story, in print, TV, and online. This is the moment every young journalist dreams of. The moment when I move to the front page.

After fifteen minutes of dictating I feel like I've recorded everything I need. I put my key into the ignition and look out the windscreen, and that's when I notice Max. He is standing at the window of his office and gazing out into the distance. For some reason, the excitement I am feeling drains away and is replaced by a heavy and uncertain sensation. I sit with that feeling for a moment, and then something tips over inside of me, and I realise I need to talk to Max.

I lock my car doors, walk to the office block, and a minute later I am standing in front of Sheila. She greats me warmly and tells me she'll ask if Max is free. A moment later she shows me into Max's office. He's still standing by the window, a pint of beer in his hand.

"Hi, Liz," he says. He doesn't seem surprised to see me. "Can I get you a drink?"

"No thank you, Max. I just need to tell you something, and then I'll be heading back to London."

He motions to a chair and we both sit down, Max placing his chin on folded hands behind his desk. I place my Dictaphone onto his desk and we both look down at it. "I've made a recording from memory of what just happened in that meeting, as the basis of a story I would write for my paper."

Max nods. "Mmm," he says.

"But I'm not going to write that story – not now, anyway. It's too raw. Whatever is happening here, it's not something I feel I should be writing about at the moment."

Max puts his hands on his knees and takes a deep breath of air which he expels. A smile grows slowly across his face, and he nods and gazes straight into my eyes. Max picks up his pint glass, takes a large sip of beer, and then pushes a button on his phone. "Sheila, can you please pop in for a moment."

A few seconds later Sheila is standing next to me. "Sheila, sweetheart," says Max. "Human resources should still be open this time of day. Can you please take Liz down there and have them make a Henderson Nautical photo security badge for her. And can you please give Liz the code for the front gate."

"Of course, Max," says Sheila.

He looks at me. "You're always welcome at Henderson Nautical." Max reaches across the desk and takes both of my hands in his for a moment, and gives them a little squeeze. He looks tired, his eyes glassy, and I wonder how drunk he is. "Thank you," he says. There is this very genuine expression of gratitude in his eyes, which I'm not sure I deserve.

"Well, thank you, Max," I respond.

He lets go of my hands and there seems to be nothing more to say, so I follow Sheila out of the office and down the stairs, and I have this strange sense that something really important has happened, but I'm not exactly sure what.

CHAPTER 24

Dom pulls his BMW S7 up to the curb outside 417 Hackney Road. He looks through the yellow glow of London street lighting at the decrepit housing estate, the graffiti against the worn brick walls, the rubbish on the pavement. Memories come to him of the years he'd spent living and grifting in a neighbourhood like this one. He doesn't really want to be here, but there is a job that needs doing so there is no point bitching about it.

Dom approaches the building and waits outside the front entrance, his back turned to the door so he can avoid security cameras and keep a watch on his car. He pulls sunglasses from his suit coat pocket and puts them on. A couple of minutes later an old black man comes out and he catches the door before it closes. The man gives him a wary look and scuttles down the street.

The dilapidated elevator groans as it works its way to the sixth floor, and a few moments later Dom is standing outside Room 618. He listens, but can hear nothing, and he notices the peephole. Dom removes his sunglasses, forces a smile onto his face, and knocks. A few moments later he hears a bolt slide over and the door opens a crack, still on its brass chain. Dom quickly jams his leather shoe into the door, removes a compact bolt cutter from under his jacket, and cuts the chain. A woman lets out a sudden gasp, and he pushes his way into the apartment.

Dom glares at the woman and hisses, "Shut up, if you want to live."

The woman stares wide-eyed, a hand brought up to her gaping mouth. Dom closes the door quietly and slides the bolt over. The room is dimly lit, a smell of cooked meat hangs in the air, and a man is sitting on a couch, dressed in a cheap suit. The man appears stunned and immobile, his gaze locked on Dom. Dom pulls his Walther P-99 out of his shoulder holster and points it first at the woman's face, and then the man's. "Don't say anything," he whispers to the woman. "Go sit on the couch."

The woman sits next to the man and Dom pulls a chair over from a kitchenette table and sits down, his back to a TV, a coffee table between them. Dom points the handgun in their direction and gazes at the woman.

"So, I know something about who you are, Candi," says Dom. "You

135

get up to some nasty tricks on the internet." Dom stares at the man, who seems to be pressing himself into the back of the couch and looks like he is about to cry. Chubby and balding, unshaven, Dom reckons he's in his late fifties. Something about the wrinkled, cut-rate suit suggests he is a low-level manager in some civil service job. Maybe divorced or with a pissed-off wife at home. Dom waves the handgun at the man. "What's your story, then?"

"I... I... look, whatever is going on here," says the man, "it's got nothing to do with me."

"What's your name?"

"Ian."

Dom puts his gun on his thigh, pulls out a pack of Marlboro cigarettes from his jacket pocket, and looks at the woman. "You mind if I smoke?"

The expression on the woman's face is hard. "Go ahead," she says.

Dom picks up a lighter which is lying on the coffee table between them, lights up, takes a long drag on the cigarette, and blows it out in the direction of the entranceway. Dom smiles at the man. "So, what do you do, Ian?"

"Inland Revenue."

A burst of laughter escapes from Dom. "You enjoy your work?"

"Not really," says Ian.

"Well, that's a shame. It's important to enjoy your work."

Dom takes a closer look at Candi. Skinny, a bloodless countenance, thinning hair dyed some bizarre shade of pink-red, makeup working hard to cover the circles under her eyes. Probably pretty at one point. She's wearing a garish and tiny dress, pale and undernourished legs and arms jutting out. There are bruises on her arms and Dom notices needle marks in the crook of an elbow. She could be anywhere in her twenties or thirties – it's hard to tell with people who have been on the gear for a while.

"Look, I don't hardly know her," says Ian, his tone pleading.

Dom takes a drag on his cigarette, blows it out, and gazes at the man. "You're a john then?"

"Yeah," the man blurts out.

"Can I please have your wallet, Ian?"

Ian pulls his wallet out of his trouser pocket and gives it to Dom. "You can have it," says the man. "There's about eighty pounds there, and some cards. Please, I just want to go."

Dom smiles and laughs. "Ian, I don't need your money."

Dom studies Ian and Candi's faces. Ian looks like he's going to piss himself, if he hasn't already. Candi continues to stare at him with a blank, hard expression. Dom opens the man's wallet and takes a driving licence out and gazes at it. "Look at that," says Dom, "your name really is Ian." He pulls his mobile phone from his pocket and photographs the licence and places the licence back in the wallet, which he hands to the man. Dom places his Marlboro between his lips and points the Walther P-99 directly at Ian's face.

"Here's what's going to happen, Ian. You're going walk out of here, calmly, as if nothing special happened. And you're not gonna report what you saw to the police or any other authorities, ever. And, if you do, I'm going to find you and I'm going to kill you. Do you understand?"

"Yes… yes, I understand. I won't say anything."

"No, you won't," says Dom, "because you're smart enough to know when to cut your losses. Dom points his gun towards the door. "Off you go."

The man jumps from the couch and starts for the door. "Ian," says Dom. The man stops and turns. "Calmly. Walk out of here calmly, like nothing happened."

The man nods and exits the flat, closing the door softly. Dom takes another drag on his Marlboro and gazes at this woman for a moment. "So, you're a real internet sensation, right? You go by Candi, but your real name is Susan Marshall."

"How did you find me?" the woman asks.

"That's not important. What's important is that I work for the man you are trying to extort for ten thousand pounds. That's not gonna happen, you understand? What is gonna happen is that you're gonna get in my car and I'm gonna take you to the man I work for."

Susan looks confused. "Why?"

Dom shrugs. "He wants to meet you."

Susan sighs heavily and looks at the table, then back at Dom. "Are you going to kill me?"

Dom smiles. "Does it matter?"

She releases a burst of nervous laughter. "Yeah, it fucking matters. I don't wanna die."

Dom looks slowly around the dimly lit room. "Well, I can't think why. But that's good. If you really don't want to die then you'll probably behave yourself, right?"

Susan looks down and grabs her arms, squeezing them hard.

"Look," says Dom, "relax a bit, okay? Do exactly what I tell you and things will work out. But if you make some sort of scene, then yeah, I'll have to kill you."

Susan gazes at Dom for a moment. "Okay." She points at the pack of cigarettes Dom placed on the coffee table. "Can I have one of those?"

Dom picks up the pack, frowns, and hands it to her.

Dom parks his BMW just outside *The Half Moon*. He'd chosen the pub carefully. It's a dank crap-hole, located on the outskirts of Portsmouth in a run-down neighbourhood. And, no security cameras. Susan had smoked about half of his cigarettes on the way down and had tried some flirtatious conversation with him, which he had deflected until she understood that he didn't want to talk.

Dom looks over at Susan, who is wearing a sweater over her skimpy dress, no doubt conscious of her needle tracks. "So you're gonna come in the pub with me and have a conversation with the man I work for. Don't do anything stupid and you'll be safe in your bed later this evening. You understand?"

Susan nods. Dom gets out of the car and opens her door. He holds her by an arm and Susan totters on high heels, sinewy calf muscles working as she clomps over rough pavement, a small shiny handbag under her arm. They walk through the pub and the place is exactly as Dom remembers it. Worn carpet which stinks from everything that's been dropped on it, cigarette burns on the tired upholstery, people eating caramelised potatoes and cheap beef drowning in salty dark gravy. They enter a back room containing a single table. Max is there, dressed in his work suit, a pint in front of him. Max gets up and extends his hand.

"Hello Ms... is it Candi?"

Susan takes Max's hand and smiles. "It's Susan, actually. Call me Susan."

Dom suffers through the next ten minutes in a state of restrained annoyance. Max is polite and receptive, apologises for the state of the pub and offers Susan a drink, which means Dom has to fetch her a glass of white wine from the bar. When Dom returns to the table and hands Susan her wine, Max is looking at her in a thoughtful way.

"I think people can do bad things," says Max. "People can make mistakes, but I don't know that there are bad people as such. The thing is Susan, I need to understand why you did that to me. Do you see?"

Susan takes a sip of wine and stares down at her lap. A moment later she looks up, a sad expression on her face. *This should be good*, thinks Dom.

"I'm very sorry, Max, about what happened. I just… needed the money. I have a Jack Russell named Bean. Sometimes I think he's my best friend. And… he's really ill."

Dom tolerates the next thirty minutes of conversation through tight-lipped irritation, sipping at a pint he brought back with Susan's wine. Susan raises her sick dog with a sick mother, and the honeytrap scam is quickly forgotten. Susan finds reasons to laugh and touch Max's arm, which looks rather clumsy. Amazingly, Max expresses interest in Susan's apparent computer skills, which leads to some bullshit story about how Susan used to work for an IT firm before they made her redundant after the 2008 financial collapse. What happens next is something Dom saw coming, and he practically needs to force a fist down his own throat to stop himself from interrupting. Max gives Susan his business card and suggests that she give him a call because he thinks that Henderson Nautical Works could use someone with Susan's computing skills. Susan is delighted of course, and there is more laughing and arm-touching.

Forty-five minutes later and Dom is standing in *The Half Moon* parking lot, having just called a taxi for Susan. She stands next to him, hugging herself against the cool night air.

"Ooofff," she says to Dom. "It's cold."

Dom puts his phone in his pocket and gives her a hard stare. "Yeah, I don't really give a shit if you're cold, Susan."

She makes a face and looks out into the glare of the parking lot lights. Dom reaches over and takes her handbag from under her arm. "Hey, that's mine," says Susan.

Dom rifles through her tiny bag. He notices a hypodermic needle, bag of heroin, a length of rubber hose, mascara, eyebrow pencil and blusher. "Look at this," says Dom, "everything a girl needs for a night out." He pulls out Max's business card and hands her the bag. Dom tears the card in two and puts it into his pocket. He looks around the parking lot and then grips her by the arm and walks her over to the edge of the lot where the lighting is dim, Susan tottering and clomping on her massive high heels.

He grips harder at her arm and glares down at her tiny form. "Ow," she says.

"Listen close, Susan, because your life depends on what I'm going to tell you. My boss doesn't understand people like you, but I do. You're going to go back to the shit-hole you came from and you're never going to contact my boss, ever. And, if you do, I will come for you, and I will shoot you and your non-existent dog. You'll just have to find yourself another sugar daddy. Do you understand me?"

Susan gazes up at Dom and smiles. "You wouldn't hurt a lady, would you?"

"No," says Dom, getting close to her face. "I wouldn't hurt a lady, but I would hurt a twenty-five-quid smack-whore who's trying to fuck with my boss."

Susan makes a face and looks at the wrecked pavement. Dom tightens his grip on her arm. "Ow – you're hurting me."

"Do you understand the plan, Susan?"

"Yes, yes... Jesus."

"And what's the plan?"

"I won't contact Max."

Dom releases her and a moment later the taxi pulls up. "Let's go," says Dom, and he walks with Susan and opens the rear door. She gets in, Dom closes the door, and walks to the driver's open window. An older Asian fellow gazes at him blankly.

"I need you to take her to London, Hackney."

"Oh no, I can't do that. I only serve Portsmouth."

Dom pulls bills out of his wallet and holds them up to the man. "That's three hundred."

The man shrugs, takes the cash, and rolls up his window.

CHAPTER 25

At 6:15 PM Margaret Williams sits at the small conference table in her Prime Minister's office and gazes at the three men sitting opposite – Home Secretary Jared, Defence Secretary Ronald, and Andrew Stubbings, the Director General of MI5. All she knows about the meeting is that there is an important update concerning the *Joan of Arc* situation. Margaret is missing her granddaughter's ballet performance and she's feeling very irritated at Max Henderson. She doesn't know why Jared had wanted to bring along the Director General of MI5, but Margaret imagines that it doesn't mean good news.

"So, what's the good news?" asks Margaret.

Jared and Ronald laugh in a forced way at Margaret's joke. "Well, yes, Prime Minister," says Jared, "I'll see if I can think of some. But I've brought along Andrew because he needs to make you aware of a development."

"Excellent," says Margaret. "I assume this is going to be upsetting, so perhaps just before we finish I could hear about a new baby panda that's been born at London Zoo, or something similar."

"I'll see what I can do," says Jared, smiling. He looks over at the Director General of MI5 before continuing. "As you know, MI5 has been surveilling Henderson Nautical Works. Andrew needs to make you aware of something. Andrew…"

"Good evening, Prime Minister," says Andrew. "Prime Minister, I have fifteen agents outside the gates of Henderson Nautical Works making observations of the grounds, keeping an eye on the people who are congregating there as well as shed 4, where *Joan of Arc* is housed. I also have one agent working undercover, inside the site. That agent took some photographs of deliveries which were shipped to the site and then transferred to shed 4."

Andrew lays out nine photographs on the table in front of Margaret. They depict wooden crates of various sizes which are being taken in turn through a large shed door by a huge forklift.

Margaret scratches her head. "So, what's this mean?"

"There's no markings on the crates which can tell us where they came from or what's inside," says Andrew. "It could be anything. But we don't like this crate here." Andrew taps his finger on a photo of a large rectangular crate. "Naval jet fighters can vary in size somewhat, but for the purposes of transport, there is normally a standard crate which is used. That crate there fits those dimensions precisely."

"So you think Henderson is buying naval fighter planes for *Joan of Arc*?" says Margaret.

"We can't know for sure and we can't prove it," says Andrew, "but, like I said, we don't like the dimensions of that crate. There's just one of that size we've seen delivered, but we can't be sure."

"What do our solicitors say about this?" says Margaret.

"They say it helps," says Defence Secretary Ronald, "but they don't think a delivery of crates constitutes sufficient evidence of a crime or grounds for arrest. Andrew is right. Those are the dimensions of crates generally used to transport naval fighter jets. But arms providers will sometimes use spare crates to ship something else. Shipping is not an exact science."

Margaret groans. "I've got so much to deal with – I just need this Max Henderson thing out of the way. Let's arrest the bugger. Cut the snake's head off and the body dies, right? If we throw Henderson in jail these nutters following him around will get bored, wander off, and do something else. Right?"

"I agree that we need to get this sorted," says Jared, "but arresting Henderson will mean this thing will be in the courts for months, and the United Nations may have something to say if they have actually made a petition for statehood. And then there's the issue of Henderson achieving some sort of martyrdom."

Margaret gazes into space for a few moments. Memories of Prime Minister's questions in parliament as well as several awkward interviews come to mind, and she feels angry at appearing indecisive and weak. Something tips over in her mind and a decision forms – not one she is sure of, but she has a sense that these moments are just part of the office. She looks directly at Andrew and taps the worrying photo.

"You're telling me there is evidence, based on the dimensions, that there is a fighter jet in that box. And it seems to me that these other boxes going into that shed – there could be military weapons in them as well." She looks all three men in the eye before continuing. "We are going to infiltrate Henderson Nautical Works and seize *Joan of Arc*. I want a plan presented to me in two days and we go in… seven days… or maybe ten… but no later than ten days."

Jared and Ronald glance at one another, silently questioning whether they should challenge Margaret's decision. A moment passes and they turn their attention to Margaret. "Yes, Prime Minister" they say, nearly in unison.

CHAPTER 26

When Dom enters Sheila's office, she looks up at him, a tired expression on her face. Dom realises he hasn't seen Sheila in a few days. He leans over and gives her a kiss on the cheek. "You look gorgeous, Sheila. How you doing, sweetheart?" he says.

"I'm getting tired of this aircraft carrier shit, Dom. Can you talk to him?"

"I talk to him all the time, Sheila."

Sheila smiles at Dom. "You know... if I was forty years younger..."

"Yeah," says Dom, "and I'd take you to the best restaurants. Course if I was forty years older my dick probably wouldn't work anymore. So we're in a fine situation, aren't we?"

Sheila laughs. "Oh yeah. That's all I need. A working dick."

Dom smiles. "So, what's this meeting about?"

"That Winston fellow wanted to meet up," says Sheila, rolling her eyes. "Something about constitutions and flags."

"I need to talk to Max about something as well. Is this meeting gonna take long?"

"Max has a busy morning," says Sheila, "so I hope not. Hedvika, Winston, and that annoying woman with the shaved head are attending. Max is on the phone and that woman... Sunshine whatever... is in the waiting room. Do you want me to make you a coffee?"

"I'm fine."

Dom gives Sheila a wink, enters the waiting room, and sits in a chair directly facing Sunrise70. He puts his elbows on his knees, leans forward, and looks directly at her, noticing the short-cropped purple hair. She glances up from her phone and then ignores him. Dom smiles, slaps his legs, adjusts his tie, and then sits in a chair right next to her, his arm touching hers.

She looks over at him, giving him a cold and direct stare for several moments.

Dom smiles. "You look like you wanna say something to me, Sunshine."

"My name is Sunrise70."

"Yeah, I know," says Dom, continuing to grin. "Sunshine is my affectionate nickname for you."

Sunrise70 continues to look directly at Dom for a while. Finally, she says, "I'm not afraid of you."

Dom chuckles. "And why would you be afraid of me?"

"I said I'm *not* afraid of you." She continues to stare at Dom, and then says, "I know your type."

"Really?" says Dom. "And what type is that?"

"Guys like you. You think you're real hard. But when you're in the shit, you run."

"Is that so?" says Dom, the smile evaporating from his face.

"Yeah, that's so."

Dom feels a sudden anger rising in him, which he controls. He turns his body and leans into Sunrise70 until he can feel the hard metal contained within his shoulder holster press against her arm. It's a trick from the old days, one he hasn't used in years. Sunrise70 doesn't flinch or appear surprised in the least.

"Is that your dick pressing against my arm?" she says.

Dom struggles for a response, thinking to himself that there's been a weird amount of conversation about dicks for one morning. He prides himself on always having a response in situations like these. A moment passes, and he finds one.

"I wouldn't have thought you'd be interested in dick."

Sunrise70's cool exterior breaks. She jumps to her feet and glares down at Dom and he sees rage in her face. He locks eyes with her and tightens his arm muscles, preparing to block a punch. "Fuck yourself, hard man," she hisses.

Dom has a decision to make, and he silently weighs the situation up, aware they are sitting in the waiting room outside Max's office. He opens his arms and smiles. "Hey, relax, okay? I'm just fucking with you a little bit, right?"

"Yeah?" says Sunrise70. "Well don't fuck with me... ever."

Dom considers his response but Hedvika walks in, a look of concern on her face. "Everything okay here?" she says.

"Yeah, sure," says Dom. "Sunrise70 and I are just getting to know each other. I think we might even be friends, right, Sunrise?"

Sunrise stands up straight and looks at Hedvika. "Hi," she says, her tone flat.

Winston enters the waiting room and no one can help but notice his appearance. His beard is still there, but trimmed now. And what really grabs everyone's attention is that he seems to be wearing a strange uniform. Olive-green trousers and shirt hang on his slight frame, and everything is ironed and pressed. He has two shining silver stars pinned to his breast pocket and wears a red cap with an image of *Jeanne d'Arc* on it. The band of red cloth is still around his arm, but sewn neatly, and there are shiny black shoes on his feet. A new brown leather bag is over his shoulder. His posture seems straighter.

Winston appears self-conscious. "Is it too much?" he says.

"Um... no. It seems fine Winston," says Hedvika.

"I didn't know whether to go with one or two stars," says Winston.

"Two... seems okay," says Hedvika.

Winston looks at his stars and frowns. He unpins one of them and puts it in his pocket.

"You make me think of that communist guy," says Dom. "You know, the one in Cuba."

"Castro or Che Guevara?" asks Sunrise70.

"How should I know? One of those guys," says Dom.

"Right," says Hedvika, "I've got a lot to do. Can you two sort out your communists later? Let's go see Max."

Hedvika knocks and enters Max's office. He's just saying goodbye to someone on the phone and waves his hand at everyone, inviting them to sit down. They all take a seat in front of his desk.

Max opens his arms. "Good morning, friends. How are developments going?"

"Well, we've got a constitution and a flag for you," says Winston. "And people are submitting applications for citizenship."

"Wonderful," says Max.

Winston pulls an enormous and professionally-bound manuscript out of his leather bag and places it on the desk. Max leans over and reads out, "Constitution of *Jeanne d'Arc*." He looks at Winston. "Wow, did you write all this?"

"I did, sir. I hope you're pleased with it."

Max looks over at his solicitor. "Have you read it, Hedvika?"

Hedvika chuckles. "Max, it's over nine hundred pages long. I've skim-read much of it, but that's all I could manage."

"What do you think?" asks Max.

Hedvika smiles. "You can't say it's not comprehensive. Covers everything you could possibly imagine – bill of rights, education, health, environmental practices, law and enforcement, separation of state powers. Well, it covers separation of state powers except there really isn't much of that. From what I can tell, the form of government is pretty much a benevolent autocracy with you as head of state."

Hedvika picks up the huge volume and opens to the contents page. She utters a small laugh and points to something. "There're forty pages on animal welfare." She puts the tome back on the desk.

Max smiles warmly at Winston and places a hand on the manuscript. "I love it Winston. Great job." Winston dips his head, an expression of gratitude running across his face. Sunrise70 folds her arms and blows out a breath of air.

Max looks at his watch. "Okay then, let's see the flag."

Winston opens his bag and places a single sheet of paper in front of Max. There is a drawing, clearly done by Sunrise70. The flag is a sea of blue with a pink heart in the middle. In the centre of the heart is a single raised fist drawn in blue.

Max examines the flag and then looks up. "What do you think Dom?"

"It looks a little less gay than the first one," says Dom.

"Hedvika?" asks Max.

She smiles and shrugs. "It's a flag, Max."

Max looks at Winston and Sunrise70. "What I like is that you two managed a compromise. I love it." He looks over at Hedvika. "Hey, this stuff will help with that application thing, right?"

"You mean the application to the UN for Statehood?" says Hedvika.

"That's the one."

"Um, sure," says Hedvika. "Why not. I was going to get the application in the post this afternoon, so I'll include the constitution and flag."

"Okay, what else?" says Max.

"To date," says Winston, "we've had 2,816 people express interest in citizenship. We've been emailing or handing out application forms, and 651 people have applied. There are about 300 people still camping out in front of Henderson Nautical, and most all of them have applied. The others have applied through a Facebook page we've set up. Many of them are Brits, but we've had applications from a bunch of different countries. We're processing all the application forms and informing people if they've been granted citizenship."

"Wow, 651 people have applied," says Max. "How many have been granted citizenship?"

Winston looks a little confused. "Well... 651."

"Oh, okay," says Max. "We need to think about getting our citizens on board before too long. I hate to think of all those people camping. It rained last night."

"I've talked to the Captain," says Winston. "We just need to get bedding and food to stock up the kitchen."

"Well, decide what you think you might need," says Max. "Then order it and get Sheila to pay for it through my personal account."

Max smiles and claps his hands. "Great job everyone… now, I'm very sorry, but I've got another meeting."

Max stands up and shows Hedvika, Sunrise70 and Winston to the door, but Dom remains seated and Winston seems to have something on his mind. Hedvika and Sunrise70 head down the hall and Winston raises his hand.

"Winston, you really don't have to raise your hand," says Max. "What is it?"

"Mr Henderson… Max. I hope you won't think I'm being impetuous, but I wonder if we could think about your… attire."

"My what?"

"It's just that… well, you're the Head of State now." Winston looks over at the giant manuscript on the desk. "I had to think about your role quite a bit when I was writing the constitution. I just wonder if we need to consider what sort of attire suits *Jeanne d'Arc*'s Head of State. So what I'm thinking is that my sister is a dressmaker. And she's a real history buff. She's perfect. I'd really like to send her over and let her help put something together which fits the gravity of your new role."

"Absolutely, Winston. Have her book an appointment with Sheila."

Winston gives Max and Dom a little bow, exits the room, and closes the door.

Max looks over at Dom. "Boss, I know you're busy, but there's something I have to tell you."

Max closes the door and sits down behind his desk. Dom sits down again. He raises his hands and there is a sad expression on his face.

"It's Peter, isn't it?" says Max.

"I'm really sorry, boss. He's gone again. I've really tried… but…"

Max is shaking his head. "It's not your fault, Dom." Max sighs heavily. "Shit."

"I'll do what I can to find him, boss. There's a couple of guys I can put on it as well."

Max nods thoughtfully. "Thanks, Dom. I'm sure you will."

CHAPTER 27

At 7 PM I knock on the front door of Sheila's small terraced home, which is in a quiet Portsmouth neighbourhood. Driving from London after a full day of work at the newspaper struck some of my colleagues as beyond the call of duty, but I felt Max's PA would be an important key to understanding the inner workings of the *Jeanne d'Arc* story, and maybe even the inner workings of Max Henderson.

Shelia opens the door, greets me, and I follow her in. She shows me to her kitchen and offers me a glass of wine, which I accept. Her advanced years have not dimmed an energy and quickness, which you notice in her tone and eyes. She takes me through to her sitting room and I am struck by the cleanliness, order, and minimalism of her small house. Everything here seems necessary. And, when I look around her sitting room, I am overawed by... the books. Her furniture is in the centre of the room, and instead of hanging pictures, every wall contains varnished wood shelves which go nearly to the ceiling, and most every inch of shelving holds books.

"Wow," I say, the word slipping out. "Do you mind if I have a look at your books?"

Sheila sits and places her glass of wine on a side table. "I'd be insulted if you didn't. Take your time."

I slowly walk around the room and notice that the books are organised by category, and there are labels on the shelves. I see *History (Modern)*, *History (antiquity)*, *Physics and Cosmology*, *Philosophy (general)*, *Philosophy (Existential)*, *Psychology*, *Transpersonal*, *Art*, *Music*, and *Fiction*. There isn't a speck of dust.

I spend a few minutes looking over her collection, touching a volume here and there. "This is an extraordinary collection you have," I say.

"I'm an old woman, I'm not into cats, and I don't have much use for a man. What are you gonna do?"

"You must love books."

"I like ideas, and you find quite a lot of that in books. Humanity's effort to understand what's going on might have some value, but if not, it's at least amusing."

I sit in an armchair opposite her, sip on my wine, and consider what to ask. "You've worked for Max for a very long time. I'll bet a woman of your experience and talent gets head-hunted by other companies. Why have you stayed all these years?"

"Max is a good businessman and he understands ships better than anyone, but he... needs me... and he never lets me forget that. Well, it's more than that. He cares about me too. I'm important to him, and maybe I need that. I don't know." She smiles and looks into space, and then continues. "There's something else, though. Max is different to me. He always seems to see the good in everyone."

I find myself laughing. "Do you realise, Sheila – Dom and Hedvika have said just the same thing."

"I'm not surprised," she says. "But it's difficult to know whether to admire or worry about Max in this respect." She waves her hand at the books in the room. "I find it hard to think like Max, but sometimes I wish I could."

"What about *Jeanne d'Arc*? Does it surprise you?"

"I don't know. It did at first. I wish it wasn't happening but I think Max is caught up in something that perhaps has been there for a long time. He seems to need to do this."

"Is it self-destructive?" I ask.

"Probably," she says. "But... self-destructive... self-creative... I think it can be hard to separate these two."

"That's a very philosophical way of understanding things. Isn't there an explanation for all of this?"

"Most likely," says Sheila, "but does Max even understand what he's doing or why he's doing it? He seems to be on some sort of trajectory, but maybe it's like he got shot out of a cannon and now he's just flapping his arms and wondering if there's a big bale of hay somewhere down there."

I'm laughing and Sheila is smiling, and I realise I like this elderly woman. Sheila takes a sip of wine and looks thoughtful. "But, joking aside," she says, "I'm worried about Max. It's like he's searching for something, but... he's on the edge."

An image comes into my head. "That makes me think of those sailors from centuries ago who wanted to discover new lands but thought they might sail off the edge of the world."

Sheila smiles and then look down at her wine glass, a thoughtful and concerned expression on her face. "Yeah," she says. "Maybe it's like that."

CHAPTER 28

Max is sitting on the plush leather couch in his cabin on board *Jeanne d'Arc*, sipping at his third pint. Captain Jean-Pierre and Aeronautics Chief Hugo sit opposite him, both with glasses of red wine. Chief Engineer Alexis is back home in France for a few days, celebrating one of his kid's birthdays.

"There was an article in *La Monde* yesterday about you," says Jean-Pierre, waving a finger at Max. "They said you are a revolutionary."

Jean-Pierre's lids are drooping and it occurs to Max that maybe the stereotype about British and French drinking is true. The French start early, about lunchtime, and then drink slowly for the rest of the day. Brits create the illusion of discipline by waiting until the early evening, but do their best to catch up as quickly as possible.

"Revolutionary?" says Max. "Sorry about that."

Jean-Pierre and Hugo laugh, and Max doesn't know what's funny. "Oh no," says Jean-Pierre. "I am making a compliment. In France, there is always some revolution going on. We all like revolutionaries, even when we say we don't."

Max considers the mixed press he is getting. Politicians and anyone involved with policing certainly dislike him. Art critics like him for some reason. A lot of people seem confused. "I don't think we are so fond of revolutions over here," says Max.

Hugo raises his glass. "Why not?"

"I'm not sure. I've been told that we don't have civil wars very often, but when we do, they're really bad."

The Frenchmen laugh and Max wants to join in with their humour, but Peter is on his mind. He wonders if he should call Dom to see if there is any update, but he called only an hour ago, so he leaves it. He wonders if his son has a place to stay tonight, or if he is on the streets. Max notices Jean-Pierre's eyes close. A couple of minutes pass and the Captain's breathing slows. Hugo takes the Captain's glass of wine out of his hand and places it on the coffee table.

Hugo jerks his head at the Captain. "His wife is mad at him. She wants him to come home and retire properly."

"Is he going to?"

"I doubt it," says Hugo. "It's all gin rummy, bridge, shuffleboard, and getting dragged to dance classes. Mostly, it's memories of a better life. It's difficult when you were an important person. You get used to that."

Hugo takes a long sip of wine. "Are you okay, Max? You seem... I can't think of the word – like you're not there."

"Distracted," says Max.

"Yes, that's it."

"I'm fine," says Max.

"I know what will cheer you up. Let's go look at the plane. We've got it out of the crate and into a hanger. And I've been tuning the jet propulsion system."

Max smiles. "Sure – why not."

Max follows Hugo through a labyrinth of grey corridors, stepping over several bulkheads along the way. At one point they emerge into the strange green glow of the shed and walk along a platform just below the main deck. A moment later they come upon one of the deck guns they had purchased at the arm's fair.

"You've had it installed already?" says Max.

"Of course," says Hugo. "I thought we would have problems, but the gun slotted into *Jeanne d'Arc*'s mount immediately. The other one is installed on the port side."

Max inspects the anti-aircraft gun closely. It's mounted on a swivelling platform and has two parallel barrels, each about five feet long. Max places his hands on the handles used to point and operate it and tries to swivel the gun, but it won't move."

"Here," says Hugo. He pulls down on a lever. "Try now."

Max swivels the gun, and he is surprised how easy it is to swing the large weapon up and down, side to side. He notices a large metal cylinder attached to the rear of the gun, which he points to. "Is that the...?"

"Yes, it's the loader for shells," says Hugo. "Fifty calibre."

"Is it...?" starts Max.

"No, don't worry," says Hugo. "The shells are in the armoury."

"Why did we buy shells?" asks Max.

"The shells came with the gun."

"Oh," says Max. "Well, it looks impressive."

"It's not so good as restoration goes," says Hugo. "Jean-Pierre thinks the gun is ex Russian Naval. The bullets are American. Not surprising, really. The Russians and Americans account for most of the guns and bullets you will find on the planet. Come on, I want to show you the

151

plane."

Hugo locks the deck gun into place and they walk back into the carrier and down some stairs. It takes another five minutes before Hugo leads Max into hanger number two. Hugo hits a light which illuminates the enormous hanger, and there, right in the middle, is the jet plane. It's painted grey and seems incredibly sleek with twin engines, twin tails, a compact cockpit, and a nose which comes to a sharp point. Max sees insignia on the tails and wings which he hadn't noticed at the arms fair. The colours of the insignia are green, orange, and white.

Max points to the insignia. "I thought the jet was Russian."

"It's Russian-made," says Hugo. "It's a Mikoyan MiG-29. The insignia is Indian. The Russians sold this jet to a lot of countries and India bought loads of them. How the plane wound up at an arms fair in Egypt I have no idea. I think this one was made in the 1980s, but she's still in pretty good shape."

"What was she used for, do you think?" asks Max.

"It's Indian. So, probably flying patrols and trying to scare the Pakistanis, right?" Hugo laughs and points at the plane. "Do you want to sit in the cockpit?"

"I'd love to," says Max. "Can we start her up?"

Hugo laughs. "Max, do you know how loud a fighter jet sounds inside a hanger with the doors closed? All of Portsmouth will hear it."

Hugo points to a rolling ladder on wheels. "Let's push that over here and I'll help you get in."

CHAPTER 29

Max notices Sheila's head appear through his office door. "Max, Constance Godfred is here – the dressmaker."

Max looks into space, an air of vague reflection in his eyes. "The dressmaker?" he says to himself.

"Winston's sister," says Sheila. "Something about a uniform."

"Okay, send her in."

Sheila opens the door wider and a thin, pale woman enters. The woman offers Max a hand. "Nice to meet you, Mr Henderson," she says, laughing and smiling.

"Please, call me Max." There is no mistaking this woman – she is the female counterpart to Winston in every respect. Nervous enthusiasm worn on her sleeve. She wears an old-fashioned brown dress which goes to her ankles and antiquated boots. It all looks rather Victorian.

"One second," says Constance. She disappears into the waiting room and reappears a moment later rolling a seven-foot rack. Sheila sighs and closes the door.

"It's very good of you to come by," says Max.

"My pleasure," says Constance. "Winston has been talking about almost nothing else. It's been *Jeanne d'Arc this* and *Max Henderson that*. Constitutions and people power. I'm telling you – he never shuts up about it." Constance spits out laughter and puts a hand to her mouth. "Oh dear, I'm sorry."

"That's okay," says Max, who is trying to remember why he is meeting with Winston's sister. "So… how can I help?"

Constance laughs nervously again and for no apparent reason, and waves at the garment rack. "Well, Winston thinks you need some sort of attire that will suit your position as Head of State."

"Oh yes, that's right," says Max.

"So I've done some further research and put a few ideas together."

"Further research?" says Max.

"Oh yes. World leaders put an awful lot of thought into their appearance. There's an interesting history to it all."

Constance pulls an opaque plastic cover off the garment rack and Max finds himself staring at a discordant collection of clothing. There must be a couple of dozen outfits. "Now," says Constance, waving at the clothing, "national leaders dress in a way which express who and what they are, or certainly how they want others to see them. It's not as random as you might think, because when you look closely you see certain themes. The way national leaders dress really falls into one of three groups – the conventional, the humble, and the splendid."

"Really? How does that work then?"

"So, to start with," says Constance, "some national leaders dress in a rather conventional way, similar to how posh businessmen and women would dress." She pulls a blue suit complete with trousers, white shirt, and dull blue tie off the rack, and holds it in front of her. "Examples of *the conventional* include Saddam Hussein, Nicolae Ceauşescu, Robert Mugabe, and a number of Western leaders. Bashar al-Assad is a very good example. I call this the Bashar al-Assad look." Constance laughs loudly at herself. "Oh dear, I'm sorry," she says.

"That's fine," says Max. "This is quite interesting."

Constance collects herself and continues. "So, in terms of appearance, you then have what I would call *the humble*." She pulls a hanger off the rack and holds up a jacket and trouser combination made of a dirt-brown rough weave of cloth. "In this group you've got leaders like Mao Zedong, Kim Jong-il, Kim Jong-un, Joseph Stalin, Fidel Castro, and Ho Chi Minh. They are all trying to identify with the peasants or rural people, and, to a man, they are all communists. They convey the idea that they too are living humble lives, just like the downtrodden masses. It's nonsense, of course. They all lived lavish lifestyles, except Ho Chi Minh, which is probably why everyone wrote so many songs about him." Constance bursts into laughter. "I'm so sorry – I get very nervous."

"No, really, Constance. You're doing very well."

Constance takes a deep breath, places the hanger back on the rack, and continues. "Which brings us to *the splendid*." Constance pulls a hanger off the rack and holds up an outfit which is a blaze of colour – a royal blue jacket featuring shining gold epaulettes on the shoulders with tassels, giant lapels with glinting brass buttons, a huge gold medallion and a collection of medals, and a garish red satin sash.

"Wow," says Max.

"There's white trousers which get tucked into some black boots which come up to your knee, and..." She reaches into a box at the foot of the rack and pulls out a large blue and red cap featuring peacock feathers and more glinting medals. "Pretty great, huh?"

"I suppose so," says Max.

"Anyway," says Constance, "there's plenty of splendid leaders – Idi Amin, Napoleon, Muammar al-Gaddafi, Catherine the Great. Not much to say about them except that they want you to know they are pretty great."

"Well," says Max, "you certainly seem to know your stuff."

"I can show you more examples if you like."

"No, no – that's perfectly alright, Constance – I think I get the idea."

Constance waves a hand at the rack of clothing. "So, do you want to try anything on? Does any particular look say, *this is Max Henderson – National Leader?*"

Max walks over to the rack and runs a hand over the outfits, noticing that Constance has organised everything into groups of the conventional, humble, and splendid. "To tell you the truth, Constance, I don't really think much about clothing. I just sort of put on more or less the same thing every day."

"Winston asked me to take some photos for him of the outfits you try on, just so he can get an idea."

"He did? Does, um, Winston have some sort of idea of what outfit I should wear?"

"Oh yes," says Constance. "Definitely – but I'm not supposed to lead you."

Max gazes at the clothing and sighs. "Well, maybe you could lead me, just a little."

Constance bursts into laughter. "Okay, so Winston really wants you to wear the splendid uniform I showed you a moment ago. He really thinks it will suit you."

Constance holds up the lavish royal blue uniform with gold epilates and tassels, red sash, and glinting medals. Max smiles. "And this would make Winston happy?"

"Oh yes," says Constance. "If you want to try it on, I can wait outside."

Max examines the lavish outfit for a moment. "Why not?" he finds himself saying.

Constance organises the clothing and boots and steps outside. Max stands in front of the mirror he normally uses to change into his work overalls and slips on the bright white trousers, and then the royal blue jacket. He pulls on the nearly-knee-length shining black leather boots, and then places the cap with peacock feathers and medals on his head.

He feels a little ridiculous but is also surprised at how well everything fits. He turns to either side and inspects the reflection, tilting his head upwards and putting a serious expression on. Max smiles and suddenly feels a little giddy. He has a sense of needing to give a speech but can't think of what to say. Max opens the door and discovers that Constance seems to have her head nearly pressed against the other side.

"Come on in, Constance."

Max closes the door and notices that Constance has both hands pressed to her mouth. "My goodness, Mr Henderson! You look so… well, wonderful."

Constance smooths out a few wrinkles in his sleeves and adjusts his hat. "Really impressive. Will you let me take a photo for Winston?"

Max opens his mouth to answer but hears a familiar shout coming from Sheila's office. "Um," says Max, "we might have a complication."

A look of confusion crosses Constance's face and a moment later Sheila sticks her head through the door. "Trouble, Max. It's Violeta. She's ranting about some magazine article. Really pissed-off. What do I do?"

Max looks over at Constance. "Sorry about this. My wife seems to be upset about something."

"Oh dear," says Constance.

"I told her you were in a meeting Max, but she's standing in the front office shouting and waving a magazine around."

Max opens his mouth to speak but Violeta is suddenly at the door.

"Idiota!" shouts Violeta as she pushes herself into Max's office.

"Mrs Henderson," says Sheila.

"It's alright, Sheila," says Max. Max gives Sheila a wave and closes the office door.

Violeta brandishes a rolled-up magazine and glares at Max, apparently oblivious of Constance. "Do you see what they say about me? *Society* magazine. It say you are lunatica and maybe I am lunatica and that I am no good singer anymore."

Violeta swats Max in the arm with the magazine. Her eyes are red and tear-stained. Violeta opens her mouth to speak and suddenly seems to notice her surroundings. Her eyes glance furtively from Max to Constance, and then she looks from head to foot at Max, her mouth dropping open. "What the hell is this?" she says, gesturing at Max with her magazine.

"Well…" says Max. He smooths his hands over his royal blue tunic, catching a finger for a moment on the large medallion, and looks up.

"Um…" says Max. "Violeta, I don't think you've met Constance. Constance is my dress-maker." Max looks over at Constance, whose eyes are wide with fear.

"I don't care who this person is," shouts Violeta. "You are like… el asno. What the hell are you wearing?"

"It's, um, well…" begins Max. "You see, Winston thinks that I need a new look."

"Winston?" shouts Violeta. "I don't know Winston." Violeta jabs a finger into the side of her head several times. "El disastre… el disastre. Are you too stupid?" she shouts.

Max feels at a loss for words and looks over at Constance, who grimaces and shrugs her shoulders.

"Imbicile!" shouts Violeta. She smacks Max in the head with the magazine and stomps out the door, shouting something in Spanish down the hallway. Max closes the door and looks over at Constance, who is picking his cap up off of the floor. A peacock feather has come loose, which Constance puts back in place. She puts the cap back on Max's head and smiles apologetically.

"I'm sorry about that, Constance. My wife seems a little upset with me."

"Yes, I can see that," says Constance.

Max turns to face the mirror and Constance stands next to him. They look at the reflected images in silence. "Your brother cares an awful lot about what's happening, doesn't he?" says Max.

"Yes," says Constance. "A lot of people seem to."

Max looks over at Constance. "Does that seem strange to you?"

Constance reflects for a moment. "No, I don't think so."

Max nods and looks back at his reflection as well as the hopeful reflection of Constance. For reasons he can't fathom, a smile grows from the edges of his mouth and then spills out as laughter and Max finds he can't stop laughing. His laughter feels rather maniacal and then Constance is laughing as well. A few moments later they finally catch their breath and Constance wipes tears from her eyes. "My god," says Max, pointing at their reflection in the mirror. "We're a pair of strange birds." Max sighs loudly. "And this uniform would make Winston happy?"

"It would. He seems to have ideas for you."

"Well, I can't imagine what that would be, but okay," says Max. He takes the hat off and hands it to Constance. "Maybe we don't need peacock feathers, but… I have something you can add. Max gets the French National Order of Merit from a desk drawer and holds it up. He points to the medal. "An actual medal – the only one I ever got."

"Impressive," says Constance. There are already so many ribbons and medals on Max's jacket Constance has to remove a medal in order to pin the Order of Merit on.

Constance stands back and takes a photo on her phone. "Bingo," she says, and a burst of laughter pops out.

"Bingo, indeed," says Max, grinning.

Constance plucks the peacock feathers from the hat and hands it back. "Good luck, Max."

She waves, opens the door, and begins to pull her garment rack behind her. Constance stops suddenly and looks back. "Oh, Max. One other thing. You know that my brother has… problems. Right?"

"Don't we all," says Max.

Constance thinks for a moment. "Um, sure. Yeah. I guess."

She smiles and a moment later is gone.

Max turns and looks at his reflection again, and then hears the office door close. He turns and Sheila is gazing up and down at him, arms folded. Max opens his arms wide. "So, am I losing my mind, Sheila?"

Sheila sighs. "I'm just worried about you, Max. You're spending so much time with this boat business, and some of these people seem… weird."

Max's face falls and he looks at the carpet for a moment. He senses Sheila move close to him and feels her bony hands squeezing his arms. "But," she says, "you look very handsome in… whatever this is."

Max gazes at her. "Violeta was pretty mad, huh?"

Sheila frowns. "I'll make us some tea, alright?"

CHAPTER 30

Margaret sits at her desk in the PM's office and gazes into space. She is having a reoccurring daydream in which she is retired from office and is being interviewed by a future biographer. The way the daydream goes is that the interviewer is male and young and a Cambridge graduate. His composure exudes admiration and deference. Margaret is now beyond the reach of special interests and there is a lightness to this sense of liberation.

The PM job can be so demanding, says the young man, pushing a wisp of dark black hair from his face. *What was the driving motivation to become Prime Minister?*

Margaret chuckles inside. *The same thing that drives all ambitious politicians. You want to be on top of the whole stinking pile, don't you?*

The young man makes a note and is about to ask a follow-up question when the Prime Minister's reverie is broken by the sound of her phone ringing.

"Hello," says Margaret.

"Prime Minister," says her PA. "It's the Director of MI5. Can you take the call?"

"Yes," says Margaret.

"Good morning, Andrew," says Margaret.

"Good morning, Prime Minister," says Andrew. "The Home Secretary asked that I contact you if there were any significant developments concerning *Joan of Arc.*"

"Yes," says Margaret.

"Um," says Andrew. "Well, there's been a development."

Margaret sighs. "I assumed as much, Andrew. Perhaps you should tell me what it is."

"Of course, Prime Minister. The people who have been camping outside of Henderson Nautical – they have all got into a queue which is facing the east entrance to the shipyard."

"What does this mean?" asks Margaret, fairly sure she knows the answer.

"Well, we can't be certain, but the east entrance is closest to shed four. My guess is that they are preparing to board *Joan of Arc.* Are there any

159

instructions, Prime Minister?"

"What sort of press presence is there?"

"What?"

"The press, Andrew," says Margaret. "It's a group of news reporters."

"Oh, yes, Prime Minister. Several outlets."

"Wonderful… just perfect," says Margaret, aware that lapsing into sarcasm is never a good sign. "Have your agents continue to monitor the situation closely and make sure I have updates if things change. I assume you've informed the Home and Defence Secretaries."

"Yes, Prime Minister."

"Good. That's all for now."

Margaret hangs up and punches at the phone, her PA answering a moment later.

"I need to speak with the Home and Defence Secretaries this morning. Have them come to Number 10 if they can. Otherwise, set up a conference call. Tell them I want an update on preparations concerning that goddamned aircraft carrier."

CHAPTER 31

Max sits on the plush red leather couch in his cabin and looks across the coffee table at Captain Jean-Pierre and Chief of Aeronautics Hugo. The fact that his naval compatriots are on *Jeanne d'Arc* and dressed in full naval uniforms which are spotless and pressed reminds Max of how important this morning is. Alexis Girard, also in full naval uniform, sits down adjacent to Max and places the four strong coffees he'd just made onto the coffee table. Max picks up his coffee and inhales the rich acrid aroma.

"That's good coffee, Alexis," says Max.

"He's an engineer," says Jean-Pierre. "He ought to be able to make a cup of coffee."

Max laughs. He feels less self-conscious dressed in the extravagant outfit which Constance had made for him than he imagined he might, perhaps because he is sitting with three men who are in full naval dress, each with some collection of ribbons and medals. They only noticed his uniform in passing when they arrived this morning. Jean-Pierre had looked Max over and simply said "Splendid," and Max thought *Exactly, how did you know?* Max was aware that when he was with his naval companions there was a lot they talked about and quite a lot which remained unsaid, and this seemed about right.

There was a knock at the door and Max called, "Come on in." A moment later Dom, Hedvika, Winston, and Sunrise70 are standing in the room, and Alexis is on his feet organising coffee. Max gets up as well and ushers everyone over to an oak table in one corner of his cabin. Max notices that Winston is wearing his 'Che Guevara outfit', which isn't surprising as he wears this all the time now. What surprises Max is Sunrise70. She normally appears in whatever she might have picked up off of the floor that morning, but she is dressed in what looks like new clothes, and she is in black from head to foot – black cargo jeans, black button-up shirt, thick rubber-soled black boots, and a black beret cap featuring a small silver pin of a raised fist. Max recalls that Sunrise70 is in fact in charge of *Jeanne d'Arc*'s security.

Alexis hands out coffees to Hedvika, Sunrise70, and Winston and joins them at the table. Dom raises his hands and smiles. "Hey, everyone's wearing a uniform – nobody told me."

"As if you'd wear a uniform," says Hedvika. "You were born in an Armani suit."

There is laughter around the table, except from Sunrise70, who is sitting next to Winston. "She's right," says Dom. "The midwives were very surprised."

Max laughs and looks over at Winston. "Okay, Winston, tell us where we are."

Winston's eyes grow large, he clears his throat and glances around the table. He tries to speak, but the words seem caught in his throat. He clears his throat again and places a hand against his chest, breathing heavily.

"Is he okay?" asks the Captain.

"He's probably having a panic attack," says Sunrise70, rolling her eyes. She whacks him on the back, which is a bit shocking and seems uncalled for. "Get it together Winston – you got a job to do." Winston is leaning forward now, gazing at the table, hand still pressed against his chest. "He's such a fucking girl," says Sunrise70.

Winston clears his throat, uttering a weird animal-like noise. "I'm okay," he spits out.

"Alright. Well, that's good," says Max.

There is a moment of anticipation, and then Winston looks up and finds his voice. "Well, it's really happening. The people who will become citizens of *Jeanne d'Arc* are ready to board. They are bringing clothing and personal belongings with them and they've formed a queue at the east gate. All the mattresses and bedding have arrived and I've had help from our working committee in making *Jeanne d'Arc*'s quarters as comfortable as possible.

"How many people are there?" asks Max.

"Not as many as I'd hoped," says Winston. "I think about 400. It's odd. Over 3,000 expressed interest in becoming a citizen, nearly 800 applied for citizenship. But only about 400 are actually here for boarding. Most of them are the same people that have been here all along. But there are also people who arrived in the last few days from overseas. Sixty-eight applications are non-British."

"Four hundred is fine Winston," says Max. "That's just how it is. People like the idea of change, but for most it's just the idea they like. So, what happens now?"

"Well," says Winston. "In a moment we'll all go to *Jeanne d'Arc*'s main serving hall. It seats nearly 400, so we should just about fit." Winston looks over at Dom and Sunrise70. "Perhaps Dom and Sunrise70 can open the gate for our new citizens and then lead them onto *Jeanne d'Arc* and to the main dining hall and get everyone seated. I've arranged for coffee, tea, juice, beer, and wine to be available. There's a long table at the head of the hall for all of us to sit when the citizens come through, except for our Head of State."

"Why isn't Max going to be at the table?" asks Dom.

"Because," says Winston, "our Head of State needs to make an entrance... at the right moment."

"An entrance?" says Hedvika.

"Yes," says Winston, who seems to be shaking as if the room were cold. He looks at the faces around the table for a moment before continuing. "What is happening has huge implications for human progress. The country of *Jeanne d'Arc* represents something new. What's going to happen in a few minutes needs to have some ceremonial importance. I'd be so grateful if you can all indulge me. When our new citizens are seated, I'd like Captain Jean-Pierre to introduce us and to welcome everyone to *Jeanne d'Arc*. And then... our Captain will introduce our Head of State, and of course that's when you enter, Max." Winston looks over at Max. "Perhaps there is something you would like to say to everyone at that point."

Max smiles. "Sure, Winston."

"And then lunch can be served," says Winston.

"What's for lunch?" asks Hugo.

"It's a recipe of my own and you're going to love it," says Winston.

"Meaning?" asks Alexis.

"It's a Vegan Garlic Pasta with Roasted Cajun Cauliflower."

Alexis blows out his cheeks and shakes his head.

"The wine is Pinot Noir from Burgundy," says Winston."

"Much better," says Alexis.

"After lunch," says Winston, "Sally, our Secretary General for Citizenry, will call each person up to the front of the hall. Where there are families, she will call them as a group. And she will present them each with their *Jeanne d'Arc* passport, as well as..." Winston reaches down and pulls a small hardback book out of his leather bag. The book has an image of *Jeanne d'Arc*'s flag with a raised fist and pink heart on the cover. The title reads, *Little Guidebook of Jeanne d'Arc*.

"What's in the book?" asks Hedvika.

"Oh," says Winston. "Just a summary of the main points of our constitution. And, if you can bear it, along with the handbook and their new passports, I think it would be very nice to also hand out one of these." Winston reaches into his leather bag and pulls out a white daisy.

"Oh, for fuck sake," says Sunrise70.

Winston looks a little panicked and his eyes flit around the table. Max looks over at his lawyer. "What do you think, Hedvika?"

Hedvika tries to keep herself composed, but she cannot help but laugh. "Max, I think we are now so far beyond normality we can hand out passports, handbooks, daisies, and helium balloons if you like."

A look of panic flashes across Winston's face. "But I haven't arranged for balloons."

There is laughter all around the table and Winston looks very confused.

"Winston, it's a joke," says Max. Max then claps his hands before continuing. "Well, there you go. It's that vegan lunch thing you said Winston, and then passports, handbooks, and daisies for everyone. Let's get them on board."

I'm standing in *Jeanne d'Arc*'s *kitchen* and everything around us is stainless steel tables bolted to the floor and pots hanging from the ceiling. I've stuffed my journalist's notepad and Dictaphone in my purse as I want to blend in as much as possible. Max and Hedvika stand next to me and all three of us are listening to Captain Jean-Pierre as he is introducing Winston, Sunrise70, Hedvika, Dom and the whole of the working committee to a dining hall which is filled with *Jeanne d'Arc*'s citizens. Well, people who are about to become citizens. I glance at Max and smile to myself. He looks very calm, almost serene, and perhaps his countenance makes his seemingly outlandish uniform appear almost normal. I peek around the corner and see a room full of faces, young and old and everything in between. Children drink juice, adults drink beer or wine, and all listen intently to the Captain.

"And now," says Jean-Pierre, "without further ado, I want to introduce the man who has made everything possible... Mr Max Henderson!"

Max smiles at me and takes my hand. As we walk into the main dining hall, I look at a sea of glowing faces and hear applause. Max leads me to the main table at the front of the hall and I take a seat next to Hedvika. The Captain hands the microphone to Max, applauds along with the others in the room, and then sits down.

The applause dies down and I scan the room, recognising many of the faces from those who have been camping at Henderson Nautical. The room is silent and I expect Max to speak, but he is looking around the room, seeming to make eye contact with the people here. He is nodding his head, smiling, and he seems very affected by what is happening. The silence continues as Max looks from one person to another, and you might think this would be uncomfortable, but it isn't.

Finally, Max takes a deep breath which he releases and raises the microphone. "I really have no words to express how happy it makes me to see you today. I want all of you to feel safe and cared for, and I need all of you to look after one another as well. And, all of you will have something special you can contribute to our new country... *Jeanne d'Arc.* This is all we need, isn't it? To feel loved and cared for, to be able to love and care for others, and to be able to express our unique and special gifts."

Several people in the room nod their heads. Max walks around from behind the table and stands by a family sitting in the front of the hall. He looks down at a little girl who is perhaps six years old and smiles at her. "What's your name, sweetheart?" says Max, holding the microphone out to her.

"Miranda."

"I bet you can do something special, Miranda," says Max. "Something you're particularly proud of. Do you know what that is?"

"Yes, I know," says the girl.

"And tell us what you can do."

"I can draw pictures," says the girl, "and I can run fast too."

The room fills with laughter and clapping and the girl smiles broadly. "You see," says Max. "Miranda can draw pictures and run fast. This is no small thing. It's very important to keep finding out what you really love to do, and to feel safe and encouraged, because then it's the greatest joy imaginable to spend the whole of life giving your gift away to as many people as you can."

Max smiles and looks around the room. "Now, I'm supposed to say something else... what is it?" He looks over at Winston. "Oh yes. Ladies and gentleman, Captain Jean-Pierre introduced you to Winston Godfred. Winston is an important person in making all of this happen, and he's going to explain what happens next."

Max returns to the table and stands next to Winston, who stands up, looking very shaky. Max hands the microphone to Winston and places a hand on his shoulder. They look absolutely bizarre standing together, Winston dressed like Che Guevara and Max like a cross between a third-world dictator and Napoleon Bonaparte, but weirdly, it doesn't seem to matter.

Winston sputters, gets his nerves somewhat under control, and begins explaining the line-up of events. He's talking about how dinner is going to be served, the presentation of passports and induction of citizenry, and then how every person and each family will be shown to their living quarters. But the words sort of float past me and I am paying attention to something else. It's the feeling in the room. People are happy. There are smiles stuck to so many faces, and I wonder if maybe this isn't as crazy as it all first appeared.

CHAPTER 32

There is a knock at Max's office door. A moment later Hedvika enters, holding a large mug of coffee. She's wearing a simple lime-green dress and silver earrings, and Max is reminded of some of the modelling images he'd seen of his solicitor in magazines from twenty years ago. Hedvika smiles, but she looks tired.

"You look beautiful this morning, Hedvika," says Max, getting up from behind his desk and motioning to a chair.

Hedvika sits down. "Thanks, Max. You wanted to see me?"

"Yes," says Max. "A letter arrived from the United Nations. Shall we open it?"

"Sure – why not?"

Max opens the envelope, removes the letter, and reads it out. "Dear Mr Henderson. Thank you for your application for recognition of Statehood for an entity you have designated as *Jeanne d'Arc*. We are writing today to acknowledge receipt of your application. Please be aware that the process of review normally takes between three and six months, and you may be asked to provide further information during this period. Yours Sincerely, Jennifer Braithwaite, PA to Ms Eerika Vanhanen, Director-General, United Nations Office at Geneva."

"It's just a standard letter acknowledging receipt of the application," says Hedvika.

"Three to six months," says Max. "That's a long time."

"If you want to hang onto that boat of yours for a while longer, Max, this is good news."

"Really?" asks Max.

"I think so," says Hedvika. "I have a friend I studied law with who works for the Home Department. She told me, off the record, that the Home Secretary and his solicitors have been working behind the scenes to convince the UN to quash our application from the outset. I was expecting that letter would tell us to bugger off. While the UN is reviewing the application, it's a little more difficult for the UK government to say that we are entirely crazy."

Max hands the letter to his solicitor. "Well, that's an interesting way to look at things. Hedvika – do you think this is crazy? Am I losing my mind?"

Hedvika smiles. "It's funny you should ask because I was just thinking about that the other day. All of this seemed very odd at the outset, but I guess what seems strange can start to feel normal after a while. I needed a break from my work yesterday, so I went and had a walk around *Jeanne d'Arc*. Have you spent much time on the ship recently?"

"As much as I can," says Max. "But I still have to run a shipyard. What did you think?"

"Well, it's all pretty organised. People have jobs, for one thing. Some people prepare meals, some do laundry, some clean. There are two classrooms, one for the younger kids and one for the older kids, and there are people who have teaching roles. Winston seems to be organising everything. He's sort of manic, from what I can tell. I saw a list of activities and a schedule as well. Things like meditation and painting."

"Well, that's good, right?" says Max.

Hedvika reflects for a moment. "Yeah, I guess so, Max."

"You don't seem sure."

Hedvika sighs. "Ignore me, Max. I'm cynical, that's all."

Max laughs. "Do people seem happy on *Jeanne d'Arc*?"

"As far as I can tell," says Hedvika. "But they don't just stay on the ship. Your loyal subjects spend a lot of time on the ship, but they come and go as well. Some will walk into town, maybe go shopping or to a pub – normal stuff. But here's an interesting thought. If by some slim chance *Jeanne d'Arc* is awarded Statehood, and if by some even slimmer chance it's recognised by the UK, your citizens might have to cross a border every time they leave the ship and step foot in the UK."

"Huh – I never thought of that," says Max.

Hedvika laughs. "Well, I wouldn't worry too much about that at the moment. There's a lot that can happen."

CHAPTER 33

Dom sits on a bench near the gatehouse of Henderson Nautical Works. He puts an unlit cigarette into his mouth and dials a number on his mobile.

"Hi, Dom," a deep male voice says.

"Any progress on locating Peter?"

"Sorry, Dom," says the voice. "Nothing at all. I've talked to about a dozen junkies and a dealer. No one has seen him."

"You check with the hospitals again?" asks Dom.

"I made calls this morning. Nothing. I'm telling you, Dom – he's not in the city. You know how it is. You follow the junk and you find a junkie. He's just not here."

"Shit. Okay, maybe we need to start looking in London."

"London's a big city, Dom. Where do we start?"

"Islington first… and then Camden. Same as Portsmouth. Talk to the junkies and anyone else. Show 'em Peter's photo. Pay the junkies for any information – but they won't need more than a tenner. Maybe fifty quid for good information."

"Okay, Dom."

Dom ends the call and lights his cigarette. He gazes at the overcast sky and listens to the sad note of a tugboat horn drifting up from the estuary. A moment passes and he notices Winston walking towards him, his skinny limbs pumping beneath the Fidel Castro uniform. He is shaking his head, and tears are streaming down his face.

"What the fuck now?" Dom whispers under his breath.

Dom shoves his cigarette between his lips, stands up, and gazes at Winston. "I can't believe it," says Winston. Dom looks around and then pulls a silk handkerchief out of his breast jacket pocket. He hands the handkerchief to Winston.

"Winston, wipe your face and tell me what's happening."

Winston wipes the tears from his face with the handkerchief, blows his nose loudly into it, and then exhales painfully. "Jesus," says Dom. "I didn't say to blow your nose. I said, wipe your face."

Winston gazes up at Dom. "Oh, sorry, Dom."

Dom takes the sodden handkerchief from Winston. He folds it

carefully, an expression of disgust on his face, and places the thing into his trouser pocket. He looks back at Winston. "Now, what's going on?"

"It's Sunrise70 and her thugs," says Winston, releasing another sob and shaking his head.

"What's she done? What thugs?"

"She's put two of our citizens into the brig," says Winston.

"The brig?" says Dom. "Like a jail cell?"

"Yeah, like that."

"I didn't know there was a brig on *Jeanne d'Arc*," says Dom.

"Well, there is."

"Why did she do that?" asks Dom.

"She says these two guys stole food from the pantry."

"Who are these guys?" asks Dom.

"Some of our citizens were probably homeless. From the look of these guys, they might have been on the streets. If they see some food, they're probably gonna take it, right?"

Dom thinks for a moment. "You said thugs. What thugs are you talking about?"

"That's the other thing. Sunrise70 has got about six... maybe eight people working with her now. They're all wearing that uniform she's started wearing – you know, dressed in black from head to foot like the SS. And they've got guns."

"Guns? What the fuck?"

"Yeah, Dom," says Winston, patting his waist. "Holsters and pistols."

Dom blows out a breath and shakes his head. "Alright, let's go talk to Sunrise or Sunshit or Sundick or whatever the fuck she is."

Dom takes Winston by the arm and they walk towards shed 4. "There isn't going to be any violence, is there?" says Winston. "Because I can't cope with violence."

"Let's hope not," says Dom.

Dom makes his way onto *Jeanne d'Arc* with Winston trailing after him. They enter the ship and begin making their way along one of the ship's seemingly endless corridors. "So, where is Sunrise likely to be?" asks Dom.

"I'm not sure," says Winston.

A family of four walk past them, a young mother and father with girls, maybe four or five years old. Dom is struck by how different the ship feels now that 400 citizens are living here. A moment later, Dom notices a young man dressed entirely in black, maybe twenty years old, standing ahead in the corridor. Dom stands directly in front of the man, sizing him up. He's eight inches shorter than Dom, ruddy cheeks, darting eyes. Dom glances at the handle of the pistol strapped to his waist and recognises the model immediately.

"I'm Dominic Delfino – I work security for Mr Henderson." Dom stands a little closer to the man and raises his chin.

"Um, okay," the man says.

"Do you know where Sunrise70 is?"

"Um… she was making the rounds, but I think she's probably in the hall now, having lunch."

Dom feels he's got the measure of this kid. He's nervous, unsure of himself. "What's your name?"

"Um, it's Mike."

Dom points to the handgun. "So, what model of weapon are you carrying?"

Mike looks down at his waist. "Oh, ah, I knew this. It's um, German, I think."

"Let's have a look," says Dom.

In one smooth action, Dom reaches down, pops off the holster clip, and pulls the handgun out of the holster. He holds it up and watches the man closely for his reaction. The man opens his mouth as if to speak, but says nothing. "This is a Sig 226," says Dom. "And you're right, it is German. Is it loaded?"

"Um, hey, that's…" the man says, pointing to his gun.

Dom directs the gun away from them, pushes the magazine release button and catches the magazine in the palm of his hand. He holds the magazine up and glances at the hollow-point nine-millimetre slugs protruding from the end. Dom examines the Sig more closely. "Jesus! The safety is off."

"The what?" Mike says.

Dom pops the safety to the 'on' position and turns around. "Winston, come here."

Winston, who had been standing about five feet behind them, stands next to Dom and looks at the young man, offering him an apologetic expression. "You okay, mate?" says Winston.

"Um, yeah, I guess," the young man says.

Dom offers the gun to Winston. "Hold this for a moment."

"Oh, I don't think so, Dom. I don't like guns."

Dom thrusts the gun towards Winston. "It won't kill you. Just hold it for a moment."

Winston's eyes widen and he accepts the gun, holding it between his thumb and an index finger as if it were a ticking bomb. Dom squeezes fifteen bullets out of the magazine, which he places into his trouser pocket. He takes the gun from Winston's hands, pops the magazine back in, and hands the Sig back to Mike.

"Um, are you supposed to do that?" says Mike.

"Look Mike, I need to know where Sunrise70 is."

"I told you," says Mike. "I think she's probably having lunch in the hall."

Dom smiles and claps Mike on the arm. "Don't shoot anyone, alright?"

"Okay," says Mike.

Dom gazes at Mike for a moment and gets an image in his head of confronting Sunrise70 in the dining hall. He reckons there will be a lot of people eating at this time of day. Dom feels a surge of anger and a need to sort her out, but he reflects for a moment and decides that a crowded dining hall isn't a smart place to deal with her. He takes Winston by the arm and walks them towards the ship's gangplank. "Let's go see Max," says Dom.

"Okay, Dom, but Mr Henderson is on *Jeanne d'Arc*. I'm pretty sure he's with the Captain in his cabin."

"That's even better. Let's go," says Dom.

Dom leads Winston down a few shining gunmetal grey corridors, down one deck, through several bulkheads, until he feels lost. "Damn it, Winston, I still can't find my way around this maze."

Winston takes the lead, and five minutes later they are standing in front of a brass plaque inscribed with *Cabine Executive*. Dom knocks and hears Max call "Come in."

They enter and Dom notices Max, Captain Jean-Pierre, Chief Engineer Alexis, and Chief of Aeronautics Hugo, sitting around a table and drinking coffee.

Max stands. "Ah, good. Dom… Winston. I'm glad you're here. You should be part of this conversation. Can I get you coffee?"

Dom notices that the naval men are in their uniforms, as is Max. Dom might grin at Max's lavish dress, but things feel too serious for that. "No thanks, boss," says Dom. "There's something we need to discuss as well."

Dom and Winston join them at the oak table. "Okay," says Max. "You first – what's up?"

"Sunrise70," says Dom, "has organised some dipshit squad of a security team. She's got them outfitted in black uniforms and they've thrown a couple of citizens into the ship's brig, apparently for stealing food."

"Oh," says Max. "I didn't know about that." He looks over at Captain Jean-Pierre. "What do you think, Captain?"

"How many are in this security team?"

"We think maybe six or eight," says Dom.

"Well," says the Captain, "that's probably about right."

"What do you mean *about right?*" says Winston, his voice a high-pitched squeak.

"Well," says the Captain, "there is always some military police presence on any capital ship. And… if someone steals food or gets too drunk or obnoxious… they probably end up in the brig. The sea provides its own justice, as they say."

Dom frowns. "Okay, that makes sense. But the security detail are wearing handguns." He looks at the three naval officers in turn. "They're carrying Sig 226s, and I think we know where they came from."

Max looks confused. "Where would they get guns?"

"Boss, the arms fair in Cairo. Remember – we made some purchases, right? *Jeanne d'Arc* was supposed to be restored properly and all that. Sig 226s were part of the purchase order."

"Oh," says Max. "They were?" He looks over at his shipmates.

"Yes," says Hugo. "Handguns were part of the order list we put together. Handguns are standard on all capital ships, but any guns we purchased went into the armoury. Sunrise70 must have got access."

Max looks over at Jean-Pierre. "Captain?"

Jean-Pierre shrugs. "I don't know how she got access to the armoury – I didn't give approval. But… a ship's security does carry sidearms."

"Yes…" says Dom, "but Sunrise is… batshit nuts."

"Well, in that case sidearms might be a bad idea," says the Captain. "What do you think Winston?"

"She's scary," says Winston.

"Alright," says the Captain. "I'll have a word with her. No guns, then."

Max smiles. "Okay, that's settled. But… Dom… Winston… we might have some other problems." Max looks over at Jean-Pierre. "Captain – do you want to explain?"

"Well," says Jean-Pierre, "there are developments. *Jeanne d'Arc's* surveillance systems are all operational, so we have been keeping an eye on three ships, two destroyers and a carrier, and we suspect there's a submarine as well. They're positioned about five miles off the Portsmouth coast. And the British special forces situated just outside Henderson Nautical must think we are complete amateurs because they haven't bothered to encode their radio communications." Jean-Pierre folds his hands and looks at Max.

"You can tell them, Captain," says Max.

"The chatter we're picking up suggests that they are coming... on Thursday morning... at 8 AM."

Dom stares at his hands for a moment, reflecting. "That's two days from now. So, what are we doing, then?"

"Well," says Max. "We can all walk away from *Jeanne d'Arc* and go back to our normal lives, we can stay put and see what happens, or we can go to sea."

"What do you think, boss?"

Max picks up his coffee cup and takes a long sip. He puts the cup down and exhales. "Y'know, Dom, I really don't know. I think we need to talk with our citizens."

There are a few moments of silence, and then Max looks over at Winston. "I don't like the idea of these fellows sitting in the brig either. How long have they been there?"

"Since yesterday, I think," says Winston.

"Okay," says Max. "Don't worry about it, Winston. I'll have a word with Sunrise70 and ask her to release those guys." Max looks over at his engineer. "Alexis, what about the engines?"

"I've added fuel like you asked, Max, so her tanks are full, and I've serviced the diesel engines as well as one person can. They haven't fired up in four years, but they seem fine and I can't see why they would be a problem."

Max nods his head slowly. "That's good, Alexis."

CHAPTER 34

Max drives his car slowly along Fort Road, down the western edge of the mouth of the Solent Estuary. He parks the car at the side of the road, looks over at Winston, and waves his hand at the view.

"What do you think, Winston?"

Winston gazes through the windscreen and across Portsmouth's estuary at Southsea Castle on the other side. The sun glints off the huge stone walls of the old castle, giving it a timeless quality.

"It's a beautiful view, Max. You come up here much?"

"Now and again."

"A place like this probably helps you think," says Winston.

Max reaches under his legs, opens a small cooler, and pulls out a four-pack of chilled pale ale. He gets a couple of pint glasses out of the glove box, pops open a can and begins pouring the beer. He watches the bubbles in his glass develop for a moment before continuing. "Maybe drinking beer and looking at beautiful old castles makes me feel a little better, but I'm pretty sure it don't help my thinking much." He grins at Winston.

Max puts his pint glass between his legs, some beer spilling onto his suit trousers, and holds up the empty pint. "Can I pour you a beer, Winston?"

"My doctors tell me I shouldn't drink. It doesn't mix well with my meds, apparently."

"That sounds like terrible advice," says Max.

"One doctor told me it encourages flight of ideas."

"Flight of ideas?" says Max. "What the hell is that?"

"I've never asked. I think it's psychiatric speak for unrealistic views."

Max holds up the empty pint glass. "Well, how about I pour you a pint of flight of ideas and we just see what happens."

Winston smiles. "Sure, Max."

Max pours another pint and hands it to Winston. They both take a large sip of chilled and hoppy beer and gaze out the window at the evening sun which is casting a bronze glow against the castle walls. Seagulls cry out and a question forms in Max's mind.

"Where do you think things went wrong, Winston?" The question sounds vague now that the words are out of his mouth.

Winston puts the ale to his lips and kills about half of his pint. "I'll tell you, Max, I've been trying to understand the historical development of nations over the past five hundred years or more. I've been trying to figure out why some nations come to power, other nations with power fall apart, and how people get caught up in all of that."

"Like, the rise and fall of empires," suggests Max.

"Well, yes," says Winston. "The history of nations is pretty much what you'd expect. Military power is closely linked to economic might. Nations that have become supreme military powers also had strong economies. And the race to become the hegemon nation always leads to wars – trade wars or military wars, and usually both."

"Hegemon nation? That's a new word on me," says Max.

"Sorry, Max. It just means the nation that is supreme at any one time. What's interesting is that when a nation loses out to another nation, it's not usually because they became less powerful."

"What do you mean?" asks Max.

"Take Britain, for example. The empire was at the peak of its power in the late nineteenth and early twentieth centuries. We were clearly the hegemon. Today, the hegemon nation is the US. But does that mean that Britain is less powerful today than it was in 1900? It doesn't. Britain has more economic and military power today than it did in 1900, it's just that in relative terms other countries have developed power much faster than us over the past century. In 1900 we controlled twenty-five per cent of world trade – today, we control three per cent."

"That's interesting," says Max. "Y'know, we used to have maybe a hundred shipyards in this country. Today we have about five or six, depending on what you want to count as a shipyard. The work went to China, Korea, and Japan. Now, there are yards popping up in Brazil and India."

"So, is that bad then?" asks Winston.

"I don't know," says Max. "It feels sad to me that Britain doesn't have the same shipbuilding industry, maybe because it's part of our history. But the world changes, doesn't it? For a few hundred years the Western nations ran the world. Other nations are stepping up now." Max looks at Winston, a more serious expression forming. "Nations... people... they want to feel in control, right? Everybody wants to feel important. So, what happens now?"

"What?" says Winston. Like, in the world?"

"Yeah, sure," says Max. "You're the historian."

Winston kills the rest of his pint and stares out the window. Max gets another can out of the cooler and pours it into Winston's glass. "Well," says Winston, "India and especially China are growing in military and economic strength many times faster than America, Britain and the other Western nations, so they are on course to become the new hegemon at some point, with China getting there first. If history goes like it normally does, there will be trade wars and military wars, most likely overseas, at least at first. The nations will leverage wealth to increase their power and influence."

Max smiles. "It's funny how we always rank countries by military or economic power. Isn't there another way? What about how happy or fulfilled the people are? Who knows – if we did things that way, maybe the best country in the world is someplace most of us have never even heard of."

Winston smiles broadly and slaps his knee. "Yes, yes – exactly Max. This perpetual race between nations to be top dog has ground people down the world over. Rulers and moneymen are afraid of sharing power with the people, so they spread lies about wealth and war. And Max... with *Jeanne d'Arc*, you are cheating the whole rotten stinking system because you are building a nation which is for the people. A nation of safety and love and personal growth. The Communists almost had it and then messed it up, but you are actually doing it, Max."

Max smiles, takes a sip of beer, and gazes across the water. "Winston, you're funny. I just fell in love with this ship no one else wanted, and then these people started arriving. You think too much of me."

"And you're too modest, Max," says Winston, his voice filling with emotion. "This is greatness, you see. True greatness. You embody that rare mix of genius, strength, and humility. Max, I can't begin to tell you what an honour it is to just sit here drinking beer with you."

Max laughs and looks over at Winston. "Is this that flight of ideas?"

"Oh no, Max – I haven't even got started on that."

They gaze across the water in silence for a while, sipping pale ale, watching the stones of Southsea Castle shift slowly through shades of gold to bronze. "By the way," says Winston, "my sister Constance is in love with you."

Max looks over at Winston, confusion written on his face. "Why?" says Max.

Winston bursts out laughing. "How should I know, Max? People just fall in love, don't they? I'm a complete screw-job when it comes to these matters, so don't ask me to explain it."

CHAPTER 35

Dom sits in front of Hedvika's desk, smiling at her. Hedvika looks as beautiful as ever, though a little tired. Dom isn't surprised, given how events have developed.

"Honestly, Dom, Max doesn't have to buy me a car. I have a salary. I can buy my own car."

"Yeah," says Dom. "But you know how he is. He feels grateful for everything you've done and the extra work. I think I'm supposed to pick out a car, wrap it in a big ribbon, and put it in your driveway. But maybe you already did some research. So, just tell me what you want, let me go pick it up for you, and that will make the boss happy."

Hedvika shakes her head and then Dom's phone rings. He notices it's one of the guys he's got looking for Peter in London. Dom looks up at Hedvika, a serious expression forming. "I gotta take this. But I mean it. Tell me what you want, okay?"

Dom steps out in the hallway and closes the door. "Any news?"

"Hey, Dom," says a deep voice. "He's gone. Peter's dead."

Dom stares at the wall opposite him for a moment.

"Dom, you there?"

"Fuck," says Dom. "Yeah, I'm here."

"I'm sorry, Dom. You know I been looking everywhere. I've talked to so many junkies and dealers I've lost track."

"Yeah, yeah, I know," says Dom. "Where did you find Peter?"

"He turned up in Islington. There was an unidentified body in the morgue at Whittington Hospital. I went down and said I thought he might be a friend of mine and they let me have a look."

"Are you sure it's Peter?"

"Absolutely. He's a perfect match for the photos you gave me. Plus, cause of death was apparent heroin overdose. It's definitely Peter."

There's a pause on the line. "I'm sorry, Dom."

"London is a big place. Come back as soon as you can. I gotta go now."

Dom ends the call and makes his way to a bench which overlooks the Solent Estuary. He sits down and sticks his E-cig between his lips. He takes a drag, makes a face, and puts the E-cig in his jacket pocket. Dom lights up a cigarette, takes a long drag, and slowly blows the smoke into the spring air. There is no wind today, which is very unusual, and Dom watches as the smoke slowly drifts out over the calm water.

Dom reflects on how Max is gonna take this. He's sure the answer is not good, but what variety of not good is what Dom is wondering about. Max seems pretty unhinged as it is, and Dom really does not want to have this conversation. He's trying to decide how to tell Max, but by the time Dom finishes the cigarette, he's not discovered any good way of doing that.

A few minutes later, Dom knocks gently on Max's office door. He hears Max call "Come on in" and he sits down in front of the desk. "Hi, boss," says Dom, his voice barely a whisper. Dom stares at Max's face and realises he can't speak. Max gazes at him for a moment, and then his face falls.

"It's Peter, isn't it," says Max.

"Yes, boss. It is."

Max closes his eyes and puts his head in his hands. Dom sits quietly for a moment and hears a low sob coming from Max.

A moment later Max looks up, his face stained with tears. "How...? When?"

Dom sighs deeply and shakes his head. "I had a guy looking for Peter in London. He found him in a hospital morgue. It was an overdose. I'm really sorry, boss."

Max gets up slowly and gazes out of his office window, silent for a while. "When Peter was about six or seven, we used to walk to this little park around the corner from us and I would be the goalkeeper and he would kick the ball at the goal. I usually let him score. Then we would go home and I would cook us bacon and eggs or pancakes. He was really happy then. I was happy too." Max turns back to Dom. "What the hell happened?"

Dom shakes his head. "I fucked up, boss. I should have gone down to London myself."

"No, Dom. This isn't your fault. This is just... shit, I don't know."

Max stares down at his desk, his work suit crumpled, his eyes filling with tears again, and he shakes his head. "Well... that's it, then. That's it," says Max.

Dom wants to say something but there are no words, so he walks over to Max and puts his arms around him, and holds him.

179

CHAPTER 36

Winston and Max stand in *Jeanne d'Arc*'s kitchen, Winston inspecting Max's uniform. Winston runs his hands over the royal blue jacket and shining gold epaulettes on the shoulders, and then straightens the collection of medals and red satin sash.

Winston checks his watch. "It's a couple of minutes before 7 PM. Do you know what you want to say?"

Max slowly lifts the pint glass of pale ale to his mouth, takes a drink, and then shakes his head. "Not really, Winston."

Winston gazes at Max's flaccid expression, concern in his eyes. "Max, you don't seem yourself. Are you okay?"

Max nods and takes another sip. Captain Jean-Pierre walks in. "Hi, Max. The citizens of *Jeanne d'Arc* are pretty much all here. We did a headcount and there are 384, so only a few of them are missing. Are you ready?"

Max nods, finishes his beer, and places the pint glass on a nearby counter. "Let's go."

The Captain leads them into the serving hall and to an oak podium, all of which Winston had prepared. Max notices that an image of *Jeanne d'Arc* is affixed to the front of the podium. The Captain stands in front of the podium and talks into the microphone.

"Ladies and gentlemen, children, citizens of *Jeanne d'Arc*: Mr Max Henderson."

Everyone assembled claps and, as Max steps up to the podium, he gazes out at a sea of beaming and expectant faces. The clapping dies down and Max nods his head, looking from one face to another. He notices Liz Burton sitting in the front row.

"Thank you for coming here this evening. It's made me happy to see how everyone has been settling in and getting on over the past week. It's been quite a time, hasn't it?" Max looks over at Winston and the Captain, who are standing against a wall. "Thank you Winston and Captain Jean-Pierre and so many others for helping us all to create something which is very... unique... very special." Max pauses and scans the expectant faces again before continuing. "I said before that feeling safe and cared for is so very important, and this is part of the reason for developing the

Nation of *Jeanne d'Arc*. So… I need to make you aware of something. Early tomorrow morning… special forces are planning to board Jeanne d'Arc. They will probably have guns and they will want to take control of the ship."

Max pauses, there are gasps, and a few people cry out "No", and "They can't do that". Max raises a hand. "Now," says Max, "before these special forces arrive, we will open the shed door, and *Jeanne d'Arc*'s diesel engines will start up. "Where is Alexis?"

Alexis, who is standing next to Dom at the back of the room, raises his hand. "Ah, there's Alexis," says Max. "Alexis is one of the finest engineers in the French Navy, and he is pretty sure that our engines will work fine. So, at 7 AM tomorrow morning we will open the shed door, start our engines, and steam out astern into Portsmouth Harbour. And then… we are going out to sea."

The reaction from the room is mixed. Some people clap and smile, others seem unsure of how to respond. Max looks over the faces and notices Sunrise70, dressed in black, standing at the back of the room with a couple of her team. She straightens up, her expression impassive. Max had forgotten about Sunrise70, and wonders what she is thinking.

"I think this was always going to happen. And maybe this is okay. *Jeanne d'Arc* is a ship, after all, and ships are happiest at sea. If we are a nation it probably makes sense for us to find our own way and our own place rather than to be tied up here."

Max pauses and looks from face to face, noting that some people seem happy, others sad, some confused, others concerned. "I feel…" begins Max, and then he seems to lose his way and stares down at the podium for a while. An air of heavy expectancy fills the room, and finally the Captain stands next to Max and whispers in his ear. "Max, are you okay to speak further?"

Max looks up, as if awakening from a dream. "Yes, yes," he says to the Captain. He looks out at the audience. "I feel such a sense of gratitude to all of you… for being here… for believing in whatever is happening… but I don't want anyone to be frightened or to get hurt. I can't possibly know what will happen tomorrow. Maybe we will go out to sea and a new chapter for *Jeanne d'Arc* will begin. But we might not make it. The government has some warships a few miles off Portsmouth, and they may not want us to go anywhere. I want all of you to know that, if you are worried, you can leave tonight. The nation of *Jeanne d'Arc* is not essentially a ship… it's not a place… it's all of you… and you are always citizens of *Jeanne d'Arc* no matter what you decide or where you might be. Please do whatever you think is best."

Max nods in a solemn and sad fashion and walks back into the kitchen. He sits down on a metal stool, picks up the pint glass he had left there, and drinks from it. A moment later he senses Winston's presence, and now Winston is kneeling in front of him, a hand on Max's knee. Max looks down and is vaguely aware that Winston wears an expression which is a strange mix of wonder and veneration.

"Max, those are the most beautiful words I have ever heard."

"What?" says Max, his eyes glassy, his voice distant.

"That was beautiful."

Max stares at Winston for a moment and then takes another sip of beer. "Winston, I'm not very well right now. I think you are going to have to take over."

"Nonsense, Max. That's impossible. My role is merely to serve your purpose."

"My what?" says Max.

A worried expression crosses Winston's face. "You are coming with us tomorrow, right? Out to sea."

"Sure… yes…"

"You're tired, Max, that's all. You've been working too hard. You need a good night's sleep."

Max nods. "Yes, Winston… that's probably it."

CHAPTER 37

Margaret walks through the Whitehall basement corridor located deep within the bowels of the Ministry of Defence. She nods to several of the servicemen and women guarding the corridor, aware of the collection of ministers, assistants, and military staff around her. A guard opens a thick concrete door for her at the end of the corridor and they enter the war room.

Margaret points to the circular table in the centre of the room. "Have a seat, gentlemen."

As they sit down, Margaret looks around the table and checks her watch – 6:45 AM. To her right is Defence Secretary Ronald Hudd, next to him is Director of Special Forces Frank Fields and Chief of Naval Staff Robert Gibbons, and across from her sits Chief of the Defence Staff Steve Millband. She glances around at the collection of deputies and assistants standing back from the table. "Where's the Home Secretary?" says Margaret.

"Jared is just taking a phone call from the solicitors," says Ronald.

"That's all we need now – solicitors," says Margaret. "Can someone hurry him up?"

An assistant nods and leaves. Margaret scans the room, trying to remember how this works. There is a huge screen at the front of the room displaying a real-time satellite image, which she recognises as shed four at Henderson Nautical Works, and a bank of computers which are staffed by various defence personnel. "If Jared is going to make us late, can we get some coffee please," says Margaret.

Another aide nods and heads out through the concrete door. Jared arrives and leans in close to Margaret's ear. "Can I please have a brief word, Prime Minister?"

Margaret frowns and leads her Home Secretary to a small room at the side of the main work area, closes the door and remains standing. "I hear you've been talking to government solicitors, Jared."

"I have, Prime Minister. Look, the Leader of the Opposition and Shadow Home Secretary are having seizures over this assault. Their view is that we should be getting approval through Parliament."

"Jared, please stop calling it an assault. We're collecting the damn boat. Anyway, what did the solicitor say?"

"He's still saying it's a grey area. There's no precedent for this sort of thing."

"Which solicitor? asks Margaret.

"I can't remember his name. You know – the chubby bloke."

"Ugh, not that guy. Everything's a bloody grey area with that one. Jared, maybe we need parliamentary approval before going to war against a recognised country. It's a stupid boat being run by a bunch of lunatics, and I am sick of everyone thinking it's all so hilarious and harmless, or whatever they're saying."

"I wasn't going behind your back, Prime Minister – I just wanted to make sure we were covering all contingencies."

"Well, your conversation with tubby solicitor hasn't made anything clearer, so let's just get on with this, and when we pull that ship apart, I want every piece packed up in boxes and mailed back to Philipe Dupont in Paris."

Jared smiles. "Okay. Glad you haven't lost your sense of humour, Prime Minister."

"I'm not bloody joking, Jared," says Margaret, leading him back to the conference table.

Margaret looks at the faces around the table and then turns to her Director of Special Forces and Chief of Naval Staff. "Frank... Robert... talk us through the logistics."

Robert unrolls a large map displaying Portsmouth Harbour and part of the English Channel, and places it over the table. "Our two destroyers are currently situated right at the mouth of the Solent Estuary. The plan we've devised means bringing the destroyers down the estuary and placing them just off Henderson Nautical Works, with our submarine and carrier remaining just outside the channel. The destroyers will take up position here," he says, pointing to the map. "Simultaneously," says Frank, "we dispatch six vans carrying eighty-five SAS ground forces who will carry assault rifles, tear gas, rubber bullets, and equipment for cutting through locks and chain-link fence. *Joan of Arc* is being held in shed four, which is here," says Frank, poking a finger at the map. "Our forces will enter shed four, by force if necessary, will secure any security staff they find there, and then will take possession of the ship. No one fires a shot unless lives are threatened. Land and sea forces will be in constant communication by radio. When *Joan of Arc* is secure, the destroyers will move directly to the entrance of shed four. We open the shed door from inside and secure *Joan of Arc* to the destroyers. The destroyers will tow the carrier down the coast to our naval facility at Plymouth Harbour."

Frank looks at his watch. "I have 0713 hours now. On your command, Prime Minister, we go at 0800 hours."

Margaret looks at Jared. "And no word from Max Henderson?"

"He's not returned our calls."

Margaret looks at the large overhead image of shed four. "Well, we have no choice. We go at 0800 hours."

"Yes, Prime Minister," says Frank.

A young woman staffing one of the computers suddenly calls out, "Mr Director of Special Forces."

"Yes?" says Frank.

"Our special agent on the grounds at Henderson Nautical just made contact. There is a loud sound of diesel engines coming from shed four. They've started up *Joan of Arc*."

"What?" says Margaret.

"Yes," says the young woman, "and our man is pretty sure he heard the door to shed four open."

Margaret stares around the table at a collection of stunned expressions. "Well done, boys – you really nailed the element of surprise on this one."

There is a moment of silence, the officials looking at one another. Finally, it's Jared who speaks. "What do you want to do, Prime Minister?"

"We go..." says Margaret. "And not at 8 AM. Now. Robert... Frank...get those destroyers and vans moving."

"Yes, Prime Minister," the men say in unison. The Chief of Naval Staff and Director of Special Forces jump from their seats and jog down to the staff operating the computers at the front of the room.

Margaret stares at the table and experiences a sense that something is missing. Something which seems important. And then she remembers. "Where's the goddamned coffee?"

CHAPTER 38

Max stands next to Captain Jean-Pierre on the bridge of *Jeanne d'Arc*, the deep rumble of the diesel engines filling shed four. He watches Alexis and Hugo for a moment, who are looking down at a bank of levers and flashing lights and discussing something in French. Dom and Winston stand next to one another a few feet away.

"She won't vibrate like this when we get her out of the shed and into open water," says the Captain.

Max nods and gazes out of the bridge windows and into the green glow of the enormous work shed. "I want to say goodbye to someone."

Jean-Pierre leads Max through a door and onto an external walkway which surrounds the bridge. Max looks down six stories to Hedvika and Sheila, who are both waving. Max waves back and recalls the conversation he had with both of them yesterday morning. With some reluctance, Hedvika had accepted the role of running the shipyard. Max remembers the email he'd sent to all Henderson Nautical staff this morning, and he wonders if that was the last email he would ever send to them.

Dear Henderson Nautical staff,

As many of you are aware, I've been a bit preoccupied with Jeanne d'Arc this past month, and I think its best that I hand over the day-to-day management of the shipyard to Hedvika Zavatsky until further notice. Hedvika will probably run things better than I did and Sheila will be offering Hedvika the fantastic support she has always given to me and all of us. I'm going on a little trip, and, to be fair, I can't say when I will be returning. I wish all of you happiness and success.

Best wishes,

Max

Max returns to the bridge and talks into Winston's ear. "How's everything?"

"It's good, Max. I did the best headcount I could this morning. I think there are nearly 300 citizens who have remained on board." Winston inspects Max's uniform, and then straightens a few medals and repositions the scarlet sash.

Max walks over to Liz Burton, who is holding a notepad and pen.

"Are you sure you want to be here?" Max says. "I know you are dedicated to journalism, but I really don't know what's going to happen."

"I'm fine, Max. I won't be in your way."

Max nods and a moment later Jean-Pierre stands next to him. "We are as ready as we can be, Max. It's going to be a fairly slap-dash departure. We've already cast off all ropes, so we are just sort of floating in the bay. Definitely not textbook. We will probably bump the sides a bit, but I don't think I'll break anything."

Hugo walks over and looks from Max to Jean-Pierre. "Captain," he says, "I've just had a look at radar surveillance. Both destroyers are entering the mouth of the estuary. I'd make their speed at perhaps five knots."

Jean-Pierre looks at Max. "Well, there you are. Not a surprise. She's your ship, Max. Shall I give the order or do we terminate?"

Max walks to the bridge windows which form a view ahead and to the left and right. He stares through the windows, looking around as far as he can. "We're in a damn shed with our diesels running," says Max. "We've come this far — let's at least get out into the fresh air for a few minutes."

Jean-Pierre sits down in a large leather chair which is elevated above the chairs Alexis and Hugo sit in. The Captain flips an orange switch and talks into a microphone. "Citizens of *Jeanne d'Arc*. Mr Henderson has given the order for us to depart, so we will be leaving Bay four and entering the harbour. For your safety, can you please stay inside the ship until further notice."

The Captain looks at a large video monitor which shows a view of Portsmouth Harbour as seen from the stern of the ship and through the open door of bay four. "Dead slow astern," the Captain shouts above the noise of the diesels.

Alexis pulls back on a lever, Max hears the sound of *chunk,* and the diesels lowering in tone as the screws engage. A minute passes and Max can't be sure if *Jeanne d'Arc* is moving at all. "Is everything alright, Captain?" says Max.

"Yes, everything is fine, Max. *Jeanne d'Arc* is a large ship. She takes a little while to get going."

A few moments pass and Max realises the Captain is right because he can see the image of Portsmouth Harbour slowly growing larger on the monitor and the walls of the shed appearing to move. "Rudders ten degrees to starboard," shouts the Captain, and Max watches as Alexis makes an adjustment at his terminal. There is a slight bump and a metallic scraping noise, and the Captain looks at Max. "A little bit of paint – that's all."

Five minutes later a bright shaft of light gradually illuminates the bridge and then, a few minutes later, Max finds that he is actually looking through the port and starboard windows at the harbour. A moment later and Max is looking down the huge deck of the carrier and he can see the whole of Bay 4 in front of the ship.

"Rudders thirty degrees to port," says the Captain, now able to speak in a fairly normal voice.

Jeanne d'Arc slowly begins her turn and the bows arc in the direction of the Atlantic. "Good work," says Max to Jean-Pierre.

"Just like backing your car out of the driveway," says Jean-Pierre.

Dom and Winston have come around and stand next to Max. Still backing around, *Jeanne d'Arc*'s bows finally face the mouth of the Solent Estuary and the English Channel. Except for the drone of the diesels and sound of the reversing screws, the bridge is silent. Everyone stares out the windows at the two destroyers which are about a mile off as they make their way down the Solent Estuary.

"Oh," says Max. "You know, for a moment, I almost forgot about them."

"Full stop," says the Captain. Alexis pulls a lever and the screws disengage.

"What do you want to do, Max?" asks the Captain.

Max turns to Winston and Dom. "What do you think?"

"*Jeanne d'Arc* should be at sea, Max," says Winston "If we are to be our own nation, we have to leave Britain."

"Dom?" says Max.

Dom turns to the Captain. "What sort of damage can destroyers do to *Jeanne d'Arc*?"

The Captain laughs. "They carry four-and-a-half-inch deck guns. They won't sink us but they could make a real mess of everything."

"Oh god," says Winston. "That sounds awful."

"Stop fussing, Winston," says Dom. "I doubt her Majesty's Naval Service wants to shoot at us – right, Captain?"

"I'd hope not," says Jean-Pierre.

Dom shrugs. "Up to you, Max, but I say we go for it."

Max turns to Jean-Pierre and nods.

"Ahead slow," says the Captain, raising a pair of binoculars to his eyes. "The destroyers are coming down the channel with about a third of the channel width between them. We'll aim to pass straight between them."

Alexis pushes a lever and the screws engage.

"Will they try to block us?" asks Dom.

"They can try if they like," says the Captain, "but if I was piloting a 9,000-ton destroyer, I wouldn't relish a game of chicken with a 42,500-ton aircraft carrier."

Dom laughs and points at the Captain. "This guy's got balls, Max."

"Not really," says the Captain. "I'm an old man without much to lose. The outcome is perhaps the same, but one's motivations are quite different."

Dom notices something out of the corner of his eye and looks back at Henderson Nautical. The road down to the shipyard is somewhat elevated, and Dom places his binoculars to his face and watches six black vans make their way to the entrance gate. Dom smiles and remembers the conversation he had this morning with his staff. *If any special forces arrive, be very polite, let them in straight away, and make them feel right at home.*

"Is everything okay, Dom?" he hears Max say.

Dom puts the binoculars down and looks up the estuary again. "Sure boss – everything is fine."

Margaret pushes the plunger on the large cafetière and then pours the coffee into her mug. She and all of the ministers and military staff are now standing and scanning the overhead satellite video feed of Portsmouth Harbour and Henderson Nautical Works. Margaret stares at the image which shows *Joan of Arc* pointing directly at the two destroyers, with about a mile between them.

"The destroyers look tiny compared to that ship," says Margaret.

"Well, it's an aircraft carrier, Prime Minister," says Robert.

Margaret wonders if the Chief of Naval Staff is patronising her and she purses her lips.

The young woman at the front of the room calls out – "*Joan of Arc* is moving... I'd estimate three knots."

As the staff try to absorb the situation, the video feed shows a line of six black vans making their way down to the front gate of Henderson

Nautical Works. The minuscule images of several men can be seen jumping from the vans and approaching the gate.

"Special forces have arrived, Prime Minister," says Frank.

"Wonderful," says Margaret.

"I appreciate that our timing is not ideal," says Frank, "but we have to make an operational field decision."

Margaret sighs loudly. "I don't know at this point, Frank – what's your view?"

"Well, they can secure shed four… and maybe Henderson's office. There may be evidence…"

Margaret shakes her head and raises her arms. "Sure… why not? Maybe the staff at Henderson will make them tea while they are at it."

"Prime Minister," says Robert, pointing to the satellite feed. "We're going to have to make a decision quickly about the naval situation."

Margaret scans the Chief of Naval Staff's face and then looks back to the monitor. "Okay, tell me what the hell is happening here."

"Well," says Robert, "*Joan of Arc* is steaming at about three knots towards our destroyers, which are steaming at five knots. The carrier looks like she will pass right between the destroyers, from what I can tell."

"It's six knots now," calls out the woman at the front of the room.

"What's six knots?" asks Margaret.

"She means," says Robert, "that *Joan of Arc* has increased speed to six knots."

"Can we block the carrier's exit?" asks Margaret.

"We could manoeuvre our destroyers so they are broadside, and that would make it very difficult for *Joan of Arc* to pass – but we can't do that."

"Why not?" asks Margaret. "The carrier will have to stop, and then we can take control of the ship like we planned."

"Eight knots," calls out the woman from the front of the room.

"Because, Prime Minister," says Robert, "when a vessel like *Joan of Arc* gets up to speed, she can't just hit the brakes. It takes quite a while for a carrier to stop."

Her Chief of Naval Staff is smiling at her and Margaret is now positive she is being patronised, and she makes a mental note to give Robert a good slap when she gets the opportunity. "Terrific," says Margaret, waving at the monitor. "So, basically, I'm looking at a big fat game of chicken right now. Is that it?"

"Yes," says Robert. "That's one way to put it. This sort of thing happens all the time in naval conflicts – the battle for the Atlantic... Trafalgar... the Carthaginians, the Athenians, the Persians..."

"Thank you, Robert," says Margaret. "Perhaps you can give us a stimulating history of ships crashing into one another some other time, but do you have any idea of what we're supposed to do now?"

Robert looks up at the monitor, noticing that the increased speed of the carrier is now apparent from the video feed. "I think your options are fairly narrow, Prime Minister. You can allow *Joan of Arc* to pass through our destroyers, or we can fire on the carrier."

Margaret suddenly notices two small dots moving over and around the carrier. "What the hell are those?" asks Margaret.

The woman at the console responds. "Those are a couple of helicopters which are with news outlets. TV news crews, Prime Minister."

"Well, they need to get the hell out of there – make some calls," says Margaret.

"Yes, Prime Minister," says the young woman.

Dom is between Winston and Max, and they are all standing behind Captain Jean-Pierre's elevated chair, which is just behind the seats which Alexis and Hugo sit in as they operate the controls. Dom gazes at the oncoming destroyers, which have grown considerably larger, and then looks down at Winston, who is stuffing the knuckles of his left hand into his mouth.

"Winston," says Dom, "you're squeezing my arm pretty hard."

"Oh, sorry," Winston says. Dom imagines Winston will let go of his arm, but he just loosens his grip.

"Speed and manoeuvring?" asks the Captain.

"We are nine knots," says Hugo. "The destroyers are 300 metres and closing. Unless the destroyers change course we should pass through with no problems."

The Captain cranes his neck and speaks. "Well, we are committed now. Let's see what they want to do. They won't be shooting at us."

"How do you know?" asks Dom.

The Captain points. "Their bow guns are still pointing directly ahead rather than tracking us."

Dom places his binoculars to his face and watches the destroyers grow larger. A moment later they are alongside briefly, and Dom scans the faces of seamen and woman who are standing on the walkways. The expressions seem stern and he imagines a little pissed off. "I get the feeling they'd love to fire those four-and-a-half-inch guns at us," says Dom.

"Oh sure," says the Captain.

Dom looks at the rear-view camera monitor and notices the destroyers beginning to make a turn as they rock back and forth in the giant wake the *Joan of Arc* has made.

A few minutes later *Jeanne d'Arc* passes through the narrowest section of the channel, between Fort Blockhouse to starboard and Round Tower to port. "When we clear the headland, we should see her," says the Captain, his binoculars to his eyes.

"See what?" says Winston.

The Captain doesn't answer. "The British carrier, Winston," says Max.

"There she is," says the Captain, pointing. "It's *HMS Prince of Wales*. I thought it might be."

They all stare in silence at the ship, which is about two miles off the coast. Finally, it's Winston who speaks. "Is it like our ship?"

"Do you want to answer that, Max?" says the Captain.

"It's an aircraft carrier, Winston, but no, it's not really like ours. It's... much larger. 65,000 tons, I believe. Captain?"

"That's right, Max."

The PM and her staff are standing near the front of the war room to be closer to the young assistants monitoring computers and communications. Margaret gazes at the satellite video feed and looks over at her Chief of Naval Staff. "Situation report."

"*Joan of Arc* is just clearing the harbour and is making ten knots," says Roger. "Our destroyers have completed their turns and are following her back up the channel at twelve knots. *HMS Prince of Wales* is off the coast by two miles with engines running and crew on high alert. But we've noticed something else, Prime Minister. There are two fifty-calibre anti-aircraft guns which have been installed port and starboard on *Joan of Arc*. They were definitely not there when the French handed her over."

"Fantastic," says the PM. "So maybe this isn't The Love Boat after all. Okay guys, this has been a great giant balls-up from the word go, so before we make anything worse, let's think for a moment. What are the principles around why we are doing this? Jared?"

"Well, Prime Minister, the *Joan of Arc* and Max Henderson are seen as a threat to national security. We've said from the start that we can't allow private ownership of a nuclear warship within British Territorial waters."

"Yes, exactly," says Margaret. "Especially since we have no bloody idea what Henderson is doing. But… we've made a mess of seizing the ship in port." Margaret leans forward and scans the satellite feed. "What's happening now, Roger?"

"*Joan of Arc* is making a turn to port, moving away from *HMS Prince of Wales*. If she is heading down the English Channel and into the Atlantic, she probably wants to give our carrier a pretty wide berth."

"Our territorial waters are twelve nautical miles – correct?" says Margaret.

"Yes, Prime Minister," says Roger.

Margaret scans the faces of her staff. "Well, the choice at this point is clear. Either we let them go and they wander off into the Atlantic Ocean or wherever they're headed, or we seize the ship as per the original plan." Margaret looks at her Home Secretary. "Do we know how many UK citizens are on board that ship?"

"We think about 400 boarded originally," says Jared. "Most of them are UK citizens, some are other nationalities, but we don't really know where the non-UK citizens are from. I had a report that some people left the ship last night. So, maybe there are 300 left on board, and perhaps 250 are Brits. But these are just estimates, Prime Minister."

Margaret looks at her Chief of Naval Staff. "Robert, if we seize *Joan of Arc*, how do we do it at this point? Please tell me we have a contingency plan."

"We do, Prime Minister," says Robert. "We land a Chinook helicopter on the flight deck of *Joan of Arc*. The Chinook will carry forty-eight special forces equipped with assault rifles, tear gas and protective armour, and ten naval personal capable of operating the carrier. Henderson and those operating the ship are taken into custody. We will also put three Apache attack helicopters in the air to offer tactical support to the Chinook."

Margaret scans the satellite video feed and watches *Joan of Arc*, still heading into the English Channel and angling away from *HMS Prince of Wales*. "Well," says Margaret, "*Joan of Arc* is a ship of fools, if you ask me. You've got Henderson and that mental health patient… what's his name?"

"Winston Godfred, Prime Minister," says Jared.

"Yeah, that one," continues Margaret. "Plus that screw-job activist… Sunshine something or other, and some bloke who is ex-London Mafia, right?"

"Um… yes, Prime Minister," says Jared. "That would be Sunrise70 and Dominic Delfino."

"Yeah," says Margaret, "and there are at least 250 UK citizens on board, and for all I know this is some whack-job cult."

Margaret looks at her Home Secretary. "Jared, is it better to seize the ship in our territorial waters?"

"I'd think so, Prime Minister. There's this business about *Joan of Arc*'s application to the UN for statehood. It's probably all a load of nonsense, but if we seize the ship in our waters, we will have an easier defence if… you know…"

"If I know what?" says Margaret.

"Well… if anything goes wrong."

Margaret makes a face. "Well, nothing better go wrong. Roger, can we take control of *Joan of Arc* before it leaves our territorial waters?"

Roger squints at the satellite feed. "I think she's only about a half-mile off the coast. We'll have time… if we go now."

Max gazes over the Captain's head and through the bridge windows. The early morning sun glints off the English Channel water and a modest breeze brings up moderate swells. Max feels a strange sensation he gets whenever he crosses that invisible boundary where the estuary becomes the open water. He looks to his right and inspects the enormous British carrier.

"Captain," says Max, "do you know why *Prince of Wales* has two islands?"

"I do. It provides redundancy in the event one of the islands is successfully attacked. Also, she has two funnels, so they can space the funnels out that way."

Max nods. "Is it okay if I call Hedvika and Sheila?"

"Sure, Max."

"Hello, Max. Are you okay?" he hears Hedvika say.

"Yes, we are all fine. Is Sheila there too?"

"Yes, Max. You're on speakerphone."

"Hi, Sheila."

"Hello, Max," says Sheila.

"Max," says Hedvika. "We're standing on the quay. We watched you go up the Estuary. You frightened us when you went through those two ships."

"The destroyers. Yes, that was a bit scary for everyone. But we are heading out into the English Channel now and the sun is shining and *Jeanne d'Arc* is running well. I just wanted to thank you and Sheila for putting up with me."

"That's okay, Max," says Hedvika.

"Okay, take care of yourselves."

Max ends the call and there is silence on the bridge for a moment, everyone gazing at the water and listening to the dull throb of the diesel engines. "So, Max," says the Captain, tapping the steering column, "where are we going?"

"I don't really know. What do you think, Captain?" asks Max.

"Well, the English Channel is a pretty silly place for an aircraft carrier. Shall we take her to sea?"

Max looks at Winston and Dom. "That okay?"

"Sure, Max," says Winston, and Dom nods agreement.

"Okay," says the Captain. "We can stay on this heading, take her to the middle of the Channel, then head west down the Channel and into the Atlantic – of course we may still have to get past the Prince of Wales and maybe a submarine that way. Or we go east, take a left at Calais, head up the east coast of Britain, take a left at John O'Groats, and then we are into the North Atlantic that way. Of course, the British have got a naval base on the Clyde, so they could send ships from there to intercept us."

Max is thinking all of this over when he hears the sound of distant but powerful engines starting up. John-Pierre stands up and looks out the starboard windows. "Hugo," he says, "can you take the wheel, please? Let's have a look."

The Captain leads them out onto the bridge walkway and they all stand there gazing at *Prince of Wales*, two miles distant. The Captain and Max raise binoculars to their eyes and then it's the Captain who speaks. "They have got a Chinook helicopter running, and I can see two Apache attack helicopters which are starting up as well."

"So, what does this mean?" says Dom.

"It means that they are going to land the Chinook on *Jeanne d'Arc* and take the ship by force. A Chinook can carry a few dozen special forces or more. The Apaches are heavily armed gunships – they'll be escorting the Chinook. That's how I would do it, anyway."

"Oh no," says Winston.

"Yes," says the Captain, "I'm afraid this is what's going to happen."

"But what about Max?" says Winston. "They won't take Max, will they?"

The engines and whirring blades begin to scream and a moment later a large two-bladed helicopter and three smaller 'copters lift off and make their way directly for *Jeanne d'Arc*.

"I was wrong," says the Captain. "It's three Apaches."

"Well," says Max. "That's it then. Captain, I think I should address the citizens of *Jeanne d'Arc*. I don't want anyone getting upset. The Captain nods and they return to the bridge. The Captain hands the intercom to Max and, when Max nods, he pushes a button.

"Dearest citizens of *Jeanne d'Arc*... I have some sad news. If you are on the starboard side of the ship, you will be able to see four helicopters approaching us. In a couple of minutes, the large one is likely to land on *Jeanne d'Arc*'s flight deck. There are probably going to be several special forces on the helicopter, and they will want to take control of our ship. We won't be offering any resistance, and I would ask that everyone is polite to these people as they are just doing their jobs and I don't want anyone to be harmed. None of you have done anything wrong, and I am guessing they will want you to just return home. But they will probably want to take *Jeanne d'Arc*. I don't know what they will want to do with me, but I don't want any of you to worry about that."

Max pauses and looks at the ground for a moment. "I'm not sure what else to say, except that, if I'm not able to see or speak to you for a while, I wish you happiness and fulfilment. Bye for now."

Max nods and the Captain turns off the intercom. "Captain," says Max, "what's the easiest way to do this?"

"Well, running a white flag up the pole may seem antiquated, but it's still what we do. But I think by the time we can get the flag out of the locker and up the pole, the show will be over. It's probably best if I open a channel to *Prince of Wales* and we surrender that way."

"Sounds sensible," says Max.

Winston emits a sob and Dom, the Captain, and Max are aware of tears rolling down his cheeks. Max puts a hand on his shoulder. "Winston, you did an amazing job and accomplished incredible things in a very short amount of time."

"Hugo," says the Captain, "please open a channel to *Prince of Wales*."

"Yes, Captain," says Hugo, as he flips a few switches.

"*HMS Prince of Wales*," says Hugo, "this is the bridge of *Jeanne d'Arc*. Captain Jean-Pierre Lavelle would like to speak with the senior officer in charge. Do you copy?"

There is a hissing noise that comes through the open channel, and

Max looks through the windows at the enormous Chinook helicopter which is positioning itself over the flight deck. He also notices that one Apache attack 'copter has situated itself off the bow, with the other two off the port and starboard beams, all with sinister machine guns and rockets pointing at *Jeanne d'Arc*'s tower. The noise from the rotors and engines is surprisingly loud.

The hissing ends. "*Jeanne d'Arc*... this is the bridge of *HMS Prince of Wales*..."

There is a sudden machine-like popping sound which can just be heard over the noise of the rotors, and the communication from *HMS Prince of Wales* cuts out. Dom notices the tail of the Apache helicopter on the starboard beam swing around wildly, the engine suddenly screaming in pitch.

"What the fuck is that?" shouts Dom.

The Captain's eyes grow wide. "That's a fifty-calibre gun."

"Who's shooting?" shouts Dom, scanning each of the helicopters.

The Apache on starboard continues to spin and its nose dips strangely, and then Dom notices several holes down its tail. Black smoke erupts from its engine as the popping noise continues.

"That's our fifty-calibre," shouts the Captain. "The anti-aircraft gun!"

Dom grabs Max's arm. "Shit... Sunrise," he shouts.

Max opens his mouth. "Sunrise70," he says, trying to understand what Dom is saying.

"The stupid bitch is firing at the helicopter," shouts Dom, reflexively feeling for his pistol through his jacket. "I'll sort this."

Dom runs through the bridge exit door and begins taking the stairs three at a time. When he reaches the deck floor, he opens the hatch carefully and peers out. The popping noise is louder and coming from his left. He reaches into his suit, pulls the Walther P-99 out of the shoulder holster, and pushes carefully through the hatch door. Dom crouches down behind a railing, but this offers little cover. The stricken Apache helicopter is 100 metres directly off to starboard and continues its helpless spin, black smoke continuing to belch from the engine. Dom can see panicked expressions on the faces of the two pilots who sit one in front of the other as they try to bring the craft under control. A stream of bullets suddenly rips through the fuselage just beneath the rotor, the copter does one final violent spin and crashes nose-first into the English Channel, the spinning blades tearing apart when they hit the water.

The popping of the fifty-calibre stops for a moment. Dom can't see

Sunrise70, but he spots the twin barrels of the gun thirty metres down the deck. The Apache is floating, but Dom can't make out if the pilots are alright because of the sun glare bouncing off the cockpit windows. He listens for a moment and then sees another Apache helicopter as it swings around and lines itself up with his side of the ship. Crouching as low as possible, Dom runs towards the fifty-calibre until he is ten metres away. He can see Sunrise70 now, standing behind a metal shield, gripping the gun's handles and swinging the barrels around towards the second Apache.

"Sunrise70," Dom shouts, holding his pistol down by his side. "Stop this shit! You're gonna get us all killed."

She doesn't even glance over, but instead looks down the sight of the barrels. "Fuck off, Dom."

Dom looks back at the Apache just as the thirty-millimetre cannon slung under its carriage begins to spit fire. Shells clang and ricochet off the ship and Dom stares in disbelief as Sunrise70 crouches behind the gun's shield and returns fire. Shells smash into the island just above Dom's head and he reflexively ducks lower. Dom feels a hand on his shoulder. He jerks his head around and then hears a voice.

"How's it going, Dom?"

Dom grabs at Max's shoulder and pulls him down closer to the railing. "Max, get the hell down – what are you doing?"

Dom pulls Max closer, wrapping his arm around his shoulder. The Apache's cannon is firing continuously and shells seem to clang and fly everywhere. "You shouldn't be here, Max," Dom shouts.

"This is my fault, Dom. I need to fix this."

Dom stares at Sunrise70, gripping Max by the shoulder. There is an expression of rage on her face but the storm of bullets means she is having to crouch low and her return fire seems wild. Dom aims his pistol at her. "Sunshine," he screams, "stop or I will fucking shoot you right now."

"Then shoot me, fuck-face," she screams, continuing to fire. Dom stuffs his pistol into his jacket pocket, shoves Max lower towards the decking and shouts, "Stay down, Max." Shells slam into the island inches above their heads and Dom is aware that the remaining Apache has swung around and is firing as well. Dom runs at Sunrise70, crouching. He grabs her around the arms, rips her hands from the gun handles and jerks her hard, the two of them crashing down on the metal decking.

"FUCK YOU!" she screams, struggling to free herself. Dom is

shocked by her strength but he grips her hard and wraps his legs around hers to stop her kicking. They have more protection from the gun's shield, but the Apaches continue to fire and shells scream as they ricochet off *Jeanne d'Arc*'s island.

Sunrise70 is shouting and trying to head-butt and bite Dom, but without success. "Dickless fuck!"

Dom tightens his grip around Sunrise70 and knows that he is knocking the wind out of her. He rolls her face-down on the decking, puts a knee into her back, and pulls his handcuffs out of his jacket pocket.

"I will fucking kill you, Dom!"

Dom puts a handcuff on one of Sunrise70's wrists and handcuffs the other to a railing. He is aware suddenly that the Apaches have stopped firing and of the relative quiet. He gives her back an extra push with his knee and then steps away. Dom looks up and manages to make eye contact with one of the pilots, putting two thumbs up. Dom knows instinctively that there is something wrong with the pilot's expression – he's panicky, talking into a radio, and not paying attention to Dom or Sunrise70. Dom looks over and sees Max lying prone and on his face... and the blood.

"Shit," he says, running to Max. Dom slips on the broad shining pool of scarlet, kneels next to Max, and sees the hole ripped through his back, blood continuing to pour out. He gently rolls Max over and Dom's face falls as he becomes aware of the bloody hole in the chest and the glassy and fixed eyes which seem to stare into nothing.

CHAPTER 39

I'm steering my Mini Cooper through Portsmouth's early morning traffic, allowing Satnav's computer-generated female voice to guide me to Southsea Coffee Company. I am supposed to be writing yet another piece for Britain Today on the Max Henderson story, but after writing articles for the past six days, I finally told my editor, *"No, let someone else do it today"*. He said, *"Liz, this is your story"*. I told him I've said everything I can at the moment, and I've got people to see.

I follow the A3 along Victoria Park, my windows down, and I can smell the brine wafting up from the English Channel. My mind drifts, disjointed images of the past week popping in and out of my head. The authorities said that Max had been killed instantly, a thirty-millimetre shell having gone straight through his chest and out his back. There were some pretty pointless debates about whether it was a straight shot or one that ricocheted off the ship. Max was killed, either way. There's been no funeral because the coroner won't release Max's body. The body is part of the government's investigation.

I stop at a light by a University of Portsmouth building and watch some students messing about on skateboards. My first article came out the day after Max died and I referred to Sunrise70, but I also made sure readers knew she had another name – Laura Beech. That felt important for some reason, and other journalists picked up on my lead. One of the Apache pilots sustained a broken arm and whiplash, but nothing life-threatening. Laura Beech has been charged with two counts of attempted murder and is currently awaiting trial at Downview, a prison in Surrey for female inmates. There are rumours that she is causing a lot of problems, but it's hard to know the truth. Some people see her as a monster and others see her as a rebellious cult-like figure. A thrash-metal band just released a song about her exploits, which is apparently doing well on YouTube.

Satnav's reassuring voice directs me off the A3 and onto the A288. It took most of the day for the authorities to secure *Jeanne d'Arc*, airlift Max's body, and generally clean up the whole mess. I was able to watch as the citizens of Jeanne d'Arc were transferred onto one of the destroyers, and I can still remember so many of the stunned and bemused expressions on their faces. There were no incidents and everything happened in this weird aura of silence and unspoken feelings. They made a record of the citizens' identities and addresses, and then released them. Dom, Winston, Jean-Pierre, Alexis, Hugo and I, on the other hand, we're not going anywhere. There was a moment when I thought we were all going to be arrested, and I later learned that this had been a real possibility. In the end, we were designated *persons of special interest* to the investigation. I have to say, they didn't make you feel at all special. I was interviewed for three hours before they released me, and I have been interviewed twice more since. They still have my passport and, until this morning, none of us have been allowed to communicate with each other. The British and French governments had quite a public row about what to do with Jean-Pierre, Hugo, and Alexis. I thought they might get detained in Britain, but they've been allowed to go home under agreement that they will return to participate in Sunrise70's trial.

Polite and patient Satnav lady tells me to turn left on Osborne Road, and it feels nice to allow someone else to make the decisions this morning. A moment later I spot Southsea Coffee Company and I'm fortunate to find an unmetered parking spot right outside. It's a small but tasteful café with large windows and turquoise trim. I realise I am desperate for a strong coffee.

I see Dom straight away when I walk in. He's sitting at a table in the far corner and I'm surprised because, rather than the trademark suit and tie, he's wearing a pair of tan khakis and a blue dress shirt. His black hair is combed back like normal, and he gives me a smile and a wave. He stands up and hugs me when I get to his table.

"Let me get you a coffee, Liz. What d'ya want?"

"Something large and strong with a bit of milk."

I sit down and watch him while he orders my coffee. I wonder if he has a girlfriend and I think about asking him, but I'm pretty sure I don't have the confidence to do that. I decide he is single and then I decide he has a few girlfriends, and then I decide I have no idea at all and that there isn't much point in thinking about it. I look at my purse but decide it doesn't feel right to take my notepad out.

Dom returns and places a large mug on the table. He's smiling at me, but there's a sadness in his expression, and he looks tired too.

"How you been, Dom?" I ask.

"I've been better. How you been?"

"The same," I say.

He nods.

"So…" I say, "it's felt really weird not to be able to speak. I can't believe the government installed a board of directors at Henderson Nautical."

"Yeah. None of us were asked to leave, but Hedvika and I resigned straight away. Sheila tried to resign but they figured out very quickly that without Sheila they wouldn't have a clue how to run that business. I think they threw a big salary at Sheila to keep her, but she's not planning on staying long."

"Yeah, I heard about that," I say. "So… what are you gonna do?"

"I don't really know right now," he says. "I think I'll take a bit of time off and then see what happens."

"Have you spoken to Hedvika yet?" I ask.

"Sure. I've spoken to her a few times this week."

"But the Detective Inspector said we weren't supposed to talk to one another."

"Well, there's a lot of things you're not supposed to do, right?"

I laugh. "Dom, do you follow any rules?"

"Sure. Stoplights. Returning library books. Stuff like that."

I shake my head and take a sip of coffee. "How's Hedvika doing?"

"She's pretty upset. You wanna hear something ridiculous? After Hedvika resigned, someone from the government's legal bureau actually head-hunted her for some lawyer's post with the Home Office. Can you believe that? After all the headaches she caused them."

"Well," I say, "maybe they head-hunted her *because* of the headaches she was able to cause them. Is she taking the job?"

"Nah," he says. "She's not gonna work for a bunch of bureaucratic stiffs. She's got a new job in corporate law. Starts next week."

"Do you think she'll be okay if I make contact with her?"

"I think she'd be happy to hear from you, but maybe wait a bit before you ask to meet up. She's dealing with a lot right now."

I nod. It makes sense. "There's something else I've been curious about. Max was… well, my impression was that Max was a wealthy man. I suppose his wife will do pretty well out of this?" I gaze at Dom, unsure how to continue. "I'm sorry," I add. "Is that too personal?"

Dom shakes his head. "Nah, it will all come out eventually. Hedvika knows the details. Max did have money, but he blew a lot on *Jeanne d'Arc*. There was everything we bought at the arms fair and fitting it out for all those citizens was pricey too. Do you know how much it costs to fill an aircraft carrier with diesel?"

"No."

"Well, neither do I," says Dom, "but probably a lot. And Max was always giving these expensive gifts to the people he loved. Hedvika told me that Max had a will. Max's money was supposed to go into a trust for his son, Peter, but of course Peter died."

"So, what happens now?"

"The will said that if Peter died before Max, his money goes into the pension funds of his employees." Dom laughs before continuing. "I tell ya, I'd give about anything to see Violeta's face when she gets that news."

I find myself laughing. "What about Henderson Nautical Works? The company must have value."

"Probably – but the government has seized any assets pending their investigation. Hedvika said it could end up in the courts for years."

I smile and we drink our coffee, both of us lost in our thoughts for a moment. "And Sheila?" I ask. "I suppose you've had a bunch of conversations with her too."

"I talk to her most days, and don't ask me how she is because the answer is *not good*. There have been some tears when we speak." Dom smiles before continuing. "Mostly from Sheila." He sips at his coffee and looks around the room.

"Dom, can I ask you something? I mean – I understand you want to take some time off. But... I'm thinking you must have some thoughts about what you're gonna do."

Dom shrugs. "Yeah, I suppose I do. I'm done working in security. I know a guy who refurbishes older cars from the seventies and eighties. He wants me to come in with him."

"You're gonna repair cars?"

"More the sales side of things."

Dom folds his hands and gives me a stare which makes me feel a little uncomfortable. "What about you, Liz? You know, I've read every article you've written this past week. You're describing what happened with Max and *Jeanne d'Arc*, but your articles aren't so different from what a lot of journalists are writing. You've been a part of the story pretty much from the beginning. So, what are *you* gonna do?"

I nod, and I understand what he's getting at. "You're right Dom. I've been describing the events around what happened, just like other journalists. Did you know I've been asked to appear on four different talk shows? I keep saying *"No"*. The fact is, I want to tell the story of

Max and *Jeanne d'Arc*, and all the people who were close to Max. But I want to get it right, and that will take a little time. Maybe you've noticed, but there are journalists writing absolute gibberish about Max. There was one article titled *Max Henderson – an absurd death for an absurd man.*"

He's nodding. "Yeah, I read that one. What a piece of shit."

"It was," I say. "Everyone is turning into some sort of analyst and projecting all sorts of nonsense onto Max."

Dom leans forward and looks serious. "You should do it, Liz. Write a book. Tell people what you really saw, from the inside. You have my permission, if that's what you want. But let me tell you something…"

Dom stares down at the table and purses his lips, and he suddenly seems emotional and a little lost – a side of him I've never seen. He looks up and continues. "When you talk about me in this book, remember to say that I fucked up – that I fucked up bad."

I'm a bit shocked by what Dom is saying. Almost every article that has come out has been praising Dom's role in events. "Dom… what you did on *Jeanne d'Arc* was incredibly brave."

He's shaking his head. "It's not what I did, Liz – it's what I didn't do. I've always trusted my gut. It's what's kept me and others safe. From the moment I met Sundick I knew she was a fat fucking grenade, and I didn't put a stop to that. I had plenty of chances."

"Dom, I don't think anyone blames you for this."

"I blame me, Liz. So when you write your book, make sure you put that in."

I reach over and put a hand on his arm. It feels like anything I might say would be wrong, so I keep quiet and look at the table.

"Right," he says, looking up. "Enough about me. Have you been in touch with Winston?"

"I've tried calling his mobile a couple of times, but it doesn't seem to be working."

"Well," he says, "I've got some unfortunate news about our boy, Winston. He's on a psychiatric ward at Elmleigh Hospital, about five miles out of town."

"You're kidding. How did you even know?"

"His sister Constance got in touch with me. It's an informal admission. Apparently he's not being detained – but, yeah, on a ward."

"How is he? I mean – have you seen Winston?"

"Yeah, I've been to visit. He's pretty medicated. I'm not sure he quite grasps the situation. You should visit."

His phone rings. He looks at it and turns the ringer off. "I got something I need to do Liz, but… let's keep in touch, okay?"

"Yeah, I'd like that," I say.

He looks at me for a moment. "Liz, I think you're a good person."

I smile at him. "Ya know, you're starting to sound like Max."

He laughs. "My god," he says. "What's happening to me?"

We stare at each other for a moment. "I think you're a good person too, Dom."

He nods, stands up, and places a fiver on the table. "I'll see you around, okay?" he says.

CHAPTER 40

Elmleigh Hospital is a small unit on the outskirts of Portsmouth, and it wasn't difficult to find. As I walk through the entrance, a nurse looks up at me from behind the reception desk.

"Hello, can I help you?"

"Yes please," I say. "I'm Liz Burton, a friend of Winston Godfred. I called earlier to ask if I could visit."

"Oh yes," she says. "That's fine. Winston is on Kingsley Ward. Um, Liz, I'm glad he has a friend to visit. Winston hasn't had too many visitors. Just his sister and a couple others. I'm sure seeing a friend will help, but we want to keep him calm, okay? If he stays calm, that's fine. But if Winston starts to get agitated, it might be best to keep the visit shorter, for his sake."

"Okay," I say, wondering what this all means.

I follow her down a corridor and we pass by a community room where I see some patients watching television. She knocks on his door.

"Come in," I hear Winston say.

She opens the door a bit. "Winston, your friend Liz is here to visit."

"Yes, of course," says Winston.

The nurse holds the door open for me and I notice this sympathetic expression on her face, which I find worrying. She closes the door and I see that Winston is sitting at a small desk which is covered in piles of paper, books, and notepads. He is still wearing his Che Guevara outfit, although it's very wrinkled. His scraggly beard is in rough shape, and there is an odour suggesting that he hasn't showered in a while. He gazes at me, his eyes glassy and mouth hanging open. I sit in a chair near him, unsure of what to say. He continues to stare and I wonder if he recognises me.

"It's Liz," I say.

"Yes, yes…" he says. "Of course it is – Liz Burton, the journalist. You're exactly who I need to talk to. I have to show you what I've been working on. Your views are extremely important." He's whispering in an odd fashion.

He looks through a disordered collection of papers and notebooks until he finds what he needs. It's a notebook which has words scrawled on the front: 14-Point Plan for the Repatriation of *Jeanne d'Arc*. He takes a large breath, blows it out, and looks at me. "It's all here, Liz, every step we need to take to put things right."

Winston pushes himself out of the chair and begins to pace the room, and I wonder if this is the agitation the nurse had in mind. "I had no idea," he says, "that Sunrise70, or Laura Beech, or whoever she is, was a government agent."

"She was?" I say, genuinely confused.

"Of course, of course. She and those thugs of hers. It's obvious now, but at the time we all missed it. And it's not surprising. Her cover was so unconventional… it was… well, brilliant."

I open my mouth to ask him how he knows this, but he is off again, still pacing the room. "The way they pulled off the kidnapping was genius."

Now I am really confused. "The kidnapping?"

"Yes, of course. It was all quite chaotic when the helicopters arrived and I don't know what vantage point you had, Liz, but I saw everything. Sunrise70 and her squad kidnapped Max and took him off *Jeanne d'Arc* on one of the helicopters, just before the naval forces arrived."

"Oh, right," I say.

Winston slaps his hand on the 14-Point Plan for the Repatriation of *Jeanne d'Arc*. He grins at me. "But don't worry, Liz, because I know just what we need to do."

Winston places his index finger to his lips and then gets a towel from the bathroom. He places the towel on the ground in front of the door and then pulls out a roll of masking tape. He runs masking around the three remaining edges of the door, sits down, and then whispers into my ear. "There is a woman who has infiltrated Kingsley Ward. I'm not going to say her name so that you'll have plausible deniability in case you get detained. But… this woman got onto the ward, posing as a mental health patient, in order to link up with me."

"Really?" I say. "How do you know?"

"Shhh," says Winston. "That nurse who seems so nice – she will be sticking her ear right to the other side of the door. Liz, this woman I'm talking about – I know she's legit because she showed me a mug with an image of *Jeanne d'Arc* on it. We were sitting in the common room the first day she arrived and she held up the mug. It was her way of signalling me."

I feel an impulse to point out to Winston that there are lots of *Jeanne d'Arc* novelty items – mugs, t-shirts, baseball caps – available on Ebay. Thousands of the things.

"She was careful at first," continues Winston. "But eventually I confided in her, and she told me that she knows where they're holding Max. I'm supposed to keep that secret for now, but it's all in here," he says, tapping his notebook again. "It's all worked out – the plan to rescue Max and then to retake *Jeanne d'Arc*. This woman – she's connected to some very powerful people who are sympathetic with those of us on the left. They're gonna help us."

I really don't know how to respond. I want to to explain to Winston that Sunshine70 was not an undercover agent, that Max died and that his 14-point plan is delusional, but I know very little about mental health and what is going to be helpful. So I don't say any of that. "How are you doing Winston? How are you feeling?"

He seems surprised by my question. "I'm fine, Liz. I just need to act the part long enough to convince these doctors and nurses that I can be released. And when they let me out, that's when we can activate the plan."

"Winston, I thought this was an informal admission."

He laughs. "Is that what they told you? Beautiful, absolutely beautiful. No, definitely not. If I tried to walk out of here, there would be alarms going off and about six nurses jabbing me full of Haldol. But don't worry, Liz, I know how to play their game."

I think things over for a moment. "Can we keep in touch?"

"Definitely, Liz. You are essential to the plan, and even though they've got Max at the moment, you're still his journalist. Don't call me through ward reception, though. They'll transfer the call to my room, but they listen to everything, and I can't risk the plan being compromised, okay? I lost my mobile, but Constance is going to bring me one soon. I've got your number – I'll contact you."

I nod, and there is a knock at the door. "Everything alright, Winston?"

"Y'see what I'm talking about," whispers Winston." He jumps to the floor, pulls the towel away, and then quickly removes the masking tape. Winston opens the door and smiles. "Yes, nurse Bailey. Everything's fine."

I stand up and place a hand on Winston's arm. "Winston, take care, okay?"

He nods and gives me what looks like a conspiratorial smile.

As I walk down the corridor, I pause by the common room because something on the TV catches my eye. It's Prime Minister Margaret Williams, standing at a podium and apparently speaking to a group of reporters. "All of the individuals who were involved with Max Henderson's group have been offered therapeutic counselling by qualified professionals."

"And do we know how many of these individuals have actually sought counselling?" asks a reporter.

"I'm afraid I don't have those figures to hand," says Margaret.

She does have those figures to hand because even I know the figures through my connections at Britain Today. Two. Two people were apparently so distressed by being a part of Max's project that they needed counselling, and perhaps their distress had more to do with helicopters firing at their ship. It's really hard to listen to the media right now. There's this pattern where the right-wing press makes accusations without providing evidence – *Jeanne d'Arc* was a sex cult, Max Henderson was a survivalist with a crackpot doomsday philosophy, etc… The government doesn't officially agree with these news reports, but doesn't deny them either, and statements coming from ministers and aides often provide subtle support.

Of course, they're making a big deal out of the jet plane and the anti-aircraft guns. Home Office Secretary Jared Philcox is the best example. He was asked if *Jeanne d'Arc* was planning any attacks on Britain. "It's very possible," said Jared. "They certainly had the fire-power to do it."

It makes me sick to watch. They ramp up notions of calamity and even terrorism that might have been perpetrated in order to rationalise the fact that their assault resulted in Max getting killed. What's sad is that it seems to be working. There are still a lot of people who support Max, but the government's spin is having an impact. Maybe what's even more distressing is that, just one week on, people seem to be losing interest. At the moment, the reporting is getting pushed off the front pages by a rock star overdose and some royals who got photographed on the beach. I'm learning that this is just how things go.

CHAPTER 41

I drive away from Elmleigh Hospital and turn onto New Road, which will take me to the M3 and back to London. I feel numb, like my mind can't quite absorb the conversation I just had with Winston. The sun is higher in the sky now but the day is overcast, and I have this sense that I am forgetting something. It's possible that what is nagging me is that I haven't made contact with Hedvika, but I'm not convinced. I take a quick left off New Road to find somewhere I can park and think things over. When I find a parking space I look up and see a pub, and it occurs to me that I want a coffee. The pub is unusual because it's covered in shiny green tiles. I look at the hanging sign and what sounds like maniacal laugh bursts out of me. It's called *The Prince of Wales*.

"You have got to be fucking kidding me," I say out loud. A part of me doesn't want to go in, perhaps out of a sense of loyalty to Max and *Jeanne d'Arc*. But a bigger part of me really needs a coffee and a place to think, and no one is going to care if I boycott this pub.

While the older guy behind the bar is making me a coffee in a 'to-go cup', I can't resist asking – "The Prince of Wales, huh? Wasn't that the name of the carrier that had that altercation with *Jeanne d'Arc* last week?"

"Yeah," he says. "That's the one."

"I'm not from around here – what's your view on what happened?"

"Bloody mess," he says. "It's just the Brits having to clean up after the French again, isn't it?"

"And what do you make of Max Henderson?"

"I like him. He's a local boy and good bloke. Been in here a few times over the years. Bit of a screw-job probably, but I suppose most of us are. A real shame he got shot. Lotta people 'round here feel that way."

I nod and take my cup of coffee over to a table by a window. I consider calling Hedvika, but I'm feeling a bit tired and recall Dom's advice, so I write her an email.

Dear Hedvika,

I'm so sorry about Max. I know you knew him for many years and my impression from speaking with Max was that you were very close. I know this is a difficult time for you now, but when you feel ready, I'd like to talk. Take care of yourself. Much love, Liz.

I send the email, take a sip of coffee, and stare out the window into the overcast light of early afternoon. I recall the image of Dom standing in line this morning as he was waiting to get me a coffee. I send him a text:

Just been to visit Winston. Oh my goodness. Thanks for the heads-up!!

A moment later, he texts back. It's an emoji of a smiley face. I smile, despite myself. I do like that man.

My phone pings and it's a return email from Hedvika.

Thank you Liz for your thoughts. Yes, it's a difficult time, but I'm happy to talk. I'll be in touch in the next couple of weeks. Take care of yourself too. Hedvika.

I still feel this nagging sense that I am forgetting something, or that something is missing. Suddenly, I know what it is. I need to see *Jeanne d'Arc* before I return to London. One of the ridiculous twists in the whole story is that the British Government ended up bringing *Jeanne d'Arc* back to Henderson Nautical Works. When they seized the ship, they towed it to Plymouth Harbour and, by all accounts, there followed very fraught discussions between the British and French governments. It looked like *Jeanne d'Arc* would be heading back to Cherbourg, but there was a developing group of French who now liked the idea of preserving and memorializing the carrier. To a lot of Brits, Max was 'a good bloke', like the publican said. To some French, however, he was becoming a symbol of revolt, and a bit of an icon. This seemed dangerous to both the French and British governments. The French government felt they already had enough historical symbols of revolt, and the British Government didn't want Max memorialised anywhere or in any way.

The details are hazy, but it seems that the French government agreed to pay for *Jeanne d'Arc* to be broken down, plus an undisclosed fee for the inconvenience related to the whole event, and the British agreed to pull the ship apart. Then, a government aide pointed out that Plymouth doesn't have the facilities to do the job, and the only other shipyard that could manage didn't want to be associated with it. So, irony upon irony, *Jeanne d'Arc* gets towed all the way back to Henderson Nautical Works.

I park my car just down the road from the main gate at Henderson Nautical and consider what I am about to do. I'm pretty sure the new senior management at Henderson won't want me anywhere near the place but, then again, no one has told me I can't come here. I open my glove box and pull out my Henderson Nautical identity card, which I hang around my neck.

I punch the code into the gate door and, to my surprise, it still works. The giant work sheds block any view of the waterfront, but *Jeanne d'Arc* is so huge I can see the top of her island poking up behind Henderson's main office building. I walk between the office block and a work shed, pass by a couple of staff who seem too distracted to take any notice, and then smell the salty brine coming off the estuary. I turn a corner and there she is, tied to the pier, about seventy-five metres down from me. I spot a bench and sit down, my coffee cup in my lap.

The sky has darkened further and it smells like rain is on the way. Gulls cry, circle, and swoop. A breeze throws up small waves out over Portsmouth Harbour and feels cool against my bare skin. There are four gigantic cranes which have been positioned over *Jeanne d'Arc*. One of them is lifting a metallic structure away from the top of the island. I can see dozens of workmen standing and walking all over the ship, and several smaller cranes. Even at this distance, there is a chaotic din of so many different noises. Metallic screeches, blades grinding, drills spinning, heavy objects dropping. It seems to come from inside *Jeanne d'Arc* as well.

I get this sense of all these people who were connected to this huge ship in one way or another, and I am struck by how severed that connection suddenly feels. I hear footsteps behind me and then a female voice. "Are you supposed to be here? I'm going to have to ask for some identification."

My heart thumps. I turn my head and see Sheila standing there.

I release nervous laughter. "God, Sheila, you frightened me." I pat the bench. "Come and sit down. How did you know I was here?"

She sits down, pointing over her shoulder. "I was looking out my office window and saw you. It's funny, I wasn't surprised to see you come back to have a look."

We watch *Jeanne d'Arc* together in silence for a moment. "I'm so sorry, Sheila, about Max," I say.

She nods her head. "Max always liked you, Liz," she says. "His judgement of character wasn't always so good, but he was right about you."

"Well, he would have been lost without you," I say.

There is a metallic screech which comes from somewhere inside *Jeanne d'Arc*, and we both look. Sheila seems to be thinking, weighing her response. "Max was lost with me."

I sigh, feeling like I've said the wrong thing. I look more closely at her, and she suddenly looks quite old. Of course she is old, but I'd always seen this energy about her, and it seems to have gone. I want her to feel better, but it's difficult. "I know all of this must seem senseless," I hear myself saying. "The way things developed, the decisions we all made, the events Max sort of fell into – it seems pointless at the moment. But... I don't know, maybe with time and perspective... maybe there is a meaning to all of this."

Sheila gazes at *Jeanne d'Arc* and for a while I don't know if she's going to respond, but then she does. "Liz, if you don't mind me saying, you've got a lot of your life in front of you. That's my polite way of saying that you're young. Let me tell you what I think. I think there is this very human assumption that a story or a life must have a point... the details are all meant to lead inevitably to a conclusion that's symmetrical and satisfying. Perhaps there's some sort of moral lesson, or maybe justice is served. The story is supposed to make us feel like our lives are enriched or that existence matters. And at the end of life or the end of the story, the tension is resolved and it makes sense, right?" She looks over at me. "But Liz... this is just what we tell ourselves."

I nod, grateful for her words, but feeling like I need time to absorb them, and mostly sorry that I had opened my mouth. She looks at her watch. "Well, I'm now twenty minutes late for the board meeting. That seems about right."

I laugh, and she reaches over and squeezes my hand. A moment later she stands up, gives me a sad smile, and then walks towards the main office block.

I take a sip of my coffee, which tastes good and still manages to warm my insides. I look closely at *Jeanne d'Arc* and realise that, aside from the small bit taken off the top of the island, she still appears to be in one piece, and I realise I don't want to watch this. Pushing myself up from the bench, I walk the path between a shed and the main office building. I open the main gate and a moment later realise that I am walking across the grassy area where the citizens of *Jeanne d'Arc* had parked and pitched their tents before they were actually citizens. It's odd to see it looking so empty, although there are small remnants which were left behind. I feel compelled to stop and look around. I see a Frisbee which is half-buried in mud, a dirty sock and some broken tent poles, and these objects give me this strange sense of unreality.

I close my eyes, take a deep breath, and release it. I then head for my car and the roads which will take me back to London.

ACKNOWLEDGEMENTS

Work with my newspaper kept me busy, so it took six months following Max's death to complete this book. In that period, there were several individuals close to Max and the events who gave their time and spoke openly to me. I want to especially thank Dom Delfino, Hedvika Zavatsky, Sheila Taylor, Winston Godfred, Captain Jean-Pierre Lavelle, Chief Engineer Alexis Girard, Chief of Aeronautics Hugo Dubois, Defence Secretary Ronald Hudd, and Officer Jennifer Stanbury.

Liz Burton

THANK YOU

I want to express my gratitude to British writer and comedian Danny Wallace. The premise for *The Edge of the World* was inspired by a six-part BBC series of Danny's called *How to Start Your Own Country*, which I'd found both fascinating and hilarious. Feeling a little sheepish, I contacted Danny 'out of the blue' several years ago and described the premise and plot of my novel. Danny responded with a good deal of positivity and encouragement, without which this story might not have been written.

I also want to thank you, the reader. Time is arguably our most precious commodity, and I am grateful you have given some of yours to reading this novel. If you enjoyed *The Edge of the World*, I suspect you will appreciate my first novel, *The Art of Impossibility*, also published by Raven Crest Books. And, having got to the end of *The Edge of the World*, I would appreciate it if you could take a moment and leave a review on your favourite sites, e.g. Amazon, Goodreads, Facebook, Twitter, etc. Also, please feel free to make contact at bwahl.ravencrestbooks.com.

Bill Wahl

COVER ART

The cover art was provided by Dixie Appleton-Wahl in exchange for one cup of coffee.

ABOUT THE AUTHOR

Bill Wahl is an NHS psychologist, stand-up comedian, and owner/head brewer of Apostles of Hop Brewing Co. He is also the author of a novel, *The Art of Impossibility*, and a collection of short stories, *Existence and other Stories*. He and his family live in Westward Ho!, England.

CONTACT DETAILS

Visit the author's website: bwahl.ravencrestbooks.com

Published by: Raven Crest Books: www.ravencrestbooks.com

Like us on Facebook: Facebook.com/ravencrestbooksclub

Printed in Great Britain
by Amazon